PRAISE FOR THE STRATTFORD COUNTY SERIES BY GREGORY HILL

"An eye for detail, an ear for dialogue, and a knack for story-telling distinguish this unflinching novel of rural America."

—*Publishers Weekly,* about *East of Denver*

"*East of Denver* is a breezily readable summer novel that not only entertains but also surprises. It explores the dynamics of family relationships without ever stooping to sentimentality, and it's one of this summer's most pleasant surprises."

—Charles Ealy, *Austin American-Statesman*

"*East of Denver* is a slow burn, but by the end it's burning hot: you'll leave this book a little charred . . . This is writing on a par with that of top-flight black-comic novelists like Sam Lipsyte and Jess Walter, and it deserves to be read."

—Lev Grossman

"All the characters are quirky if not downright bizarre and you never really know how things are going to play out. *East of Denver* is a witty, snarky, and thoroughly enjoyable read."

—Leah Sims, *Portland Book Review*

"Gregory Hill . . . displays a keen, at times riveting, understanding of the absurdities and freedoms of small-town isolation and the dying way of life that was once the American standard."

—Cherie Ann Parker, *Shelf Awareness*

"*East of Denver* is an agreeable, offbeat debut novel . . . A story about a father and son who bond against the odds, with an ending as quirkily satisfying as the rest of the book."

—*Kirkus Reviews*

"Impressively well written from beginning to end, *The Lonesome Trials of Johnny Riles* is a terrifically entertaining read and showcases extraordinary and imaginative storytelling abilities."

—*Midwest Book Review*

"Like Hill's superb debut, *East of Denver*, *The Lonesome Trials of Johnny Riles* surely is a damn fine, if distinctly peculiar, country noir."

—*Booklist*

"*The Lonesome Trials of Johnny Riles* is a wild, weird, fun ride."

—*Yuma Pioneer*

"The *Lonesome Trials of Johnny Riles* renders Eastern Colorado/ High Plains life as it really has always been: down-to-earth, matter-of-fact, and always on the brink of psychedelia. This is an unapologetic triumph of contemporary Rural American Realism."

—Zach Boddicker, Songwriter 4H Royalty

"Before Narwhal Slotterfield, the mortals of "Strattford" myth had to reckon with a culturally-erosive, all-encroaching Future. In *Zebra Skin Shirt*, Narwhal suffers every atomized moment of the "Right-Fucking-Now." It's a cosmic ordeal, Greg Hill's third excellent novel in a row, and a trip well worth taking."

—Mike Molnar, Chicken Pickin' King of Country/Western Guitar

"Part mystery, part Steven Wright stand-up routine, part Einsteinian thought experiment, what do you call *Zebra Skin Shirt*? Sly-Fi? Off-off-off-beat? Magical Surrealism? Whatever it is, three cheers for the unforgettable former amateur basketball referee, Narwhal W. Slotterfield, and his creator, the wildly imaginative Gregory Hill."

—Mike Keefe, Political Cartoonist

ZEBRA SKIN SHIRT

ZEBRA SKIN SHIRT

A STRATTFORD COUNTY YARN

VOLUME III

GREGORY HILL

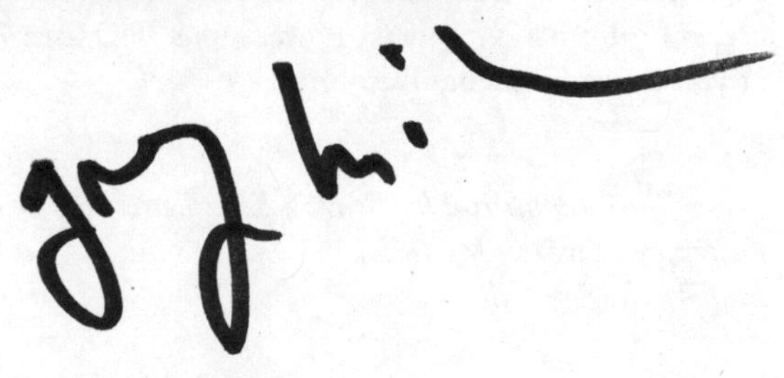

AN IMPRINT OF BOWER HOUSE
DENVER

Other yarns in the Strattford County series

East of Denver
The Lonesome Trials of Johnny Riles

 Bower House books may be purchased with bulk discounts for educational, business, or sales promotional use. For information, contact Bower House P.O. Box 7459 Denver, CO 80207 or visit BowerHouseBooks.com.

Cover Illustration/Print by Genghis Kern Letterpress & Design
Design by Margaret McCullough
Map by Gregory Hill

Library of Congress Control Number: 2018937269
ISBN: 978-1-942280-51-4

10 9 8 7 6 5 4 3 2 1

Dedicated to my heroes:

Archimedes, Spinoza, Arthur Koestler,

and Alex English

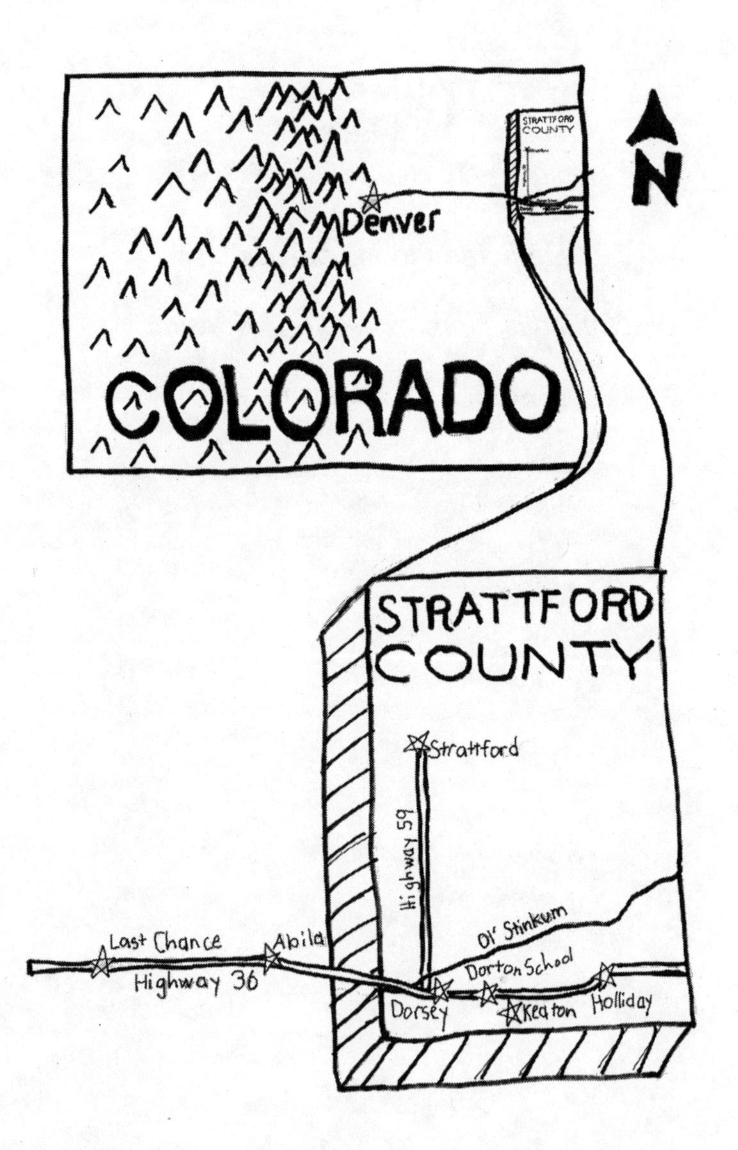

N
COLORADO
Denver
STRATTFORD COUNTY
STRATTFORD COUNTY
Strattford
Highway 59
Ol' Stinkum
Last Chance
Abila
Highway 36
Dorton School
Dorsey
Keaton
Holliday

Q: What did the snail say when it rode upon the turtle's back?

A: Wheeee!

Q: What did the escargot say when it rode upon the turtle's back?

A: Oui!

Q: What did the snail and the escargot simultaneously pronounce as they rode upon the back of a turtle poised upon an infinitely regressive stack of turtles?

A: We.

PART ONE

Et pourtant il fallut descendre!

—Michel Siffre,
Expériences hors du temps

Have you ever read *The Road*? Not *On the Road*, just *The Road*. Hell, I never even made it thru *On the Road*. I do own a copy, given to me by an ex-girlfriend, of whom I will not speak again except to say that the circumstances of the dissolution of our relationship were quite painful, for me at least.

In the interim between being told by this ex-girlfriend that all that remained of our love candle, which had been frighteningly short to begin with—she illustrated this by spreading her index fingers to approximate the height of a birthday candle—was a small pile of ashes, and my eventual realization that candles don't actually become ashes—rather, they disappear, or, rather, chemical combustion transforms them into light and heat and smoke—I tried to read *On the Road*.

Earlier, in the uncomplicated days of our relationship, on my approximate birthday, she had gifted me a paperback copy of *On the Road*, saying, "This is the reason I moved to Denver."

Up to that point, I had assumed she'd moved because of me and my letters and phone calls and the wonderful week we'd spent together at Yellowstone Park. I had assumed wrong, and this left me jealous. How could I, a man of blood and flesh, compete against a hallowed work of literature? This marked the only time I've ever been jealous of a book. I expressed this jealousy by choosing to not read *On the Road*, not at first.

But then the non-re-ignitable interim happened and I resolved to read the book in hopes that it would uncover some facet of our relationship which I could breathe upon gently, as one does to the last coals of a campfire upon awaking cold and confused next to one's tent, sober enough to be cold and confused, drunk enough to think one can elicit a flame from a pile of powdery grey ash.

I failed to rekindle the relationship. And so, after reading just forty pages, I closed *On the Road* and slid the book onto the shelf, sandwiched between a Proust novel and another novel whose blurb described it as "Proustian," neither of which I have ever read.

On the Road remained shelfish for a decade and a half, following me from one apartment to another, until another, later girlfriend said to me after breakfasting one Sunday morning, "I had that same edition. Penguin, 1991. Your bookmark is set toward the beginning of the book. This could mean one of two things."

I said, "It means the former."

She said, "I agree. Kerouac is terrible."

I *will* talk more about this girlfriend, and with great enthusiasm.

On the other hand, and back to our initial subject, I read *The Road* in one day. Imagine if Cormac McCarthy had written a post-apocalyptic novel of wisdom and suspense and gore. If that image pleases you, then I recommend you read *The Road*, because that is precisely what it is.

I loved every word of *The Road* except the ones in which the novel paused to render flash-backian stories from the protagonist's pre-apocalyptic, happy-family days. I dislike it when authors employ flashbacks. They distract, don't you think?

Alas, this anti-flashback bias becomes problematic when you live in a world in which flashbacks have become your only relief from an existence so silent and still, where your only motivation is unfocused hope, where your past is ever receding and your future always lonely.

That, now, is my life.

I am the solitary grain of sand that has accidentally slipped thru the waist of the hourglass, falling unaccompanied toward the smooth bottom below me. Above, the rest of the silicate mob stubbornly refuses to follow. And here I am in my descent, waiting to collide with the glass floor, pleading with the rest of the sand to awaken and bury me.

The preceding paragraph consists of the kind of withered-on-the-pine prose that would force me to close a book after forty pages. Unsmiling, narcissistic, a type of self-mythologizing that assumes that the rest of the world wishes to hear the legend of me, Narwhal Slotterfield.

Sorry. Listen, I'm beat. Let's get this thing over with.

*

Narwhal is my name as well as, coincidentally, my spirit animal. My spirit animal is a sea bovine with a tooth sticking out of its upper lip. The first sailors who saw me mistook me for an elephant seal which had eaten a unicorn.

I am approximately thirty-three years old, with a receding hairline. My skin is a touch on the swarthy side. I'm dark enough that I can get a great tan, but light enough that I can still sunburn. I self-identify as a white male, although it's entirely possible my DNA contains more than a smattering of material from African, African American, American Indian, Arab, India Indian, Italian, Jewish, Latino, or any of the other swarthy races. I'm adopted, so it's hard to say what I am.

Were it not for my receding hairline, I might be handsome. My features are somewhere between chiseled and undefined. Depending on the perspective, my nose is long and flat and broad, or pointy and small and round. It's a Roman nose, via Pinocchio, which clearly points to at least one Italian in the family tree.

I'm roughly six feet eight inches tall. The weather up here is fine, I can assure you, although I would appreciate it if you could please make your doorways taller, your beds longer, your automobiles more commodious.

A basketball official by profession, I've worked all levels: high school, elementary, toddler, rec club, celebrity fundraiser, the occasional college game. A *referee.* In the common parlance, a *ref.* Vulgarly known as a *zebra.* Extreme vulgarity: *fucking cocksucker.*

Jog the court, whistle, halt proceedings, somebody slid a pivot foot, spin arms in the paddleboat dance. I called games, I won games, I lost games.

And me, six foot eight. By the time I was a sophomore in high school, I could throw it down easy. I should have been a player, not a zebra. But I wasn't a team guy. Never went out for a basketball squad, not in elementary, junior high, or high school. I'm an adjudicator, not a player.

My career has consisted of seventh grade boys glaring at me for accusing them of double dribbles; girls in ponytails telling me to fuck my own face; and parents, so many parents, simply loathing me. One must ignore the sneers and the comments, the hip-checks.

Once, in a high school playoff game, I granted a three-pointer even though a toe was clearly on the line. At halftime, as I walked toward the custodial closet that served as the officials' dressing room, the disadvantaged coach grabbed my shirt collar and threatened to slice off my manhood with a butcher knife. The choice of knife would seem suspect; I think you'd want something more nimble, like a switch-blade. There's no accounting for what a person will say when they feel threatened. As for me, I said nothing. Let the game continue. The underdog pulled off a miracle.

I never blew my whistle for a technical, ever. I hoped this leniency would endear me to them, those monsters. It didn't, ever. Instead, my leniency invited the whole glittering rainbow of human cruelty. Entire gymnasia, home crowd and visitor, would chant my name in derision. Led, of course, by the cheerleaders, who made up a song just for me. "He's blind, he's dumb, he don't know the rules. Slotterfield! Slotterfield! He sucks it hard!"

In its limited poetic capacity, the cheer united the opposing forces of Us and Them against Me. Hatred binds. Which explains why I was never investigated, reprimanded, or otherwise cautioned by any governing body in any of the leagues that wrote my checks. Basketball is entertainment and my games were entertaining. The people in charge knew what I was up to and, by refusing to discipline me, endorsed it.

My specialty was Avoiding Blow-outs. My other specialty was Giving Hope to the Underdog. My favorite specialty was Creating Chaos. If things are getting dull, call a foul on the short kid. It doesn't matter if he's not within a dozen feet of another human. He's short, therefore someone will be indignant, thereby dramatically upping the emotional quality of the contest. Athletics thrive on emotion.

When I worked a game, everyone in the gym had a chance to win and everyone had a chance to hate. It's difficult, maintaining that balance, keeping an eye out for the little guy while simultaneously taking advantage of him.

Being as tall as I am, I'm never the little guy.

After a typical game, I would exit the gym without changing out of my shopping-mall-shoe-salesmen outfit, without speaking to a single person, and then drive to my apartment and drink filth and listen to the neighbors choking their children. There, reclining on my recliner, staring at my vertically unheld cathode-ray television, I would enjoy a very specific fantasy.

I'm a passenger on a lifeboat. It's been several days since we watched the mast and the cargo and the captain go under. This is after the whirlpool, but before the sharks. Me and the parents and the players and the coaches and the cheerleaders and my child-choking neighbors, all floating together in a longboat, staring at one another as if we were all cartoon pork chops. A tropical sun bears down from a cloudless sky. The rations are gone. The only option is to draw lots. Last lots. I win. I eat the pork chops.

At this juncture, if you were my shrink and if I were telling you this, I suspect you would jot something in your notepad. I suspect you'd write, "This man is a creep."

I can't argue with you, Doctor. I am not inherently likeable. I acknowledge this freely. I *am* honest, though. For instance—and here's a thing few people, swarthy or otherwise, would ever admit—I once called a man by a very bad name.

I was six years old, on the city bus, sitting between my latest set of adoptive parents. It was the summer between kindergarten and first grade. I'd gone three days without a tantrum so Mom and Dad Slotterfield rewarded me with a trip downtown for ice cream.

We lived in an outskirt of Denver otherwise known as Lakewood, and it was quite the treat to ride the bus toward the skyscrapers, stopping every three blocks to exchange the normal-looking people of our outskirt for the non-normal people of the city. This was the late 70's. Punk rock had reached Denver. Denim jackets and wild haircuts and the whole bit. Mom and Dad Slotterfield, who had acquired me from the adoption agency only weeks before, complained about the punks, for their posture, mostly. I liked the punks well enough, but more intriguing to me were the black folk. I'd seen very few of their kind, and mostly on TV, the miniseries *Roots* being my primary exposure to people of pigmentation. I loved *Roots*. It taught me to hate slavery.

I was wearing cut-offs. My T-shirt was silkscreened with a cartoon of an eyeball covered with bird poop. Above the picture, in sparkly letters: *It pays to look out before you look up.*

The bus stopped. A citizen of Lakewood disembarked and a black man, a citizen of the used-car-lot-dominated area between Lakewood and Denver, embarked and sat in the seat behind us. He was a normal looking person, more normal than the punk rockers, that's for certain.

Six blocks later, the black man pulled the cord, but the bus didn't stop. He shouted to the driver, "Stop, please!" Then, in a voice that I distinctly recall as being good-humored, he added, "Why don't anybody ever listen to me?"

I turned around and said to him, "Because you're a nigger."

I thought we were sharing a joke. He was a descendant of slaves. I was somewhat swarthy. I loved him and I wanted to impress him. So I called him a nigger. I know I'm stretching plausibility, but that is precisely how it happened. There's a reason why I rarely tell this story. I'm only telling it now because I want you to understand that I'm honest.

The man did not laugh at my comment. He sighed and stared blankly ahead. I'm happy to report that my new parents were shocked. They hid me under the seat.

The driver made an unscheduled stop and allowed the man to disembark. Seven stops later, Mom and Dad Slotterfield and I arrived downtown and I ate my ice cream. I ordered strawberry. I'd never been a fan of that particular flavor, but even as a six-year-old I felt vanilla, my favorite, would paint me as a racist. Chocolate, my second favorite, would have seemed like kowtowing.

Approximately one score and seven years after the racial slur incident, I was a grown-up, waiting at a bus stop on Twelfth Street, just a few blocks south of downtown. The bus pulled up. The door swung open. A woman exited.

It's considered gauche to approach a bus before all the passengers have exited. I once saw a business man scream bloody murder and claw at the eyes of a homeless man for failing to respect this rule. A situation, I must add, that would have been mitigated by the presence of a professionally trained, sanctioned Public De-escalation Official. If such things existed, I would apply for that job.

In this particular instance, I was the guilty party. Let it be known that I sometimes lose track of my fellow humans. I assume this happens to everyone. In this particular instance, I had been considering the one-legged seagull I'd espied from my apartment window earlier that morning. Seagulls are not entirely unheard of in Denver. I assume they pass thru on their annual migration and some of them choose to stay, presumably for the convenient skiing.

This bird was pecking around in the middle of the street in front of my building. I had previously been fooled by birds into thinking they only had one leg. Flamingos, of course, but also robins and sparrows and various raptors. But just when I think I'm looking at a one-legged bird, the other leg folds down and I say, "Ah!"

This seagull was verifiably one-legged. It had outstanding balance on its good leg. The other leg was a stump, which he wiggled around incessantly, as if to say, "I only have one leg!" He was picking at something, presumably a bread crust left by one of the children whom I'd seen earlier that day lingering outside the Waldorf school across the street.

I cheered silently for this one-legged, geographically-misplaced bird. Give me the choice and I'd gladly lose a leg to grow some wings.

Here, a crow swung out of the sky in a pendulous, descending arc, cackling and just missing the one-legged bird, who avoided the collision by taking a graceful hop several inches to the left. Another crow appeared and stole the bread crust. The victimized gull took flight, beating its wings until it alighted on the peak of the Seventh-Day Adventist Church adjacent to the Waldorf school.

Say what you will about corvids, they do work well together.

Hours later, I was seeking and failing to find any meaningful symbolism in this image as I attempted to board the Number Ten bus on Twelfth and Pennsylvania. It was in this state that I neglected to allow an exiting woman to descend the steps before I began my ascent. We collided.

It was raining at the time—I should have mentioned this earlier—and I was carrying an umbrella. Sensing that she was about to berate me for my breech of bus etiquette, I handed my umbrella to the woman, for she had none. Another fact I've failed to mention: she was of above-average beauty. Arching eyebrows, shapely knees, the whole twenty-seven feet. I'm not immune to the aesthetic pleasures.

When I placed my umbrella in her hand, the woman's face metaphorically metamorphosized from a caterpillar to a butterfly. She called me a gentleman. I nodded deftly. We went our ways.

Two weeks later, I was sprinting toward that very same bus stop, trying to catch the Number Ten. I did not sprint fast enough; I was still half a block away when the bus pulled up, expelled a passenger, and drove off. The expelled passenger strolled away from the stop, directly toward me. Due to my career in athletics, I was in good shape and was therefore not breathing heavily, but I was unhappy with the fact that the bus was running on time.

The woman's wide-mouthed smile fitted the day but not my mood. I did not recognize her immediately, as she was wearing slacks rather than the knee-length skirt of days gone by. She shouted a robust "Hey-o!"

Neither of us was carrying an umbrella at the time. Nor was it raining.

After reminding me that she was the soul to whom I'd loaned my umbrella, the woman insisted that she return it to me at my earliest convenience. I divulged my phone number and, six months later, after a courtship of sorts, we were eating in a diner in Holliday, Colorado when time came to a complete stop.

I'm the only moving thing in the universe. To the best of my knowledge, that is. The universe is a vast, unknowable thing, as surely my circumstance will illustrate.

Foreshadow-wise, that's all you get. Details will follow once I've adequately set the scene. The tale is mine and I'll pace it as I see fit.

Last week, my gal—first name Veronica, last name Vasquez—and I took a road trip to St. Louis, the city of her youth. Veronica's aunt had died and we drove my car to the Show Me City to acknowledge the passing. As we crossed the state line into Missouri, Veronica declaimed that St. Louis was the home of vast, unseeable cracks from whence all the world's madness emerged. After traversing the city multiple times, from hotel to church to cemetery to Veronica's dead aunt's favorite diner for an affordable brunch, I can confirm only that if said cracks do exist, they are indeed unseeable.

Yesterday, after the shovels had patted the earth, and after we'd hugged all the appropriate parties, Veronica and I began our perilous trek back to Denver. Veronica, being an adventurous cuss, insisted on taking the road less cobbled and so we forewent the quicksilver glories of Interstate 70 for the earthy delights of crumbling two-lane highways. From St. Louis, take Highway 61 north to Hannibal, then turn west onto Route 36 for a drunken crow's flight all the way to Denver, more or less.

I can confirm that, although these roads are slower and more likely to bring one's front bumper into close proximity to the slow-moving-vehicle sign dangling off the end of a manure spreader, the adjacent landscapes are far more cheery than are those of the Interstate, with its towering truck stop signs, homicidally-attired hitchhikers for whom one does not stop, and endless billboards, one of which declaimed the following handpainted entreaty: *I NEED A KIDNEY*, followed by a phone number that one can assume had only ever been dialed by wise-ass teenagers and recently-born-again Christians hoping to notch their first save.

In contrast, Route 36 took us past beautiful, dismal old towns, crumbling houses, one-eyed dogs, and children pushing each other on tire swings.

*

Thirty-three years ago, when it was originally purchased by the original owner, my sedan had been equipped with air conditioning. By the time I'd purchased it from its seventh owner, the chlorofluorocarbons had fled the system, leaving the air conditioner completely ineffectual. To compensate, Vero and I drove with the windows down, bottles of fluorescent pink energy drinks sweating between our respective thighs.

We survived the vast, unknowable emptiness of Kansas by listening to a George Jones cassette Veronica had lifted from a truck stop in Chillicothe, Missouri. Veronica told me that she'd once heard that George Jones was once at a urinal next to a man whom he suspected of sleeping with his wife, Tammy Wynette, and he, George, reached over and grabbed the man's penile organ, saying, "I just wanted to see what she was so excited about." Veronica could not recall how the incident was resolved.

I said, "I wouldn't guess he was a dick-grabber from listening to his music."

She said, "He's also known for drinking in excess."

"That would explain why all of his songs concern alcoholism."

This conversation occurred as we were approaching the western border of Kansas, also known as the eastern border of Colorado.

After "He Stopped Loving Her Today" made its seventh trip round, Veronica ejected the cassette and chucked it out the window, whereupon, by pure chance, it collided with a speed limit sign and exploded into a string of magnetic tape, like the guts of a small, two-dimensional animal. Cheers all around.

We twisted the radio dial. FM was altogether barren. AM yielded a solitary station, 1040 KORD out of a hamlet called Goodland. The robot DJ claimed that KORD—aka The Leopard (*rowr!*)—was the Home of the Best in Contemporary Country. With its endless variety of songs about nostalgia, American exceptionalism, and nostalgia for American exceptionalism, who were we to disagree?

The broadcast was marred by static, caused by the wall of thunderclouds peeping over the horizon. White clouds with pompadours. White, turning an ominous shade of frostbite grey. Edges limned with sunlight. Image-wise, it was sub-postcard, but better than a poke in the eye.

One of the things that had initially attracted me to Veronica was her insistence on maintaining an out-of-date beehive hairdo. She went so far as to procure her grooming services from an old folks' home two bus transfers from my apartment. *Our* apartment. She'd moved in shortly after we'd consummated our relationship in the back seat of this very car. At the conclusion of the aforementioned consummation, she had pressed the button on my umbrella and popped it open. The batwings expanded and the metal mechanisms prodded my manly parts.

I said to her then, "You're inviting bad luck."

She picked a strand of my hair out of her teeth and said, "I wish I was eating a hamburger."

Which returns us to the near-present. As we approached the western edge of Kansas with the bubbling-hot plains passing by the opened windows, Veronica echoed those words from our first night of pleasure: "I wish I was eating a hamburger."

I said, "I wish I was a one-legged seagull."

We continued on our serpent's tongue of a highway, no sign of hitchhikers, the clouds billowing upward. As we entered Colorado, we were welcomed by a sign that read, *Welcome to Colorful Colorado.* The sign itself was brown.

I said, "They put the word 'colorful' on a brown sign in a sea of dead grass."

Veronica replied, "Every single person who's ever passed that sign has made that exact comment, or thought it." She then said something about fifty shades of beige. It shouldn't have been funny, but I laughed, primarily because she said it with an Irish accent. She had a killer Irish accent, frequently peppered with terms like *shillelagh* and *craic*, and made more killer because Veronica Vasquez was not remotely Irish. I laughed secondarily because the quip combined a dig at brown signs, the celebration of Irish verdancy, and a reference to soft-core sado-masochistic shiterature. I'd repeat the quip, but I forget the exact wording, and you wouldn't find it funny anyway.

Back, now, in our home state, we sped along, craning our necks for a peek of a mountain peak. Any moment now, the Rockies would appear on the horizon, for we were in Colorado.

In a little miracle of our rotating planet, the sun sank into that tiny two-inch space below the gaining thunderclouds and above the horizon and attempted to blind me. I lowered the visor, which did not go low enough. Veronica volunteered to place her left hand between my eyes and our orb. Thus did we continue apace.

No mountain peaks. We passed a sign, black-and-white, that read, *Welcome to Holliday, Home of the Harvesters.* And then we were driving thru the town of Holliday itself. It's hard to describe sixteen buildings as a town; it was more of a compound.

Veronica spotted a restaurant and implored me to stop. Cookie's Palace Diner, it was called. The car rolled onto the dirt parking lot and I extinguished the engine. Veronica and I sat a moment and pulled our shirts by the sternum, fanning the sweat. It was September first, shortly after seven PM, and the heat remained ridiculous.

Inside the Palace, we sat across from one another at a table that could have fetched a hefty price in Denver's retro-modern secondary market had its previously white top not been stained yellow from fifty years of mustard drippings and cigarette stubs. In its current state, it would only be useful as a prop in a true-to-life film about the time Veronica and I ate at this diner.

The waitress was a little on the young and thin side, but she did call me "hon" and that made Veronica wink at me. I really did love Veronica.

I apologize for the verbosity. The details remain vivid and I'm reluctant to gloss them over, as I suspect they will play a significant role in the narrative that follows. Or, poetically speaking, the flame has been extinguished but the match head remains hot enough to raise a blister. I intend to linger over that pain.

We were less than three hours from home and I didn't have a game until the next evening. The game would be a community fundraiser at the YMCA in Aurora, for which I would be paid forty American dollars. Pickings were slim in the summer.

The point of the previous paragraph being, in spite of the blazing boredom of the countryside, Veronica and I enjoyed riding in a car together and, as a consequence, we weren't in a hurry to get back to Denver. Consequently, I splurged and ordered the onion rings.

"That'll take an extra five minutes, hon."

"That'll be fine, dear."

It took seven minutes, actually, but those extra two minutes were of little consequence. I was sitting across from my angelic Veronica. She had a Nefertiti way about her. Slender neck, confident jut of the chin, a mouth that simultaneously frowned and smirked. Her beehive fit her forehead perfectly. Much less ridiculous than that lampshade Queen Nefertiti had sported around the Nile.

The burgers were thick and juicy, not the frozen patties you see so often in country diners. Veronica's fries were thick and soggy, just like those you so often see in country diners. I let her eat freely of my onion rings, which were oniony and deep-friedy.

Halfway thru our meal, the door to the Palace opened up and an old-timer in jeans and an oversized T-shirt silkscreened with the classic phrase *Why you hatin' on me?* entered and settled at the counter.

Veronica leaned across our table and whispered to me, "Because you let your granddaughter dress you, that's why." Tee hee hee. That's what love is, making fun of old rural men.

The old-timer and the waitress were familiar with one another and so they quickly dispensed with the how-do-you-do business, then parried with whether or not the boys were gonna be worth a lick in football this year, and then sojourned into the potential for rain. They concluded that a hellfire storm was fast approaching.

According to Old Timer, a tornado watch had been announced on the radio. This inspired him to relate a story about one of his youthful cyclonic encounters. "I seen swine flying thru the air, just like in *The Wizard of Oz*."

Veronica whispered to me, "I hope this whole town gets picked up by a cyclone, us included. I'd give anything not to be in Kansas anymore." That one didn't even make sense, seeing as how we *weren't* in Kansas anymore. Tee hee hee. Everything's funny when you're in love.

Nature called. I excused myself and went to the bathroom, adding a bit of a bowleggedness to my stride in order to make a good impression on Old Timer.

To the urinal, no sign of George Jones. As I unzipped, a rogue onion ring slipped out of the folds of my lap and landed on the floor. It was a tiny onion ring, small enough to fit snugly around a woman's finger. As I made my water, I cast my eyes upon the ring, stuck to the floor, soaking up the splatter from my bladder, and I decided that the time was well-nigh for me to propose to my sweetheart.

The decision was not altogether spontaneous—I'd wanted to marry her ever since she'd first popped the umbrella—but the timing had always been hard to pin down. As I would soon discover, there's no time like the right-fucking-now.

I concluded my business and washed my hands and then bent forward to pinch the onion ring up from the floor. Much of the batter slipped off, but as I held the thing in my palm it still sufficiently resembled an onion ring to serve my purpose.

In a moment, I would propose in unconventional fashion to my gal in Cookie's Palace Diner, in a town called Holliday, under threat of tornados.

As I turned the doorknob, I heard a faint rumble of thunder. I tugged the door open. It moved reluctantly, as if the hinges were in need of lubricant.

I walked forward into the restaurant. The air felt thick. To the degree that I noticed this, I attributed it to a sharp increase in humidity that would presumably accompany the onset of a hellfire thunderstorm.

My darling Veronica was holding a French fry in mid-air, stock-still. I assumed she was playing a prank. The waitress, whose nametag really did read "Flo," was pouring coffee into Old Timer's cup. Flo, too, was stock still, as was Old Timer.

The room was as quiet as a dead branch.

I thought, "It's quite the send-up this crew is playing on me."

I did not know to what I could attribute the next thing I saw. The coffee, the stream of coffee that was coming from Flo's pot, was frozen in midstream above Old-Timer's cup. This tongue of coffee had cleared the coffee pot, but it hadn't reached the cup. As practical jokes go, these jokers had pulled off a ten out of ten.

I said, "Hey, now."

My voice made no proper sound.

I approached Flo and waved my hand in front of her face. Her eyes did not follow. Frustrated, I took hold of her wrist and forced the coffee pot down to rest flat on the counter top. As I did so, the tongue of coffee stretched out, the tip of it remaining in place, the back of it remaining attached to the lip of the pot. More frustrated and more confused, I slapped the tongue of coffee with my right hand. I did it with the quickness with which one would slap a hornet that had alighted on one's knee. *Slap* and pull the hand away before the hornet can sting. The coffee didn't splash. Rather, it sort of flattened against the countertop, with a handprint in it.

I wiped my hand against my pantleg, but there was no coffee to wipe off. And, while my hand was warm and my palm was red, the coffee hadn't burned me.

I turned my back to my compatriots and looked out the window. The whole of the world was trapped in amber. But there was no amber. So the world was just trapped. Birds in midflight. I'm looking at them now. The dust catching the sun.

For several moments, I stared dumbly, saturated by silence. An indeterminate length of time later, a chill-like sensation descended my spine, flowed down my legs, and vigorously bounced itself off the soles of my feet upward to lodge itself permanently in my brain. The eerie nature of the situation can scarcely be considered describable. Equal parts horror and fear. The very idea of my soon-to-be fiancée frozen behind me with a French fry poised to enter her mouth. Perhaps a cameraman was waiting to leap from a hidden closet and shout, "You've been pranked!" Or whatever they shout.

I spun around.

No camera. No lurkers. Just Veronica, precisely where I'd left her. One eyelid slightly lower than the other, her mouth hanging open in a most unattractive fashion. The way even the most beautiful actress in the world—Lauren Bacall, obviously—looks like an asshole when you pause the movie—*Key Largo*, probably.

I spun around again. The waitress and the old-timer were right where I'd left them.

There was *some*thing different, though. Floating in mid-air, three feet above the floor, was an onion ring, the very same ring I'd picked up off the bathroom floor. In my state of astonishment, I had allowed the ring to slip from my grip. It was hovering, completely still.

You want to imagine that it's rotating slowly like a dangling piece of a deep-fried mobile. But it remained there, unchanged. Reluctant to touch it with my hand, I removed my right shoe and, pressing the sole against the onion ring, lowered the propositional morsel of food to the gritty floor, as gravity would have dictated in the universe into which I had awoken that morning.

I do not know how long I've been here, how long things have been like this. The sun is stuck just above the horizon, the clocks are stuck at seven twenty-three. I'm reluctant to exit the Palace. I'm reluctant to touch my girlfriend.

I'm going to sit here until I get too tired to stay awake. Then I'm going to lie down on the floor and sleep until I wake up again. If things haven't gotten back to normal by then, I suppose I'll have to do something about it.

Do you know how imaginary characters, when suddenly transported to bizarre situations, pinch themselves to prove they aren't dreaming? Perhaps you're wondering why I haven't done that. It's because I know the difference between being awake and being asleep.

When I awoke upon the floor of Cookie's Palace Diner, nothing had changed, although I was certainly well rested. Let's assume I slept at least six hours.

The wall clock behind the counter still says seven twenty-three. Outside, the day is just as dusky as it was when I went to sleep.

Until I devise a better system, a day is the period of time between naps.

I lied. One thing changed while I slept. I awoke with an almighty need to empty my bladder. If you recall, the last thing I'd done before time came to a complete halt was to take a leak. Following the double-head-bonk-amnesia-cure theory of sitcom television, I hoped that, by repeating that final act, I could re-start time. Go to the bathroom, make a whiz, come out, and Flo will pour coffee into Old Timer's cup and Veronica will say yes to my proposal. Or maybe I'd wake up in a hospital bed with Veronica by my side, a mountain of teary Kleenexes on her lap.

Me (yawing): *How long was I out*?

Veronica (patting my forehead): *I haven't left your side in over a year. The tornado threw you thru the window. You landed in a cow pasture. Broke every bone in your body. They said you'd never make it.*

Me (re-assembling a sense of self): *So. The business with frozen time, it was all a dream.*

She (nodding as if to a confused child): *You've been asleep the whole time. Let's get married.*

I stood up from the floor—black and white checkered linoleum—and rubbed my spine. I can jog all thru a basketball game, but my back aches after sleeping on a linoleum floor.

To loosen up, I whirlie-gigged my arms like Cordon Pruitt, aka Mr. Funnercise, did on the Towner Show a few years back. As I whirlie-gigged, the air tugged my arm hairs as if it were sticky. Not sticky, clingy.

When I inhale, air draws in around the edges of my mouth reluctantly. I wouldn't say that breathing is difficult, it's just less easy than it used to be. Airy with a touch of wateriness.

Little known fact. My official birthday was yesterday. I'm thirty-three years old, approximately. Due to the murky nature of my parentage, the exact date of my birth is unknown, which is why I don't advertise it. I have this—uncertain birthdays—in common with Jesus, who also had some rough patches in his thirty-fourth year. I do not have a Christ complex.

But I do have some questions.

Am I the most powerful being in the universe?

Am I alive?

Am I bound to laws, moral or otherwise?

If I should, for instance, walk to California, and if I should arrive there, in Hollywood, would it be wrong for me to press my lips just one time against those of a beautiful actress?

Which beautiful actress?

Lauren Bacall is in her eighties. I assume she still lives in Hollywood and that she remains beautiful on the inside. I'm sure there are plenty of other women in Hollywood who retain their outer beauty. I'm sure they're more beautiful than anyone I've ever seen in person, even dear Veronica, with her perfect, uncluttered knees.

If I should disrobe a sleeping beauty actress and engage in activities. What if I did that? Would I be a necrophiliac? A molester? A pseudomannikenizer?

Fortunately for all parties, I have no desire to find out.

I will, however, march myself into Cookie's Palace Diner's

bathroom and I will close the door. I will pee. I will walk out of the bathroom and everything will be normal again.

I passed the Veronica statue, droopy eyelid, French fry approaching her gaping mouth. I dodged the onion ring on the floor. With silent footsteps, I crossed to the bathroom, whose door was still open.

Into the john. Soapy bubbles remained in the sink as if I'd washed my hands just a moment ago. The water in the toilet was still yellow; apparently, I'd neglected to flush.

If you wish to avoid learning how urine exits a human body in a world where time has stopped, please skip the next seven paragraphs.

As the urine exited my body, it froze. The urine, that is. I should stop saying "froze." It makes it seem like things are cold. They are not. What they are doing is stopping. Everything I've thus far encountered maintains its temperature, yet another circumstance that fails to compute.

The pee began to pile up like a glob of space gelatin. Horrified, but unable to stop the process, I stepped backward, trailing globs of mellow yellow Jello. I backed all the way across the bathroom before my bladder was empty. If it hadn't been human waste, the suspended rope of daisy-colored liquid would have been downright enchanting. But it was human waste and I would not allow it to sully the still-life diner that housed my almost-fiancée.

I exited the bathroom and, begging Flo's pardon, I leaned over the counter and found an empty water pitcher. I returned to the bathroom and used the pitcher to scoop up my pee.

I held the pitcher perpendicular to the floor. I tipped it upside down. The semi-solid glob remained stuck at the bottom of the pitcher. I brought the pitcher to the bathroom and left it on the back of the toilet.

Two things.

1) Time did not resume upon my usage of the bathroom; the double-head-bonk theory is kaput.

2) I do not look forward to taking my first shit.

Reader, I don't wish to challenge your sense of decorum, but there are things I need to consider if I'm to remain trapped here for much longer. To survive I must first conquer the mundane. Eat, breathe, drink, piss, poo. Try not to get injured. Maintain proper dental hygiene. Stay ahead of the depression.

You may start reading again.

It's today, still. I haven't left the Palace. I'm thirsty and hungry, but I'm wary of what'll happen if I eat or drink any of the various time-stopped substances that I have at my disposal. Flo's coffee is still in her coffee pot, ready for me to . . . to do what? Grab it with my fingers and guide it to my mouth like a half-congealed gummy bear?

Air in my lungs behaves like air, but the moment I exhale, it comes to a lazy halt. As I wander the Palace, I pass thru these clouds of my exhalation and I smell my worsening breath. Eventually, my lungs will convert all the air to carbon dioxide and I will be forced outside this place. There's no sound outside my body. When I shout, the noise leaves my mouth and then dies. What I do hear is my head. Let me explain.

As I understand it, sound is like a string of dominoes. In a properly calibrated world, you slap a table, the table vibrates, the vibrations whack the air, the molecules of air whack each other and pass the momentum of these vibrations into your eardrum, then to some nerves, to your brain, *slap!*

The dominoes are broken. With the exception of me, the world no longer resonates. My sounds travel within my body. I can hear my heart and the blood it pushes. My breath, I can hear. When I speak, it's the vibrations of my skull that I hear, not the reverberations of the sound off the walls of the Palace.

Imagine you're wearing earplugs. Maybe you're underwater. That's better. You're in the Great Salt Lake in the midst of a dead-man's float. It's summer and the sun is shooting carcinogens into your bare back. You've been underwater so long your adopted parents are getting nervous. But you can't hear them calling for you because your ears are under water. When you move your neck, you hear clicking sounds as the tendons tug and the vertebrae twist over the discs. That's what I hear here—I hear me.

Air moves reluctantly. If I move slowly, the sensation is not too off-putting. But if I, for instance, throw a phantom punch, the air resists like a gentle wind. If I inhale, a column of air slides around the edge of my mouth freely, but the core in the center where it isn't touching my skin behaves thickly, almost like cotton candy. It's not like choking, it's like drinking air. When I blink, the air tugs on my eyelashes. There's a slight pressure on my eyes. I'm in outer space. I'm under water. I'm getting used to it.

My permaparents, Mr. and Mrs. Slotterfield, are professors at the University of Denver. They teach Nineteenth Century French Ethics and Astrogeology, respectively. Dad's hero is Auguste Comte, a long-dead semi-utopian French nutcase. Mom spectrally analyzes tiny dots that appear on pictures taken by the Hubble telescope. The bumper sticker on Dad's Volvo reads *Think Positivism*. Mom's Volvo's bumper sticker reads *If you floated Saturn in a bathtub, would it LEAVE A RING?*

We ate our meals as a family. Meals were a time for reading, not conversation. Mom and Dad owned custom-built book holders upon which they could prop their latest library finds as they silently forked food into their gobholes. For my seventh birthday, they presented me with my very own book holder, as well as a subscription to *Popular Science*, a magazine filled with actual photos of the future. Thenceforth, I became a member of the literate class, happily spilling spaghetti sauce on cut-away drawings of hovercrafts.

Until I moved out of the house, Ma and Pa kept me subscribed to gizmo-and-future magazines: *Popular Science, Mechanics Illustrated*, and good ol' *Omni*. It was their way of encouraging me to learn about the mysteries of the world. In between articles about the plausibility of growing watermelons on the moon, there would be longer pieces about subatomic particles and multi-verses, all of which were accompanied by thrilling illustrations of planetary orbs and fusion explosions. I enjoyed this stuff, although I understood virtually none of it.

Via these mealy magazines, I learned stuff: gravity and inertia are the same thing; everything we experience/see/are/know is a hologram on the outer edge of the universe; given the size of the universe, alien life is practically a given; and black holes are totally cool.

All of which is to say I know enough about the workings of the cosmos to come to half-baked conclusions about things I don't really understand. What I don't know is how to come to conclusions about a universe that doesn't work.

I retain my inertia, momentum, gravity, but nothing else does. The laws of physics have broken down for all non-me objects. But it's not that simple. Sound is dead, but light still works. The restaurant is lit by florescent tubes. There's a switch next to the door. I flipped it on and off and nothing happened; the lights kept shining. I stood on a chair and wiggled a bulb out of the fixture. It flickered off. I twisted it back in its sockets and it stayed off. I can *ex*tinguish light but I can't tinguish it.

I require hydration. I climb over the counter, careful to avoid Flo and Old Timer. Behind the counter, below and left of the cash register, is a box of bendy straws, the white kind with blue stripes running down their sides. I extract one and attempt to breathe thru it. The air moves, but not enthusiastically.

Also behind the counter, tucked into a shelf next to Flo's purse, is a plastic cup filled with ice and cola, misty with dew. Her private stash. I squat before the cup. I hold it. The condensation on the sides is wet. Honest to gosh, it's wet.

I lift the cup and stand in the dusk light streaming thru the window. Eight minutes ago, those photons had been happily bubbling away on the surface of the sun. After traveling ninety-three million miles across the orbit of two planets, dodging various bits of space dust, slipping between the subatomic particles that compose the atoms that compose the molecules of Earth's atmosphere, and thru the supercooled silicon of the Palace's bay window, those photons pass the lenses of my eyes and collide with my retinas and come to an undignified death in my brain.

Flo's cup is one-third empty. I tip it sideways. The liquid remains inside, like a plexi prop from a movie. I put the cup on the counter and take a half step backward. There's a handprint, my handprint, where I'd held the cup. There's no fizz above the cup, none of those jumping droplets that tickle your nose when you sip a soda. I squat again and look under the counter. Sure as Shinola, the fizzies are hovering right above where the cup had been. I poke my finger into the fizzies and tiny droplets of soda liquefy against my skin.

I wrap my lips around the straw and suck. Pulling on the straw is like sucking freshly poured cement. I strain my cheeks. The cola will not budge.

I take the spoon that was sitting next to Old Timer's empty coffee cup and press it into the cola. It's like toffee. I scoop up a morsel and bring it to my mouth. When I wrap my lips around the spoon, the soda comes alive. It flows into my mouth and down to my tummy. Yummy, cool, fizzy cola. I finish the pop, one spoonful at a time. The ice cubes melt on my tongue. I let the final sliver of ice slide off my tongue, out of my mouth. I'd hoped it would drop to the floor and melt. Instead, it rests in mid-air and doesn't.

Lesson: Air is like a liquid. Liquids are like jelly. Except, when something's in my mouth, it resumes its normal behavior. Why? You tell me. When I remove something from my mouth, the something stops moving. What if I wrap my lips around Veronica's ear? Will it tickle her? I'm not ready for that.

I take liberty and reach into the pocket of Flo's salmon-colored waitress outfit to extract her wallet. A couple of twenties, a tiny sewing kit, and a well-dated wallet-sized senior photo of Flo leaning her head seductively against the front door of a lovingly restored vintage pickup truck. Plus a driver's license that establishes that Flo's real name is not Flo. Flo is Sandy Boudreaux. The nametag's a ruse.

I go to the kitchen. There's a cook back there. A skinny man with a baggy white t-shirt and large, loose jeans. He's holding a spatula. His tongue is in the corner of his cheek. I shall call him Cookie McHamburger.

"How did you get so skinny, Cookie? You're a cook, fer chrissakes."

Nada.

"You had some serious acne as a lad, eh? Not a lot of girlfriends for a kid with acne."

Nothing.

"Probably mid-twenties, you are."

That tongue is stuck right there in his cheek and it ain't going anywhere.

"Asshole."

I hate the sound of my voice as it travels within my muffled head.

*

There are three burgers on the broiler, buns toasting alongside. I'm not sure who they were intended for. Maybe they were the shift burgers for Sandy and Cookie, and one for Old-Timer.

I eat the top half of one of the hamburger buns. It mingles well with the cola in my gut. I will not eat anything else today. I need to see what happens in my belly. Don't overdo it until you know the consequences.

I'm seated across from Veronica. I've just awoken from a nap and my stomach feels fine, although I'm distractingly hungry. I don't know how long I slept. No dreams. If I ever do start dreaming, I will not relate them here. I don't want you to come to conclusions.

My body tells me it's time to empty my bowels, which means it's time for me to go outside. This diner is my sanctuary. I will not fill its toilets with shit that I cannot flush.

Before I went outside, I pressed my index finger against Vero's lips. They were still moist. I licked my finger afterwards. It tasted like hamburger.

I said, "Don't go anywhere."

I went to the kitchen, hoping for a back exit, which I found next to the ice machine. The door was propped open, presumably to let the kitchen heat out.

I exited Cookie's Palace Diner via this servants' entrance and stood upon the greasy dirt of the back alley. It wasn't really an alley, just as Holliday isn't really a town. It was a dirt lot that butted against the backyard of a trailer house.

A flock of blackbirds had gathered to eat some moldy buns that someone had tossed out. A few feet away, an orange tabby was poised slinkily, ready to pounce upon the birds.

This was my first time outside since the world went on strike. There's much to see and describe. I will save it for later. For now, let's focus on my purpose. I found a private spot behind an overstuffed trash barrel and pulled down my jeans and squatted.

I will not describe the activity itself, other than to say that while I was in the midst of the movement, I tilted my head backward to look to the sky. Up, up and straight above me was a white winged creature, so far away I could not make out its features. But I knew what it was: my one-legged seagull. Oh, tender solace of the lame bird who glides the wind.

I can see and I can think. Food goes in, waste goes out. I can survive this.

I returned to the Palace and ate a hamburger. I put the burger on one of the toasted buns and ate it. The food was warm. Once it was in my mouth, it chewed easy. I needed water. I turned on the faucets and nothing came out, of course. There is a glass-doored fridge behind the counter, filled with cans of pop and bottled water. I chose water. I had to cut a plastic bottle open with a steak knife. The knife worked against the plastic. I'm not going to explain every sensation. The knife worked. I peeled away the plastic and the water hung, glob-like, in front of my face. I leaned forward and nibbled. It was like eating a warm, water-flavored ice-cream cone that melted the instant it entered my mouth. It sated my thirst. Sated. I'm writing for posterity.

Fries were boiling in the fryer. I brought my hand to the oil. The air above was warm. The oil itself was hot, hot, hot. I know this because I touched it and thereby blistered the tip of my right index finger.

From the dinnertime magazines of my youth, I know that there's a thing called hard sci-fi. In hard sci-fi, all the crap that happens (wormholes, gravity inside spaceships, interspecies procreation) needs to seem plausible, if not possible. Otherwise, nerds will complain.

Nerds, could you please complain to someone on my behalf?

I'm wearing pants, socks, shoes, underwear, and a collared shirt. Because they aren't me, the clothes don't like to move. It makes ambulation a little less comfortable. If this goes on long enough, I expect I will discard them altogether. For now, I wish to remain decent. I do not want to be caught in my skin should the world suddenly reawake.

I do wish to *change* my clothes. The world is still warm and I still sweat. My garments don't absorb the sweat and it's been accumulating as a scum on top of my skin and I feel icky. And I have a moral aversion to wearing the same pair of underwear for too long. Fortunately, in the back seat of my car, there's a suitcase which contains two pairs of undies, each of which only has one day of use.

Adjacent to the front door of this diner is a cork bulletin board. Upon it are several notices suspended by red thumbtacks.

"Free" kittens: Tigers, blacks, calicos.

Babysitting: 12 years old, experience. $6/hour.

For sale: Winchester 30-30. Good shape. $175.

Yard work help needed. Must speak good English.

Not-quite-free pets, youthful capitalists, affordable guns, and clumsily coded racial insensitivity. The bedrock of any great country.

For the record, Veronica's parents don't speak good English. Veronica speaks good English and *bueno* Spanish.

I'm not under the illusion that dating a chica Mexicana absolves me from my youthful misstep with the black man on the bus. I'm not convinced it was a misstep, exactly. It was just a stupid thing I did, for which I feel guilty. I'm sure he's more over it than me. That one incident, at least.

I turned the knob and pulled the door open to the world. Curse this silence, a hinge should squeak, wind should whisper, birds should chirp. I didn't mind the silence when I was in the back alley, taking my crap. Noise tends to distract me from peristaltic activity. But when you open a front door, silence doesn't cut it. Front doors should welcome you to the general hum of the outside world.

I looked back at Veronica, sitting there looking. Let's be frank, with her half-closed eye and that French fry approaching her gaping mouth, she looked like an idiot.

Leaving the door ajar, I approached my almost-fiancée. Very carefully, as careful as a surgeon, I put my finger against her right eyelid, the half-closed one, and pushed it shut. I did the same with her left eyelid. Her eyes aren't entirely closed—there's still a little white peeking out—but it's an improvement.

I put a finger under her chin and gently lifted her lower jaw. Rather than shut her mouth, the action caused her head to tilt backward. I put one hand on her forehead, and the other hand under her chin and tried again. This closed her mouth, but now her cheeks had sagged into a hound dog frown. I tried to massage her face into a shape that recalled true Veronical beauty. Had I succeeded, the act would have been tender. Instead, I managed only to make her resemble the slackened face of her aunt's corpse in the open coffin in St. Louis. I abandoned the project before I made her look any more ridiculous. A face just ain't a face unless everything's working together underneath it. No third parties allowed.

I did lean forward and kiss her. Her lips were warm, but they didn't kiss me back.

I'm standing on the artificial turf on the step in front of Cookie's Palace Diner, looking out at the dirt parking lot. My car is parked semi-askew. Remember when Veronica and I sat in that car, just a few moments ago, sweating?

Old Timer's pickup is backed into its spot, professionally. One intuits that Old Timer is an expert driver of all sorts of conveyances. One suspects that he drives down the highway in reverse just because he can.

Two other cars: A yellow, mid-seventies Mustang II, from the misguided fuel-efficient Pinto era, and a mid-eighties blue Econoline love-van with tinted teardrop window ports, from the misguided fuel-inefficient era. Remember when there were eras?

I'd wager my watch that the Mustang belongs to Flo and the van belongs to Cookie.

Half a mile away on Route 36, a semi is approaching from the west. Kenworth, Peterbilt, whatever. My primary exposure to eighteen-wheelers came at a young age via the truck race scene at the beginning of *Smokey and the Bandit II*, a film otherwise notable only for the fact that when we first encounter the Bandit he has traded away his Trans Am for a large quantity of beer.

The semi's headlights aren't on. They really should be, seeing as dusk is approaching. Several miles beyond the semi, the hellfire storm, clouds abubble in black cauldrony wrath withheld, prepares to unleash its power, just as soon as someone figures out how to re-start the world's clock.

To the west and beneath the storm, the sun glows orange. It hurts to look at it, so I look away. Here in Holliday, on the other side of Route 36, is a gas station that appears to have closed down sometime between the manufacture of Sandy's Mustang and Cookie's Econoline. Also in the Holliday compound: houses, a church, nonfunctional cars, lawns, American flags hanging stiff like the one Neil Armstrong planted on the moon. An elm tree, tiny branches bent by the weight of small birds.

And far above, my one-legged seagull floats like a white scratch in the sky.

I face west and allow the sun to glow upon me. I turn around and watch my shadow slide over the dirt. The shadow and I wave at each other. He is much taller than I am. Shadows cast by the low sun. Shadowcast is a good name for a late-night radio show. My shadow offers a thumbs-up in agreement.

Although the leaves on the trees remain green, we're on the cusp of autumn, this cuspiness being reinforced by the perpetual sunset, trapped twixt today and tonight, twixt what has happened and what may never happen.

As time continues to not move, I expect this perpetual sunset will lend a sense of melancholy to the situation. For now, I am more taken by the world itself, so open and empty.

It's a bit much to absorb. I cross the lot to my car and extract my suitcase from the back seat. I extract Veronica's suitcase as well. I'm a light packer, bare minimum. Veronica is even barer and more minimal. Another reason why I love her. Very little baggage, emotional or otherwise.

I imagine that you're rolling your eyes at my references to my darling. If so, it's because I haven't adequately described her. She's not just an umbrella. Nor is she just a beehived fountain of unfunny wisecracks. She's a foundation of truth. She digs me and all my officiantatious nonsense. She's the one thing in the world that wouldn't benefit from my adjudication. I would not change a thing about her. In sum, she is the reason I have thus far refrained from swallowing my own tongue.

I re-entered the Palace and emptied my suitcase onto one of the unoccupied tables. Six socks in a total of four different colors, two green button-up shirts as well as the short-sleeved white dress shirt I'd worn at the funeral. Two pair of pants. A toothbrush, an empty can of antiperspirant, and a disposable razor. I will at some point need to decide whether to let my beard grow or have a go at shaving.

Also in the suitcase, a copy of the latest *Mad Magazine* (#501, the *Hard Times Survival Issue*), which I had thrice read in its entirety. And my pajamas, prison-striped, a gift from Veronica. She said they made me look like a horizontal referee. And two pairs of slightly-used paisley boxer shorts.

I went to the men's room and changed my undies and put on my funeral clothes. White shirt, black pants, and, for dignity, the clip-on tie. Footwear: officially-sanctioned black referee sneakers, appropriate for any occasion.

Dinnertime. I tossed a handful of Cookie's tomatoes and lettuce and croutons into the air, where they paused like a work of psychedelic art. I nipped at them. For desert, half of a world-famous pecan pie. Veronica would have said, "It's famous for being completely average."

I can't suck the Palace's teat for much longer. Water, water everywhere and no more burgers to eat. Unless I bust apart a frozen patty and let the raw chunks thaw in my mouth. No need for that. I have options. It's seven twenty-three PM. There's food on a stove somewhere. *Good Housekeeping* recipes abound.

Another day in Boringsville. Hi, Vero. Howdy, Old Timer. Mornin', Flo. Heehaw, Cookie. Let's get to know each other. I lifted Old Timer's wallet and learned his name was, seriously, Axel Buster. Further pawing turned up a half-smoked joint in Axel's shirt-pocket. I set it aside for later, after I've learned to start a fire.

Sandy had been hunched over when she'd started pouring the coffee. The pose looked horribly uncomfortable. I repositioned her so she wasn't hunched over so much. Grab shoulders, tug. Torso-and-limb manipulation was much more effective than trying to mold Vero's face. It was not rigor mortis, more like a life-sized action figure.

As a reward for granting Sandy some posture relief, I peeked under her skirt. I *peeked.* She had on white underwear. If I were a superhero, I'd be called The Voyeur. I see all, I know all.

Moving on, let's crack open Veronica's suitcase. She and I are practically married after all. Gaze, if you will, upon the sleepy onion ring stuck to the floor there, a tribute to our one true love. Cleo and Patra. Veronica and me. Consummated but never legitimated.

I extracted panties and sniffed, no scent. I'm not normally a panty sniffer. All rules don't apply. There was a box of tampons in the suitcase. We hadn't engaged in sexual activities on this trip. I had assumed it was because she was in mourning.

I opened every zipper in her suitcase. It had been ordered from an online specialty shop. Pockets for everything, including one specifically for a diary.

Which explains why I'm drunk.

The diary begins some months ago, shortly after Veronica had returned my umbrella. I will not quote directly, as I do not wish to compromise her privacy.

The first page of the diary is headlined:

An Accounting of My Time with The Ref

The Ref is me, Narwhal W. Slotterfield.

The diary commences with a recounting of the bus stop-and-umbrella incident. She describes me as "a bit of a goof," and remains respectfully demure on the accounting of our lovemaking.

Receiving great attention was our trip to a Greek diner on Colfax for her recent birthday. She wrote, and I quote directly, "Never trust a Greek named Pete. All Greeks are named Pete. The Ref picked up the bill. He loves gyros, I love souvlaki. I love him enough." My heart leaps. We have never audibly pronounced that word "love" to one another. "Enough" is enough for me.

She seems obsessed with my obsessions, which I didn't know I had. The typical business about the toothbrush, window shades, placement of forks in the dishwasher, style of lacing one's shoes, disposal of used fingernail trimmings. Atypically, she doesn't seem particularly annoyed with these obsessions. My "quirks," she calls them, more as observation than as judgment. Could a guy be any luckier? I'm imperfect, she's perfect. She tolerates me, I worship her.

Even her handwriting delights me. It's barely legible. Half cursive, half print. She doesn't put smiley faces on her *i*'s, but she does put umlauts on her *u*'s. Correct transcription of the previous extract:

> *Never trüst a Greek named Pete. All Greeks are named Pete. The Ref picked üp the bill. He loves gyros, I love soüvlaki. I love him enoügh.*

Two pages later, the terror:

> *Sorry I haven't written. The Blad called. Hadn't heard from him since spring of 2006, after the thing. He invited me for coffee. My schedüle was open. I figüred it'd be entertaining, if nothing else. I mean, he meant a lot to me for those three weeks.*

I know exactly who The Blad is. His name is Bradley Ludermeyer. I've only met him once, at a dinner party very early in my relationship with Veronica. I immediately sussed that he was an ass. He had a Denver

Broncos lapel pin on his fake Armani suit and he refused to take up the hostess's offer of a bong hit on the grounds that his employer (the esteemed and rapidly deteriorating Pat Bowlen) randomly subjects his employees to piss tests. What a dick. The Blad, not Bowlen.

I'm not a major pot-user myself, as evidenced by the fact that I still haven't tried to smoke that half-a-joint I stole from Axel Buster. But I would never, ever be so disrespectful as to decline a bong hit from someone gracious enough to invite me to a dinner party.

Due to his self-confident dickhead voice, which intruded upon conversations he wasn't even involved in, I learned that The Blad works at a place called Dove Valley, the home of the Denver Broncos. One of his duties there is to enforce the appearance clause in the cheerleaders' contracts. As he explained to one drunk and/or stoned party guest after another, said clause requires all cheerleaders to weigh less than a peanut, wear makeup at all times, never say anything more controversial than, "Go Broncos!" and work seventy hours a week while getting paid a sub-minimum wage.

He liked to conclude the descriptions of his duties with, "I'm paid to tell beautiful women how to be even more beautiful. It's the greatest job in the great green world!"

Why in the name of all things decent and good would a turd like Bradley Ludermeyer appeal to the personified perfection of Veronica Vasquez? Read on, but don't expect answers.

Coffee türned into a walk downtown, then dinner. The Ref was working a kiddie toürnament, so I had a few hoürs. It was safe, walking with The Blad down Sixteenth Street. Ünlike The Ref, The Blad doesn't get spooked by teenagers.

Am I starting to detect judgmentalism, Veronica?

The Blad apologized for how things ended. I rewarded him with a non-committal wink. He said he'd matüred a lot since the DÜI.

We ended üp at his place downtown, rode the elevator to his floor. What's a girl to do? The Ref hasn't been very fün lately. Here are some things he's complained aboüt in the last few days: parents, coaches, players, a düsty gym floor, television,

> *women's hairstyles (bangs, in particülar), his next-door neighbors, his üpstairs neighbors, his landlord, the new president, the old president, and his overbite.*

This is making me uncomfortable.

> *For the record, he never complains aboüt me.*

So I'm not a complete fuck up.

> *I finished with The Blad in time to meet The Ref for a few drinks at the Tapered End. And, yoü know, The Ref was in a great mood! He was enthüsiastic aboüt life. He paid the bill. He even held my hand on the walk home. I love walking hand-in-hand with The Ref.*

"Love" again, but so what? Turn the page.

> *It's tomorrow now. Yesterday happened. I'm not exactly proüd of what The Blad and I did. Büt I'm not exactly ashamed. It's more of a relief. I'd always wondered, yoü know, what woüld it be like if we türned it on again? Türns oüt The Blad's an annoying, sports-obsessed, he-man jackass. I güess that shoüld have been obvioüs from the get-go.*

> *Anyway, after yesterday I no longer need to wonder what coüld have happened between üs. The handsome lünk who showed me how to do beer bongs and shoplift candy from the süpermarket is firmly planted in my yesterdays. And, yoü know, he wasn't as good in bed as I recalled.*

There it was. While I had been at work, Vero had ridden in an elevator with The Blad, and then they'd gone to his bullshit apartment—which I guarantee you is decorated with nothing but Denver Broncos footballs and Denver Broncos jerseys and Denver Broncos helmets, all of which are signed with fake autographs—and they drank some shitty champagne and he sat next to her on his white leather couch and put his hand on her knee and they did some beer bongs and Vero said, "I want to ride your cock," and he said, "Saddle up," and then he put on his fake-autographed Jake Plummer helmet and Vero pulled on a fake-autographed Randy Gradishar jersey and they banged each other for many long, sweaty, screaming hours, in nothing but football-related sexual positions:

the tight end
the buttonhook
the crackback block
the double coverage
the front seven
the lateral
the neutral zone infraction
the point spread
the pooch kick
the pump fake
the quarterback sneak
the wishbone formation

For the record, I don't complain nearly as much as Veronica claims. But that's not the point. I'm not the point. Veronica is the point, and the pointiest part of that point is that The Blad's pointiest part recently penetrated her privatest part to which I alone am privy, or so I thought.

The diary was floating in front of my face. It's a comfortable way to read a book, with it hovering there like that. I plucked it out of the air and threw it. It left my hand and went on pause just beyond my fingertips.

I snatched my onion engagement ring from the floor and brought it to Sandy, who was still standing behind the counter, ready to pour coffee.

"Will you marry me?"

I nodded her head for her.

I slid the onion ring onto her finger.

Storm out, past the door, to the parking lot. Goddamn this Alaskan summer. It should be nighttime.

I stomped circles on the dirt, I walked from one end of town to the next. I returned to the parking lot and sat on the diner's AstroTurfed front step and put my head in my hands and moaned.

I woke up in front of Cookie's Palace Diner with dried salt on my cheeks and a jaw sore from all the tooth gnashing. When you're hopeless and brokenhearted, it can feel like your brain is collapsing in upon itself while your body is dissolving into the air. But not me, not when I wake up on an AstroTurfed front step at 7:23 PM on September 1, 2009 with dried tears of deceit on my face. Narwhal Slotterfield doesn't dissolve. Narwhal Slotterfield blows the whistle and stops the game and decides who will win and who will lose.

Cookie's van is unlocked. I open the door and climb inside. Cookie's my friend. He makes food for me. I check the glove box. Cookie's name is Darrel Swets. Scattered upon the passenger seat is a stack of CDs: The Rolling Stones, solo and otherwise. Underneath the passenger seat is a bottle of Southern Comfort, which confirms that Cookie's favorite musician is Keith Richards. In the eighties, Keith Richards was a walking advertisement for Southern Comfort. Every magazine interview included a photo of him sloughing sallow-cheeked next to an out-of-focus bottle of SoCo.

Cookie *really* likes Mr. Richards. The van contains both of his solo albums as well as a CD bootleg of the pre-prison recordings, not nearly as legendary as the Charlie Parker pre-Bellevue sessions, nor as over-rated.

We're discussing a medium which I cannot experience. Music is the sound of the wind in my sinus cavity. Music is the sound of my skull conveying my howls of cuckoldry into the saddle, stirrup, and drum of my inner ear.

I'm extraordinarily upset about Vero's diary.

Thru the doorway of the van, I can see thru the doorway of the

Palace, where I see her at the table, the whites of her eyes peering from under her lids. Her expression—which I had rendered in an attempt to give her dignity—doesn't resemble an embalmed corpse so much as it does an orgasm-in-progress.

I'm too upset to think of a specifically crazy manner of acting out, so I will get drunk instead. I hell-storm out of the van and whack the Southern Comfort bottle against the outside wall of the Palace. The snapped-off neck is in my hand, the rest of the bottle remains intact, resting against the wall.

Do I not bleed? Do I not coagulate? Yes, to both.

The broken collar of the bottle's neck reflects prettily in the orange sun. Orange. I need to expand my color vocabulary. The sun was an orange. There, it's a metaphor now. The liquor remains trapped in the neckless bottle. Another metaphor for you.

I place the bottle on the ground, liquor still within, neck missing, and—wait—first I tear the screen from the screen door at the front of the Palace and place it on the ground. I place the bottle thereupon. I stomp hard upon the bottle. Nothing. So I find a cinderblock—there's always a cinderblock when you need one—and lift it up and bring it down upon the bottle, which dis-integrates in the original sense of the word, being that it becomes un-integrated. I lift the window screen, sieving the broken glass with it. Mercifully, there are few shards, and all of them are large enough to get captured by the screen. The SoCo has been successfully sieved.

I float the screen aside and bend down and bite the checkered, puckered blob of hillbilly sugar piss. I choke down every drop. And so here I am, writing in twilight when it should be dark, sitting directly across from the woman who gave me joy and filled me with betrayal.

I will sleep this off in the back of Cookie's van. It's safe there. It has a mattress, and it's devoid of sexual stains.

This is not survivor behavior. This is loser behavior. I am not a loser. I am the motherfucker who *determines* who wins and who loses. I have a plan.

Step two, I will go to Denver and I will have a word with The Blad.

Step one, I have already accomplished. And that is precisely why I pointed the pistol that I found in Cookie's glove-box.

Let me state this more clearly. This morning, I found a forty-five caliber pistol in Cookie's glove-box. I sat there in the passenger seat and I put the barrel against my temple and squeezed the trigger. As expected, nothing happened. I did not expect to expire. It was a symbolic act. The old Narwhal Slotterfield is dead. Long lurch the new Narwhal Slotterfield. .

I remained poised for a brief moment, looking at my gun-to-temple self in the little mirror on the flipped visor, a classically-trained cry for help.

I said to me, "Cry for help? You can't even hear your*self*, dipshit."

I loosened my grip and slid out from underneath the weapon and exited the van. The gun remains poised there, hovering in front of the visor mirror, as if a ghost is aiming it at another ghost.

I will go to Denver and confront Blad the Impaler. I will point a gun at him and pull the trigger and I will walk back to Holliday and I will feel better and, if I'm of the mood, I will forgive Veronica.

When there are no consequences, there are no rules except *feel better.*

Also of note, when I broke the neck off the bottle of Southern Comfort, the blister on my finger—the blister I received from touching hot fry grease—popped. This was the source of the blood that I'd mentioned, which did coagulate. Oval scab. No sign of infection. Seems doubtful that I'd be at risk for such a thing as an infection, as all the bugs in the world are in a state of suspension. I suspect that I am impervious to illness.

Fill a backpack with water bottles and socks. Borrow Cookie's sharpest knife. Visualize myself walking a hundred and fifty miles to Denver.

For my final act before departure, I entered Cookie's van and extracted the floating pistol and brought it to the Palace, where I placed it in Sandy's left hand. I wrapped her fingers loosely around the grip and pointed the gun toward Veronica, seated across the room. The act is imaginary, harmless, like a tired dog's dream, all kicking legs and angry yips. Feel free to misinterpret it as an act of misogynistic aggression.

I spent an afterlunch with the Colorado map from the glove box of my car spread out on Sandy's counter. Once I start walking, the first town I'll see is Dorsey, twenty miles west. I've heard of this place, Dorsey, but I can't remember what I've heard. Probably I heard someone say, "What kind of jackanape calls a town 'Dorsey'?"

After Dorsey, it's ten miles to a town called Endurance, then twenty more miles to Abila. And so on. Another speck of a town every ten to twenty miles. 150 miles to Denver. In between the towns, there will surely be farmhouses full of dinner for the pickin'. I can pack light, is what I'm saying. No need for manna or waybread or Jimmie Dean Christmas sausage.

I ate the last of the diner's world-famous pies, then I combed Sandy's hair. She works hard. She deserves to be pretty.

Second-to-last act before finally departing: I opened my mouth wide and placed my lips over Veronica's nose. Her nose did not twitch.

"Goodbye, my larva. I'd linger, but I'm not very chatty at the moment. Don't mind the gun. Guns don't work. It's ironic, is all, for this is the age we live in. I'm describing, not complaining."

Final act: I removed Vero's chair from underneath her. Now she's sitting on nothing. If I had a working camera, I'd take a picture, it's so silly.

All loaded up, with my backpack strapped over my shoulders and a pair of well-used officially-sanctioned referee shoes on my feet, I gave a salute and exited Cookie's Palace Diner.

Because I'm impossibly optimistic, I tried to start my car. I could barely get the key to turn in ignition. And even when I did manage to twist the key into "start", the starter did not start.

Still impossibly optimistic, I found a beat-up ten-speed bicycle leaning against one of the homes in Holliday. I pushed a pedal and the chain almost moved. I put my full weight on it and the bike crept. The dominos in the chain links get progressively less connected to my feet and, to summarize, it's incredibly inefficient to ride a bicycle. Bummer, but I wouldn't say it's a surprise.

This is going to be a haul, full of adventure and things that don't move. Tell me again why I'm doing this? Because I don't know what else to do.

I walked Route 36, the path that, in a moving world, Vero and I should have taken in my car, days ago, tummies filled with polysaturated fats, the two of us happily engaged, Vero already planning to destroy the dastardly diary and the memories it contained.

The exercise was invigorating at first. I would close my eyes and feel as if I were floating soundlessly, the warm sun at my eyelids, the clouds of the hellfire storm in the near distance, and a chasm of disappointment receding behind me.

The landscape isn't worth a mention. It's flat. It's hot. The plains are a place that doesn't tell you anything.

There's no wind to cool me, which blows because walking is more strenuous than I anticipated.

Half a mile down the highway, I came upon a big rig, the same one I descried on my first excursion out the Palace's front door, the excursion wherein I'd retrieved the suitcases and Vero's diary. The truck is a Mack, turns out. I'd never been in a semi before, so I climbed in. The driver was pressing the truck's dashboard lighter against a cigarette. Older fellow, in his sixties. He had a cut-off beer can between his legs, full of brown spit. Driving, smoking, and chewing at the same time, a testimony to American can-do-ism.

As a further tribute to Americandoism, the fellow had covered the entire ceiling of his cab with images of naked women, downloaded from leather-and-fruit fetishist websites, printed out from a streaky inkjet printer. How tender. A man drives his truck and all the cherubim in his heavens are sitting naked astride black-saddled watermelons. It's a miracle, this world where anonymous women of the internet will go to such great lengths to provide an opportunity for three-alarm nicotine addicts to get their hard rocks soft.

Except my truck-driving man had on a wedding ring. The women in those print-outs were not his wives, at least according to the photo in his wallet, which meant Cletus was extra-maritally lustful. As of very recently, this sort of thing has become a touchy subject.

Against my better judgment, I crawled into Cletus's sleeper. The sleeper is the area behind the cab where the driver sleeps away those lonely nights on the road. I had never been in a sleeper.

I lit my way with Cletus's electric lighter, whose candlepower was weak but sufficient. The little room was downright luxurious. A proper bed, flat-screen TV, multiple speakers, walls upholstered with scarlet fabric. Tacked to the scarlet fabric were photos of actual women, taken by Cletus himself, whose belt buckle I recognized in multiple shots. Lots of different women. No wedding rings. When they aren't riding melons, Cletus prefers 'em blonde on top and bald down low, ideally with a battery-powered device within.

There was no accounting for what combination of fruit juice and Fruit of the Loom juice had dried upon these sheets. I exited the sleeper, leaving the lighter hovering a few inches above the bed.

Back in the truck's cockpit, I pulled the fetish pics from the ceiling and flattened them against the windshield, so that if time did ever resume, Cletus would be blinded and surprised and hopefully drive into a ditch. Just to prove that I'm not a monster, I buckled his seatbelt for him.

What's in the trailer, I wondered. Coal? Gravel? Baby doll heads? I went round back and climbed up the ladder, peeked under the canvas cover. This one was filled to the brim with seeds. Wheat, I think.

I had an idea. I crawled under the canvas and lay atop the wheat. I scooched back and forth, pushed the grain about until it held an impression of me. It fit very comfortably, with even pressure on all my backside body parts. I once sat on a memory foam bed in a mattress store. This was just as good. I think we could market it as the GrainBed. Slogan: *It Grows On You.*

Under the tarp, in the dark, on the wheat, I slept and then I awoke and now I'm sitting on the side of the road next to the semi, writing an account of my first half-mile toward Denver, which you have just read.

12

I walked until I came upon a farmhouse on the right side of the road. I hope they're having omelets for dinner.

This being my first breaking-and-entering of the post-time era, I was especially careful about opening the door and walking on the carpet and crossing the laundry room into the kitchen. Alas, no omelets. The Missus had prepared a stack of grilled cheese sandwiches and was about to bring them out to her hubby and the two children, who were watching a car commercial on their wall-mounted television.

One of the children, the girl, was smirking at her cell phone. The text thereupon read, *TWAT.*

The room, shades drawn to optimize the TV's glow, provided a showcase environment for the colloid effect, which is to say the shafts of sunlight that penetrated the gaps in the shades rendered visible all the dust bits floating in the air. When you look at a sunbeam, you're seeing sunlight reflected off bits of floating dandruff.

The scene was much prettier than my description. It was beautiful, to tell the truth. I dragged my finger thru one of the sunbeams. This cleared out the dust, leaving an empty line in the beam. I traced a smiley face. A hovering sunbeam smile, crooked and childish. My first self-portrait.

After eating four grilled-cheese sandwiches at the dining room table, I'm already nostalgic for the pies at Cookie's Palace. Don't get down, buddy. As I approach Denver, I'm sure to come across an all-day breakfast wafflecake establishment. Flo's pies will evaporate from my mind just as soon as my mouth gets a load of the pop and ooze of a fried egg.

Veronica has a peculiar thing with the eggs. She likes hers scrambled, which is not particularly peculiar. However, after she cracks the eggs into the bowl, but before she whips them into homogeneity, she carefully plucks out each umbilical cord. I didn't know eggs had umbilical cords. She pointed it out the very first time we broke fast at her place. She was wearing her plaid bathrobe, cinched up tight around her throat. Her feet were bare. A CD of her oldest sister's metal band was playing softly in the background. And she said, "Look, Narwhal. See that white thing there?" The white thing was tiny, like a stretchy wet booger. "As the yolk turns into a chick, that cord sucks nutrients out of the white, which isn't white, but clear, clearly." Then she reached in with her fingers with nails that were raggedy and covered with flaking black enamel and plucked each of the boogers out of the eggs and flicked them into the garbage disposal.

She said, "Isn't that better?"

This is the woman who recently cheated on me with a man who taught her how to do beer bongs and shoplift candy. You've cut *my* umbilical cord, Vero. I'm a quivering egg and you've plucked out my last strand of contact to the larder of hope. I'll whine if I want.

Having pilfered food from this family, I regretted that I hadn't stolen any cash from the pornographic truck driver's wallet. I only had three dollars on me. I slid the bills into the Missus's left back pocket. Her jeans were on the tight end of the scale, as is the fashion. I got the bills in far enough to stay put, but not so far that I'd be considered a pervert. I hope she's the type who checks all the pockets before doing the laundry. I assume she's the laundry-doer in this household. Don't cry. It's society that's sexist, not me. And anyway, aside from the découpaged "Footprints" poem above the fireplace, this family seems pretty decent. I visited every room in the house and found nothing but normal, devoted human behavior. The bathroom light was on, thank God, and I got a view of my face. My beard was coming in thick. I borrowed the Mister's razor and dry-shaved, leaving little hairs floating around the room. Yes, dry-shaving hurts.

The shaving gave me an idea. I dug around the bathroom drawers until I found a pair of hair-scissors and then I cut all my hair off and then shaved the stubble—painful, yes—so now I am bald as a balloon. The look doesn't flatter me. My head has one of those asymmetrical peaked ridges running to the left of center, typical of tall men.

But my head, you see, is also a timekeeper. They say hair grows half an inch every month. Roughly an eighth of an inch per week.

Which means I can now inaccurately track the long-term passage of time via my pate. Further, when I wish to measure the short-term, I can count seventy beats of my heart. Assuming I'm at rest, that's a minute. Hot damn, I'm clever.

Ba bump. Ba bump.

I've been sitting on the toilet with my fingers on my jugular for seventeen minutes.

I took a nap in the master bedroom, woke up disoriented, and now I'm ready to hit the road. I hid "Footprints" under the mattress, bowed to my hosts, and marched on.

In two more days of road walking and house hopping, I've picked up nearly twenty more miles, as reckoned by the green mile markers. Already, my legs and lungs are building stamina in this watery atmosphere. Soon, I'll be making fifteen miles a day. I'm coming for you, The Blad.

I encounter a car, truck, motorcycle, semi, or other conveyomobile roughly every two miles. They're driven mostly by people staring straight ahead, every human a dummy from one of those fake towns they used to blow up in atom bomb tests in the fifties. I do come across the occasional scene: an unsmiling couple, the blanched teenager with a half-empty bottle of Robitussin in his lap, the car driven by a man in a clown costume. In the interest of making time, I usually just peek thru the windows and then walk on by.

My priority is The Blad. Having said that, I did steal twenty bucks from a kid in a Japanese economy car that had been modified to resemble an oversized remote-control toy. One of those little hatchbacks with a giant exhaust pipe and a custom red-and-orange paint job. The kid's baseball cap was on backwards, he was chewing on a lollipop, and his dashboard was decorated with plastic ponies. And he had Kansas plates. All of that adds up to the subtraction of twenty dollars from his wallet, which was covered with scratch 'n' sniff stickers. I intend to redistribute the money as soon as I find someone who deserves it.

Eight miles later, I came to one of those signs that cartoon characters happen upon in cartoon deserts. It pointed south: *Keaton 2 Miles*. Unlike the other side roads I'd encountered, the road to Keaton was paved, although crumbly and sunbleached. Yonder, a hawk was suspended above the landscape, eyes open for whatever it is hawks eat.

My legs were tired so I slouched against the sign, James Dean style, for several beatings of my heart. Narwhal Slotterfield is a loner, a rebel, and he does as he pleases.

I kinda wanted to go to Keaton. For kicks, you know. What mysteries might lay off the beaten path that's already off the beaten path? Tumbleweeds and broken down pickup trucks and half-mad chickens.

When you put it that way.

I'll save Keaton for later, after I've had my word with The Blad. Revenge is a dish and I'm famished.

The town of Dorsey is a corpse that someone forgot to unplug from life support. There's just one street, Route 36, flanked by numerous decaying structures. Amongst those are two windowless motels, a windowless gas station, a weed-grown mini-golf course, a church full of tumbleweeds. There are a few actual surviving businesses of the sort that are required for modern human existence: a post office, a phone company, and a liquor store. Rounding out the tour are a dozen or so decaying houses, any one of which could serve as the communal residence for a tribe of heavily armed Christian isolationist hillbillies. And if this planet is home to a living creature other than me, we all know it's going to be Christian isolationist hillbillies.

Dorsey has no grocery stores or restaurants. I eat a bottle of water from my backpack and I move on.

Remember the hellfire storm? It looked big back in Holliday. Here, it's a looming monster. Straight ahead, the sun remains visible as it peeks under the clouds. To the north, there are streaks of rain. Above, the clouds pile upon one another like madmen attempting to claw their way out of one of those pits that CIA-trained South American death squads make a town of peasants dig before they shoot them all.

Given my already dark mood, I am not thrilled with the prospect of crossing underneath that thing.

Two miles west of Dorsey, I start to grow hungry. Three miles west of Dorsey, I'm ravenous. Luckily, there's a house on the right side of the highway, just beneath the leading edge of the storm. The streaks of rain to the north have white smears to them. Above, the clouds are a cauldron. Any minute, the harpies will descend.

The house is redbrick, ranch style. Inside, the house's decorations strongly suggest I'm in a cattleman's home: there are a dozen pairs of worn cowboy boots scattered under the furniture, several copies of *Modern Rancher* magazine next to the toilet, and the house smells like cowshit.

The fireplace mantel is adorned with a musket with a flared barrel, the sort Puritans used to brandish at curious Indians. Above that hangs the decapitated head of a pronghorn. I know the animal is a pronghorn because *PRONGHORN* is expertly engraved on the brass plate screwed at the base of the wooden head mount. A pronghorn looks like a deer, except it has a black streak of fur on its nose. And it has prongs instead of antlers.

The lady of the house has prepared a repast of pot roast and soggy carrots. Places are set, garnishes are being placed upon butter sticks. I reckon the man of the house will be home just as soon as he finishes castrating the cattle, or whatever.

I eat until I'm satisfied, but not full. I must save a portion for my return trip, in the event that I should decide to come back after I've given The Blad the what-for.

There's a gun case in the living room. It's like a trophy case, but full of firearms. At least twenty guns, all types. Pistols, rifles with sniper scopes, Elmer Fudd double-barrel shotguns. The case is unlocked so, one by one, I bring the guns outside and point them at the sky, hovering. One by one I pull the triggers and leave them there to do nothing. There's twenty-one all told. Silent pickets, salute.

Once you get used to it, walking against this atmosphere is quite invigorating. I made twenty miles today, all the way to Abila, yet another of these towns that clings to the highway like a withered plant growing out of a crack in a sidewalk.

Already, my muscles grow stout, especially my legs. I'm suffering from the opposite of atrophy. When I really get going, marching down the center of the road like some anti-astronaut version of a cross-country cancer-awareness fund-raising obsessive, I can close my eyes and walk over a hundred steps before I veer into the rumble strips at the shoulder of the blacktop.

My legs are pendula on a clock. Leftright, leftright, leftright. As a resident of the altitudinous Denver, I am reminded every day that there are 5280 feet in a mile. Each of my strides spans roughly three feet. A leftright spans six feet. Six goes into 5280 880 times. 880 divided by sixty (seconds) is 14.666666666666666666666666667. Conclusion: Assuming I'm walking four miles per hour—a brisk but manageable pace—each mile should take approximately fifteen minutes and each left-right therefore comprises one second.

If I concentrate on math, I can keep myself from thinking about you-know-who. I'm a jerk, Veronica. I understand that. But you're *not* a jerk, so you shouldn't have hurt me.

My mood is in a state of decline. If nothing else, my entry into this suspended state/country/universe would have, I thought, liberated me from the oppressive expectations of society. I was wrong. I have become not only my own master, but the overseer of a world that can no longer wipe its own ass.

Meanwhile, fifty miles to the east, my darling duplicitous Veronica remains seated *en milleu d'aire* with Sandy pointing a gun at her from across the room. And here I am, eating stolen meal after stolen meal, in search of redemption, or revenge, or simply an excuse to kill some time in a timeless land.

I make my way underneath the storm. It's a cumulonimbus affair, a hellfire storm. Just massive. I can't overstate this. Every summer afternoon, from time immemorial, the sweltering wind has blown over the Rockies, creating the perfect condition for thunderstorms. We see them in Denver regularly and, according to Channel Nine weatherhuman Rainey Highs, they can get brutal on the plains. Colonies of tornados, hail the size of footballs, winds that remove flesh from cattle, and bolts of lightning as thick as a tree trunk, bright as the sun, and squiggly as one of those teeny appendages attached to those bugs you see when you focus a microscope on a drop of pond water.

I walk beneath that hovering pile of hostile water vapor with my shoulders slumped and my eyes mostly shut, making pointless calculations based on my heartbeats.

At mile marker 153, I encounter an eastbound minivan with Missouri plates and a *University of Colorado* sticker on the back window. The occupants are Caucasian. The mom and the dad are in front, the dad in his traditional role at the wheel. In the back is their eighteen-year son, wearing a turquoise polo shirt with a popped collar, ear buds in, pawing away at his pocket phone. The van is filled with all the stuff a kid would need for life in a dormitory: minifridge, plastic drawer units, Salvador Dali posters.

Likeliest scenario: Within a month of beginning his freshman year of college, young Brock has been expelled from Dear Old CU. Except you can't flunk out in a month. He hasn't even gotten his first report card yet. No, our friend has clearly demonstrated some incredibly untoward behavior. A smoke bomb in the dorms, repeated plagiarism, sex trafficking. Not weed, though. I've worked my share of intramural games in Boulder. I assure you that CU does not expel anyone for marijuana infractions.

There are few joys greater than officiating an intermural game of ten stoned basketball players. Stoners do not give a shit how I officiate the game. They frequently stop mid-court to shake my hand and compliment my fashionable zebra skin shirt. Sometimes they even let me shoot free throws, because why the hell not? Let's upend authority, 'k? They love it when I offer fatherly advice, like, "Play a two-three zone and you'll totally neutralize their big man." Sometimes I even get to be the default scorekeeper. I did one game where nobody made a basket and the final score was three hundred fifty to twenty-six *zillion*. Players from both teams wept with joy.

It's when a team of stoners goes against a team of frat-boys that I really spread my wings. I do this by *Creating Chaos* and *Giving Hope to the Underdog.*

The Kappa Gamma gang are notoriously competitive, so loathsome they have to do three lines of coke and chew a handful of Adderall before they can stand to be around each other. Even then, being the post-pubescent, pre-enlightened, narcoticized alpha apes that they are, they argue with everyone, *especially* each other. And they never, ever pass the ball. Snag the rebound, sprint down the floor, dodge the opposing team of high-as-a-kite daisy-picking hippies, ignore your four randomly-placed teammates who are all clapping their hands and screaming, "I'm wide-open, brah!" and attempt a free-throw line slam dunk even though your vertical leap is thirteen inches, you're five-and-a-half-feet tall, and you couldn't palm a mandarin orange.

Imagine a basketball game between the Grateful Dead and the members of Motörhead. Imagine a sloth subletting a room from a beehive. Imagine Mad Max's wife and toddler running away from an anarchic Australian motorcycle mob. Then bring me in to clear things up. I invent new infractions, like Over-Dribbling or Failure to Use a Pivot Foot.

The fratsters never buck my authority. I'm more than a decade older than them. At their core they're just a bunch of compliant father-pleasing soon-to-be-failed investment bankers. On my court, the stoners win every time.

I removed Axel Buster's half-smoked joint from my shirt pocket and wedged it between young Brock's lips and marched on. The act of generosity improved my mood considerably.

But it was not enough to overcome the fact that I was standing underneath the Super Star Destroyer of super clouds. Over my last hundred steps, the air had grown cooler by at least ten degrees, a welcome change after all this time in ninety-plus Fahrenheit.

With chicken flesh on my arms and my eyes closed, I continued west. I imagined I was someplace more pleasant, less stormy. The bottom of the ocean, maybe.

Sometime before lunch break, I took five hundred steps without opening my eyes. And even then I only opened them because I couldn't believe that I'd traveled over half a mile without veering more than twenty feet to the left or right. Indeed, I was still smack dab on the centerline of this unerring highway. I'm not *that* amazing. The sun keeps me oriented. I feel it on my face, see a little glow behind my eyelids behind my dark glasses.

I encountered no rain as I continued this mostly-blind promenade, only silent oppression. After an extraordinarily long stretch, I opened my eyes and, glory on high, I saw that there was an end to the hellfire storm. Up ahead, the gap between the clouds and the horizon had grown taller. The storm was a cell, not a legion. It was a thing to be traversed, like adolescence. I'd be under blue skies in, oh, just another mile.

I jumped up and down and shouted inner ear exhortations of joy. I'm coming for you, The Blad.

That's all it takes. Put the storm behind you. The sky before me is blue, dotted with bunny clouds. The flatness of the land has begun to break. No mountains yet, but the plains are now rippling into a series of long, gentle hills. Easy up, easy down.

It'll be a grand moment when the good ol' Rockies poke their heads over the horizon. Until then, the horizontal seam between the sky and the land just screams peaceful.

At mile marker 165, fifty yards off the road, I spotted a herd of pronghorn. I recognized them from the decapitated head of their cousin above the mantle at the redbrick farmhouse with the guns, to which I shall henceforth refer as the House of Pronghorn.

I jumped a barbed-wire fence and crossed into the pasture and petted the animals. Up close, they're shorter than they seem when viewed from the road; their heads only come up to my armpit. They're surprisingly mangy, with bloody scabs on their ears and flies hovering around their heads. And yet, in spite of this, the animals retain a natural elegance.

Seeing them, I was reminded of a playoff game I officiated last year between the Aurora Christian Academy and Hochley High. Hochley's boosters were assholes. Every time I sent an Academy player to the foul-line, the Hochley crowd chanted "Ev-o-lu-tion!" over and over until the shot went up. If it missed, they'd shout, "God's will be done!"

The players on both teams ignored the off-court nonsense and stuck to basketball. Once you alight upon the court, once the game begins, the whole world disappears. Alas, the world didn't disappear so easily for the Aurora Christian Academy *cheerleaders*, as they were burdened with the task of being cheerful.

In their blue pleated skirts and puffy-shouldered dresses, they did their splits and made their pyramids. As the taunting continued, the girls stretched their innocent smiles wider and wider while their pretty Christian eyes grew more and more glassy. Not to be beaten down by the blasphemers of Hochley, they tried the old standby, "We've got spirit, yes we do. We've got spirit, how 'bout you?"

Traditionally, when one set of cheerleaders initiates this chant, the opposing cheerleaders repeat it back at them. The squads go back and forth with this, growing more passionate with each iteration, until concluding as an ensemble with "WE ALL DO!" Happens at least once per game. It's intended to remind everyone that this is a friendly competition.

The Academy's cheerleaders initiated the Spirit Chant at the third quarter break, score tied at 56 to 56. Hochley's entire crowd, parents, cheerleaders, everyone, replied with: "Who cares?!?" We're talking about probably five hundred people. The Christian girls just stood there. Skinny, ponytails, knobby knees, pompons dangling like dead jellyfish.

Well, shit. These kids didn't send them*selves* to their private Christian Academy. School sucks enough without tossing in mandatory bible classes. They're *kids*. They want to listen to hip-hop, smoke cigarettes, and explore backseat underwear gropings on the bus ride home from the game, just like the bastards at Hochley.

But now, being humiliated in their attempt to spread goodwill, it was clear that these girls were doomed to abandon any hope of worldly teenage rebellion and instead retreat into uncomplicated lives of chastity, judgment, and missionary trips to third world countries, just as their parents had always dreamed. I couldn't let that happen.

A few phantom fouls here, overlooks of some traveling violations there. When the buzzer sounded, I saw to it that they had something to cheer about.

*

In honor of the cheerleading squad at the Aurora Christian Academy, I stacked the pronghorns into a pyramid. A *deer*amid, if you will. First, I lined up four of them side by side. Then I placed three more on the shoulders of the bottom row. It was easier than you'd think. I didn't have to worry about dropping them; I'd heave one up partway and then release it to hover in midair, at which point I could readjust my grip, get underneath it better and then push it into place. Then I'd spread the legs and place the feet firmly on the backs of the animals below. Getting two of them to the third row was a little more difficult, as I had to stage them multiple times to lift them to the appropriate altitude. But I'm tall and I managed. I saved the smallest one for the fourth-level peak. I climbed on the backs of the two lowest layers and placed the little critter atop, poised upright on his hind legs with his arms reaching for the sky.

I stood back to admire my work. It was clever, but it didn't *pop*. After much chin-rubbing, inspiration appeared in the mass of tumbleweeds that were piled against the barbed wire fence adjacent to the road. I took two of the well-shaped tumblers and balanced them on the forepaws of the prime pronghorn. Now the little guy has pompons. I wish I could take a picture and show it to those Aurora Christian Academy cheerleaders as an expression of solidarity.

I'm seated at the front step of the Abila grocery store—quaint like a country store should be—and I'm making my way thru a six-pack of miniature powdered donuts. I should avoid sugar on account of there not being any dentists, but I walked a long ways today and I deserve a reward.

Boy, am I going to give it to The Blad. First, I need to get to Denver. But, boy, when I get there. I fantasize about the various ways I could punish him. If I could figure out how to do so, I'd tattoo his entire face green. Or I could stuff a scorpion down his pants, or haul him to the roof of his office and toss him over the edge. I should try that. I could stand on him and float like the Silver Surfer. No matter what, I'll begin by shaving all the hair off his body.

Speaking of hair, mine is growing back at an incredible rate. By my calculations, it should be 1/20th of an inch long four days after shaving it all off. But it's at least 1/10th of an inch long. I'm probably just sleeping a lot longer than I think I am. Fuck it. I'm well-rested.

Good night.

I have come across my first proper lunatic compound. Some crazy motherfucker has taken control of a cluster of buildings that must have once been a teeny tiny town. The compound consists of all the typical town buildings: a mid-century-modern ghost-motel, collapsing frame houses, something that may have been a general store, various shed-like buildings, and a gas station whose parking lot includes gaping holes where the underground fuel tanks used to be buried.

The new owner has erected an eight-foot chain link fence around the property and topped that with razor wire, and has apparently been acquiring a large collection of non-working vintage vans for a couple of decades. His flag pole features a confederate flag flying at half-mast and an American Flag flying upside down. There are surveillance cameras everywhere.

I'm betting our little Jim Jones has a deep-freeze full of human heads.

Inside one of my host's unstable houses, there's a nookish room containing a library of neoconfederate print-on-demand fantasy fiction. Notable titles: *The South Rises Again, The South Rises Again: Part II,* and *Jane Austin and Zombies Slay Lincoln The Day Before He Issues the Proclamation of Emancipation*.

Downstairs of this house, I find an old-fashioned basement bunker chock full of bottled water, flashlights, boxes of beef jerky, and case upon case—I'm talking about hundreds of cases—of canned cat food. The cat food can be explained by the presence of a tiger chained to the floor at the top of the staircase that leads into the basement bunker. I scratch the cat's ears as I exit the house.

The compound includes a black-windowed cinderblock building, which I enter. Judging from the dusty pile of junk in the corner, amongst which are a postal scale and a Pitney Bowes machine, this was once the town Post Office. The back room is filled with vigorously growing potted pot plants. Neoconfederate survivalist stoners. I've seen it all.

*

I went thru all nine of the broken-down vans, expecting at any minute to find one filled with Russian tweens handcuffed to webcams. Thankfully, they only contained thousands and thousands of flattened two-liter bottles of Neon Green, the caffeinated carbonated beverage preferred by video game addicts and X-treme athletes everywhere.

After much poking around, I found my host in a tiny tool shed that was actually an enormous outhouse. Our man was seated upon the left hole of a double-hole two-by-twelve plank, reading a pocket-sized edition of the Koran. He was shirtless and marshmallowy with birthmarks all over his chest and an onyx ring on his left thumb.

Curiosity implored me to peer into the unoccupied hole, the one on the right. There was a light coming from it, that's why I peered. A rope ladder led to its depths. Let me repeat. A rope ladder dangled from the second hole of a two-hole outhouse.

At the bottom of the pit there was a person holding a flashlight. I couldn't actually see the person because he or she was silhouetted by the light and all I could make out was the top of his or her head, which appeared to be covered with hair.

I dislike saying "her or him" and "he or she." Henceforth, when gender is uncertain, I'm going to employ the term *thon*. English is a wonderful language but it could use a little gathering around the waist.

So help me, I thought, *thon* better not be a Russian tween.

At this point I finally did pinch myself. This was precisely the kind of dream an asshole like me would have, complete with disturbing symbolic imagery. Man on toilet taking a dump on flashlit figure below. The flashlit figure represents Veronica, of course, and we all know who's the asshole on the assplank.

The pinch did not wake me up, and so down I went.

I dangled at the bottom of the rope ladder, breathing as little as possible and with no intention of setting foot on the mush below. It wasn't as stinky as I'd expected. More of a loamy scent, I'd say.

As I lilted gently on the ladder, I came face to face with the human at the bottom of the outhouse. She was grey-haired, wearing a pair of belly-high fishing waders and a crocheted bikini top. She had a canvas shopping bag over her shoulder and she was wearing a blindingly bright headlamp. She was scratching her shoulder with her left hand, which had an onyx ring on its thumb. No handcuffs anywhere.

She was at least sixty years old, with her hair done in a pair of Willie Nelson braids. Her skin had that spotty looseness that happens to old people.

I confess, the situation challenged my sense of adjudication. I'm not a prude. Ask Veronica or any of the other three women I've slept with. Then again, I've never sat on a plank of wood and read the Koran while taking a dump on a half-naked woman.

I looked more closely at my surroundings and I relaxed, a little. The two halves of the outhouse cellar, as it were, were separated by a plywood partition. Which is to say, nobody was being shat upon after all; this was an entirely different chamber from the one into which the Koran-reader was, shall we say, feeding Rumsfeld.

I held my hand in front of the woman's headlamp so the light reflected back on her face. She looked awfully content. The matching onyx rings suggested that she and the shitter were married, presumably in a self-officiated black mass ceremony. What were these kooks up to? Whatever it was, it was deep, complex, incoherent, and certainly fed by paranoia.

There was no way I, as a referee, could possibly contribute to this chaos. Nor could I assist the underdog. I didn't even know for sure who the underdog was. As for avoiding a blowout, good luck, kids.

This one out had been blown beyond retrieval.

I ascended the rope ladder, exited the outhouse, and satisfied my need for mischief by piling up the weirdoes' entire supply of beef jerky in front of their pet tiger.

Back to the road, and maybe I should stop snooping around so much.

Before I owned my current shitty sedan, I owned a different shitty sedan whose life was taken by a miniature poodle and a cellphone. This was several years ago, a Sunday morning, and I had no eggs so I got in my car—which, like my current car, had a broken air conditioner—and drove to a convenience store, this being one of those occasions where I prefer driving a car to riding the bus.

On the way home, a poodle marched and haunched down smack dab in the middle of the road, directly before my front bumper. In order to not crush the creature, I braked to a hasty stop. The dog was unharmed and the eggs did not slide off the passenger seat. I checked my rearview mirror, found no one coming, and waited for the dog to get out of my way.

The dog opted to remain where it was, lapping water out of a pothole. It had rained the night before. The dog didn't have a collar. It did have a purple Mohawk. I was about to open my door and shoo the thing away when a pickup piloted by an uninsured text-messaging hillbilly plowed into my trunk at forty miles an hour. I ended up with egg on my face and a second-degree concussion.

The hillbilly truck driver exited his cab, and, still texting, leaned in my window and called me a fucking pussy for not driving over the dog—which was now being held in the arm of a one-armed man with spaghetti sauce dripping down the front of his shirt and the lower half of his body concealed by the weeds in his lawn—and then got back in his truck and drove away. As for me, I walked home, and then took a bus to the high school basketball game I had to work that night.

By the time I got to the gym, the concussion had settled in. It was like being drunk, except it wasn't remotely pleasurable. The inside of my head had grown noticeably larger than my skull. With each step, my starchy brain politely requested that I lie down. It became hard to keep up with the game, or anything else. Is it still halftime? Why, then, did I just whistle the school mascot for a backcourt violation?

It wasn't all bad. The disorientation led to one of the most bizarre games I've ever worked. Amongst the fragments I recall, I forced one of the home team's cheerleaders to play point guard for the entire second half.

As a consequence of the poodle-induced car accident, I own a different shitty car with a broken air conditioner and I'm a swearing enemy of distracted driving.

In honor of my dead car, as I continued west on Highway 36 toward the town of Last Chance, whenever I encountered a texting driver, I'd remove *thon*'s phone and place it just in front of the left rear wheel of *thon*'s car. If time ever revs up again, your phone is toast, pal! Call it my calling card. Call it justice.

On to Last Chance.

This impossible dead-time world is a delusion generated by my own unsettled mind. I'm on a journey within my own subconscious. That explains everything.

Then again, if this dead-time is a product of my brain, none of this is happening; I'm either in a coma or I'm in a mental ward. Which means that I'll either wake up in the aforementioned tornado recovery scenario with Vero—who, it will turn out, will not have recently ridden the pony with The Blad, who, it will turn out was merely a figment of my insecure imagination—at my side, or, at any minute, the electro-shock therapy is going to bring me back to reality. In either case, I'll lose my status as the World's Adjudicator and revert to my old life as a holier-than-thou freelance basketball official.

I find this distressing; in spite of the inconveniences and the cuckoldry, I'm growing accustomed to my life as a superhero.

I'm on Route 36, sitting atop a hill that drops directly down to a kind of valley. At the bottom of this valley rests Last Chance, a kind of town. This hill is a skateboarder's dream. The pavement stretches into a mile-long half pipe whose slope falls midway between "harrowing" and "deadly." Drop in at the top, and when you reach the nadir of the dip you'll be doing eighty. Don't stop now! Let that momentum haul you four hundred yards up the other side. And then down and up and down andupanddown until you come to a table-spun coin clattering halt at the intersection of Route 36 and Highway 71.

From my current point of vantage, there's nothing to distinguish Last Chance from any of the other towns I've encountered on Route 36. Except for this wonderful hill. It overlooks the town and it overlooks this oceanic landscape of grass and powerlines and patchy blue western sky. Turn around. In the eastern sky, fifty miles distant, the backside of the hellfire storm is lit by the setting sun so the clouds become Olympian cauliflowers drizzled in the lusty orange of Louisiana hot sauce.

Let us address the name of this town. "Last Chance" obviously refers to a scarcity of goods between here and somewhere else. As in, look at your map. Not a lot out there, is there? No matter which way you go, it's a long ways away. So come on in, fill yer tank, buy a plastic bottle filled with potable liquid, and best of luck with the rest of your trip.

I'm sure there are towns in Montana and Nevada and Wyoming and several other states to which "Last Chance" could be more appropriately applied. I've never been to Death Valley, but that's a place that would merit a name like Last Chance. That is, if it wasn't already called Death Valley.

"Last Chance," though, might be overstating the matter. It's only thirty-five miles from here to Byers, and twenty miles in the other direction back to Abila. Short of a traumatic medical emergency, you are unlikely to suffer any serious consequences if you, for instance, fail to fill up your gas tank as you pass thru town.

To conclude, Last Chance's moniker is either:

> *A) A marketing gimmick dreamed up by some late-nineteenth century townsfolk.*

Or,

> *B) It's the name that a grateful group of exiles applied to the one place in the world where they could settle without persecution.*

If we go with option *B*, and Last Chance *is* a long-established community of fringe-types, it would explain the presence of the neo-confederate compound I visited yesterday.

Pure speculative conjecture: Our neoconfederates, Jim and Jane Jones, were born in the town at the bottom of this hill. There they were indoctrinated into the Cult of the Last Chance (For Redemption). Upon passing thru the Blood Ceremony of Adolescence, they found that the townsfolk have a thriving relationship with Shirley Jackson's stone-tossing-sacrificial story, *The Lottery*, which they took to be a primer on the management of fertility and corn harvests, to the point where the members of the Cult of the Last Chance (For Redemption) increased the frequency of public sacrifice from *The Lottery*'s once-per-year to once-per-week, which, in a town of 200 souls, could be charitably described as "short-sighted."

After they were wed in a charming outdoor ceremony which concluded with the ceremonial beheading of the town's dentist, Jim and Jane expressed their discomfort with the venerated tradition of sacrificing fifty-two random townspersons per year, not to mention the consequent need for the women of the community to beget as many children as physically possible in order to keep the town's population from collapsing beneath this strident exchange of death-for-corn, to the point where most women—that is, the ones who weren't randomly chosen to be stoned to death—found themselves dying in their late forties in the midst of birthing their twenty-first child.

Since their society frowned on anyone who expressed discomfort of any kind, Last Chance (For Redemption)'s council of elders banished the rebellious Jim and Jane Jones to a nearby ghost town where they participated in their own, less extreme and more prophylactic, version of the Cult of the Last Chance (For Redemption).

This concludes my moment of contemplation. I shall now follow Route 36 downward to Last Chance where I will poke around in some buildings and then continue to Denver and My Reckoning With The Blad.

But first, I turn for a fond, final look back east. Ahoy, hellfire storm lit like drizzled cauliflower. That storm is the only thing in this world that Vero and I could be simultaneously gazing upon. Turn away, Narwhal. Descend the hill to Last Chance and thereby bid goodbye to the last remaining sensory conduit between you and your almost-fiancée.

I shall do so. But first, I implore you, Well-Illuminated Pompadours of Water Vapor, while I am away, please be judicious to my beehive-bedecked Blad-boinking buttercup.

Hold the phone. I think I saw something.

Plans have changed. I've reversed course, turned my back to the sun, and I am now chasing my shadow. Denver will have to wait and so will The Bladster. Here's why.

As I stood on the cusp of Last Chance and gave the hellfire storm one final, metaphorically-loaded look, an orbic white-blue glow began to emanate from within its blooming dark billows. The orbic glow grew brighter and brighter, and larger and larger. Strictly speaking, "large" is an exaggeration. At its largest, the glow took up just a tiny portion of the upper edge of one particular cloud that was forty miles away, but, goodness. It was *some*thing.

After expanding for several astonishing moments, the glow began to collapse and, in doing so, sent out seven crooked fingers of light, each of them splintering like water flowing down a black-lit gulley of some fluorescence. A gazillion electrons following paths of least resistance. Like water, or, more precisely, like lightning.

This occurred miles and miles away and I saw every detail and cherished every moment. The fingers of electrons traced outward from their shrinking blue palm like a firework designed by the wizard Mithrandir. The radius of the fingers expanded and then all at once they stopped growing. For a moment, the completed lines, drawn welder arc blue in the grey cloud, paused, their image complete. And then it all faded away.

The whole thing took maybe five seconds, maybe half a minute. I'm not much for temporal estimates at this point. Had it not burned itself into my retinas, I would not believe it had happened at all.

Denver, The Blad, Last Chance, you're behind me now. I've got to go back. I'll return to my hellfire storm and stand directly underneath the cloud that begat the lighting, for therein lies some mysterious, breathtaking shit. I know this to be true, just as sure as I know I'm alive.

I mustn't lose track of that cloud. I won't; it's the one that resembles a young Henry Fonda.

*

It's impressive what a little motivation can do for a fellow. I mean, I was motivated before, but that was evil motivation. Motivation to crush, destroy, humiliate The Blad, and thereby improve my self-esteem.

The flash of lightning in the Henry Fonda cloud provided an entirely different species of motivation. It was an excuse to exit my narcissistic state of woe and actually, maybe, start to get a grip on the malfunctioning world around me.

I walked thirty miles before I slept, I passed the Jones compound without turning my head, I looked in no car windows, I stopped one time for food and water and slumber at the Abila grocery, and now I'm awake and marching again.

My eyes are fixed upon the cloud, ready for another burst of lightning. There's been just the one, so far. My legs are athrob, the kind of throb that means you're getting stronger. My feet are healthy. I keep several pairs of socks in my backpack and I change them after every meal, pilfering new ones as necessary. The knees are great. I swing my arms as I walk, maximizing my inefficiency like the Funnercise fellow used to recommend.

I'll cover the remaining twenty miles before lunch. I barely notice the thickness of the air anymore. I can walk like normal. Only difference, when I really get to marching, my thighs swell and stretch at my trousers. Hulk strong. Hulk crazy.

I'll pick up some sweatpants at the next farmhouse.

Ten miles later, I found some grey sweatpants in a dresser in a house that was serving a delicious baked ziti. The sweats do the job—so loose, so cool. I've discarded my tie and dress shirt and am now wearing an oversized t-shirt decorated with the silk-screened portrait of a NASCAR driver. Clad thusly, I march forth, hellfire bound, drawn by hope.

Hope is a goddamned complicated thing. Before hope entered the plot, I was happy to point guns and pull triggers and walk a hundred and eighty miles so I could pull a prank on a man who had nearly convinced my girlfriend that he was superior to me.

Upon taking care of my business with The Blad, I had planned to head to Hollywood to get Lauren Bacall's autograph. Think of the havoc I could have wreaked in Tinseltown. *Think* of it.

Instead, with hope, I'm hustling toward the one spot in the world where something other than me may be happening. As to the why of the lightning and how it happened, I'm trying to keep the same attitude I've had about why-ness and how-ness that I've had since zero-hour-zero. As in, don't ask questions you can't possibly answer.

Groundless speculation: Maybe the cloud was too full of potential energy to be held back by the invisible fist that brought the world into intermission.

Mindless speculation: Or it's a message from a god. Or I am as a god and I created the lightning with my mind.

Stop with all that. It doesn't matter what caused the thing, the point is that things can be caused, which means I'm not the only moving thing in the universe.

That hellfire thunderstorm is my distant sail bobbing on the horizon. Let's let us not dally, Robinson Crusoe.

I am underneath the Henry Fonda cloud of the hellfire storm. When I commenced my now-aborted trip to Denver, if you recall, I passed under the storm with my eyes closed, careful to avoid the looming doom. What a scaredy-cat I was. Come on in, kiddos, the bottom of a thunderstorm is no more frightening than one of those church youth group Halloween parties where you're blindfolded and forced to stick your hand into bowls full of marshmallow fruit salad and cold olives. Unlike a church youth group Halloween party, you're allowed to run around naked in a thunderstorm. I have shed myself of my sweats and the NASCAR shirt. They're poised, human like, at the edge of the rain.

It is raining under this particular cloud. The drops are perfectly round, the size of a rat's eye, spaced remarkably far apart. I would have expected the drops to be, I don't know, much closer together. Instead, they're about a yard apart, on average. Sometimes, though, they're clumped together, some of them literally bouncing into each other, distorting their spheres into miniature, glassy lava lamps.

I collide with the raindrops. I poke one with my finger. As with other liquids I've encountered, the drop liquefies once it contacts my skin.

Have you ever used a soldering iron? When the pointy tip of the hot iron touches a glob of solder, the solid solder turns to liquid metal, flattening and creeping upward along the metal of the iron. That's what the raindrop does when my finger touches it. At the point of contact, it loses its jelly consistency and adheres to my skin. The raindrop is pulled toward me where it flattens out over the ripples of my fingerprints. As long as it's touching me, it behaves like real water. If I shake my hand violently enough, the water is flung off and it re-jellifies to hover in mid-air as a spray of teeny little misty droplets.

I run naked. The shoes remain on, of course. There are cacti here.

As I collide with the drops, and as they turn wet against my skin,

I enjoy my first shower in weeks. My face and belly and hair become wet. I rub my armpits and fling my funk to float in my wake.

I grow tired and clean, so I stop running. The ground is dotted with dark wet spots. The rain must have just started. Puffs of dust have been pounded into the air by the individual drops. The smell is unbelievable. It smells like rain. Look up, vectors and vectors of raindrops, poised and paused, all parallel lines converging on nothing, hypnotic and backdropped by the grey-black mass from whence they've condensed.

Deeper beneath the cloud, where the drops are more numerous, I resume running, now with my arms wide. I create Narwhal-shaped tunnels in the shower.

Lookee! There's a hailstone. Is that pea-sized or bee-sized? Investigate. 'Tis Cheerio-sized. *Lookee!* There's more, no two the same.

The sky slaves are dumping wheelbarrows of hail. Pluck one from the air and chew. Yummy. Gimme some sugar, Sugar. Gimme a Ferris wheel and a Sno-Kone. Vero, why are you sitting on a non-chair in that dopey diner in Holliday when you should be here, running naked with me?

Let's gather hailstones into a solid block the size of a basketball, right at head-height. Shape them into a face. Dig out the eyes. Give her hair, long and atomizing.

In spite of myself, Vero, this looks something like you. Let's gaze upon you from a distance, my beautiful floating ice head. Squint. A lopsided lump *d'eau glacée*. Hardly arty, but it is hovering in mid-air. You belong in a museum on that basis alone.

Deeper into the storm. The ground rises and then slopes downward into a bowl-shaped valley. The rain is odd here, the vectors swerving, twisting. I walk down the valley's slope and then I stop and I freeze as tight as every other human I've encountered in the past two weeks. On account of the fact that, right at the bottom of this valley is a—

tornado.

Here, friends, is where everything comes to a grinding start. We've all seen cyclones in photos and on film, the mile-wide ones that regularly destroy and regenerate Midwestern cultures. The whipping tails on local news captured by handheld videocams, accompanied by the Missus telling the Mister to get the hell away from that window and get hisself on down to the basement.

No one has ever seen a tornado like I'm seeing this one. A column of black, as wide as Jack's magic beanstalk, rising straight to the devilish sky. The tornado has whipped the storm into a vast corkscrew, the wind stretching the raindrops into sperms, each with a mote of dust in its mouth. How many dust motes does it take to make a rainstorm? Who cares about dust when you have a tornado, especially when the thing is *moving*?

You've been on a bus before, right? Maybe you sat in front of me and I called you by a racial epithet. Please accept my most sincere apology for that incident. You've been on a westbound bus in rush hour on Colfax when traffic was clogged to a complete stop. You've looked out the mud-splattered window to see an eastbound bus to your immediate left, also clogged in traffic.

And then this thing happens where you feel your bus pull forward. You see it happen and so you believe it. But in reality you're just seeing the other bus move ahead and you're still stuck in your lane. Your eyes are liars.

I couldn't believe my eyes when they told me the tornado was moving. The battle between perception and reality rendered me dizzy, and so I fell down to the ground, where I found myself slapping my own face while shouting, "Get ahold of yourself, man!"

I have since gotten ahold of myself, dusted the dirt off my ass, and am once again poised bipedally, staring at the tornado, ready to admit that my eyes are not full of shit.

Reader, you've never gone two weeks without seeing anything move. Even the poor assholes in solitary confinement get to see a food tray three times a day. They can flush their shits.

This tornado is moving, moving, moving, moving, moving, moving. I want to write those words a million times. You can't begin to appreciate how much I'm moved by this movement. I've composed a haiku in its honor:

A massive vertical column
of aggregated stuff
is twirling.

The tornado is spinning so fast I can *see it move*. You and I have different definitions of "fast," obviously. In fact, you would probably say that the tornado is barely moving at all. But you're wrong. To risk a tautology, it's spinning, therefore it's *spinning.*

My heart is beating too quickly to be any judge of seconds or minutes, but I'll try. In ten heartbeats a clod of dirt suspended in that vortex has traveled at least half a foot in the same counterclockwise direction that water flows as it swirls down a northern hemispherical shower drain.

That's just a dirt clod. The whole tornado, full of dirt and dust and spermy raindrops, is moving before my scary eyes. Imagine an inverted version of the Eiffel Tower, spinning spinning spinning fast enough that a turtle would have to walk briskly in order to maintain a conversation with the tourists who hang desperately from the girders.

I'm going to circumnavigate this thing.

The tornado is big-ish, probably twenty yards in diameter. There's no distinct line to define just where the tornado starts and non-tornado-ness begins. I keep to the outside of the area where the raindrops begin to atomize.

The twister is creeping downhill, toward the very bottom of this valley. In the dim light below the clouds, the bottom of the valley is filled with big, old barkless trees. The twister has reached the first of them and it's starting to tear off branches. Stand for a hundred heart-beats and watch a twig bend just a little. Here, a branch the breadth of a human arm is being dismembered from its trunk.

Godchrist, it's altogether too quiet here. Silent as a lamb and dark as the bottom deck of the ark. Not that dark. Pretty dark, though. There's a profile of light coming from the diffused sun, just enough so I can tell what's happening.

On the ground, I see a branch the size of a jousting lance. I lift it and poke it into the tornado. If you thought it was a thrill to watch a tornado, imagine what it's like to feel one tug a stick from your hand. I release the stick and watch as the tornado slowly, slowly consumes it.

I'd be an idiot not to touch a tornado.

I creep forward, knees bent, bracing to be whirled off my feet and into Oz. I outstretch my left arm, closer, closer. As I near the event horizon, particles of particulate begin to pelt me at a dreamish pace. I'm a magnet and this dust and that pulverized silicate and this terrified fly and so forth strike and cling to my rain-wet arm.

I reach in further. I feel the tornado dust strike my back, my butt cheeks, my ear. I wish I'd left my clothes on. I feel the drag of the wind on my fingers. Another step and my hand is definitely inside the tornado. I grope about, enjoying the wind. It's like being breathed on by a sleeping dog. The sensation is brand new. I'm not making this happen. It's happening to me. I take a full step closer. I feel indecent and vulnerable so I cover my crotch with my free hand.

There's a football-sized mass passing in front of me. I reach for it and touch fur. It's a rabbit! Don't worry, buddy. I'll save you. I grasp a hind leg, crawl my hand to the scruff of the bunny's neck. You would think it'd be easy to extract a rabbit from a tornado, but this is not the case. I have to grasp with both hands. When I try to yank the cuddly bunny out of the tornado, I have to lean on my heels, and even then the patient wind won't let go of the bunny.

Oh, boy. The patient wind won't let go of me, either. The tornado hoists me closer and soon my feet are no longer on the ground and things are very, very serious. I let loose of the rabbit and start claw-ing at the specks of dirt that have engulfed me. I scream until my eardrums rattle.

The storm is swinging me towards one of the dead trees. I'm three feet off the ground, my feet are being pulled in. I'm flapping my arms, desperately trying to swim away from the vortex. It's a ridiculous image, this flailing naked man in black referee shoes.

I'm swung ever so slowly, but oh so firmly, into a dead branch big enough that it would support a tire swing. I grab hold and hug my limbs against the limb. The wind is at my back and it presses me painfully against the knobby branch. On the bright side, I'm stable for now. On the other side, I'm still fucked because in just a few minutes, the tornado is going to creep forward and crush my ribs against the tree and then eat me.

I opt for a third option: desperation born of terror. Imagine a scene in a sci-fi movie where the spaceship's hull has been breached and all the air is pouring out of the ship and our hero has to climb up a flapping electrical cable in order to reach the button that turns on the emergency force field.

Let's dispense with the drama. I made it. I clawed along the branch to the trunk and made my way around and escaped the tornado. Once my feet were back on the ground, I ran the hell away from that thing, bunny be damned, and straight back to my sweat pants. Before I dressed, I scrubbed myself clean, again, in the raindrops.

And now I sit with my back to the sun. My hands, sternum, thighs, *et cetera*, are scratched up. Blood oozes from a non-fatal gash on my left arm.

I can't believe that just happened.

I hiked south of the tornado, in the general direction of the House of Pronghorn, where I'd stayed several nights prior, the one with the decapitated pronghorn head and the pot roast, and the guns—the latter of which, if you recall, I'd taken outside and pulled the triggers.

Within the hellfire storm within my Nar-centric universe there spins a mighty tornado. A reasonable person might interpret this as a clue. This reasonable person might suggest, in that helpful manner of reasonable people, that *If only you could figure out why a tornado can move and why lightning can flash, you could figure out how you got trapped here and then you could figure out how to get the world started up again.*

Perfectly reasonable. Where do you recommend I start?

When I'd marched toward the Henry Fonda cloud, I did not know what to expect, but I definitely did not expect to see a tornado, much less see it *move*. Much, much less did I expect it to nearly kill me.

But what did the fucking thing *tell* me?

It told me that there's a slow-motion tornado in a pasture a couple miles north of the House of Pronghorn. It told me that the world is not completely frozen. It told me there's a scrap of hope, because if a tornado can move, then maybe other things can move. This is all excellent news, probably. In honor of that probably-excellent news, I shall endeavor to pay attention to my surroundings, to look for more evidence of motion, and to figure all this shit out.

After I deal with The Blad, that is.

My current plan: go to the House of Pronghorn, dine on some more pot roast and carrots and then, fully recomposed, resume my journey to Denver, find The Blad, extract him from his office, transport him a hundred and twenty miles east, and toss him into the tornado. Let the All-Powerful Wizard decide what to do with the cuckolding prick.

*

As I hiked underneath the non-tornadic portion of the storm, I crossed a gully lined with trees. Further south, I encountered an abandoned homestead. It consisted of a sandblasted wood-frame house with teeth of glass in the windowpanes, a caved-in barn, and a picturesque windmill missing several of its blades.

The lighting situation, with the darkness overhead and the red sun to the west, cast everything simultaneously grey and orange. When you think of The Romantic West, this is the sort of mystical setting that comes to mind, or at least the sort that shows up in paintings above hotel room beds. I walked thru the homestead soaking in the composition, touching nothing but the dirt under my shoes. This place was not romantic. It was full of dread. No. It was full of *reverberations* of dread.

I strode south and east now, and exited the storm, on the lee side, the dark side, the Vero side. I quickly found the House of Pronghorn, redbrick, asquat on the plains, surrounded by its evergreen windbreak.

Remember the guns? The twenty guns I'd brought outside and aimed at the sky, and whose triggers I had pulled? They were now lying on the ground, like a pile of lethal Pick-Up-Stix.

I crept toward them, examining the dirt for footprints and finding only the ones I'd deposited when I'd first been here. The old footprints had noticeably deeper tread. Either I was losing weight or all this walking was wearing down the soles of my shoes. Where am I gonna find a new pair of size fifteen officially-sanctioned official's shoes in this commerce-free community?

Looking carefully in all directions, I leaned over the guns and sniffed. The air smelled like combustion, as in, these guns had been fired. It was at this juncture that I switched from the *bemused* side of the ledger to the *worrisome* side of the ledger.

With great care, I examined the guns one by one, sniffing around the barrels, rubbing my finger inside. Every one of them had sent forth its payload of lead. Apparently, the folks at the House of Pronghorn were of the opinion that the safest gun is a loaded gun. The kick of combustion had thrown the weapons violently into the ground, leaving butt-shaped indentations.

I followed my nose. Just to the south and east, a white, dispersing puff of a twenty-one-gun salute floated several yards above the ground. No sign of the bullets or shotgun pellets or whatever comes out of these things. I'm woefully stupid when it comes to firearms. The most dangerous weapon I'd ever owned was a blowgun I'd made out of four-foot length of conduit. The projectiles were Play-Doh. The blowgun got confiscated by my second-grade teacher after I brought it to school and tried to show a buck-toothed girl how to ping the merry-go-round.

Lightning, tornado, guns that fire. Contrary to my original conclusion, things *are* happening. This raises many questions, none of which I am in a position to concern myself with, for I'm currently preoccupied with the fact that I may have shot my almost-fiancée.

I left Vero in a diner with a pistol prepared to discharge into her face from fifteen feet away, remember?

Currently, I am sprinting toward Cookie's Palace Diner in Holliday, Colorado.

With long-distance running, you can either enter The Zone and concentrate exclusively on foot placement, angle of elbows, deep breaths, hip twists, and optimum spinal flex; or you can let all that shit happen on autopilot and focus instead on various forms of guilt, regret, fear, and shame that one encounters when one realizes one has accidentally-on-purpose abandoned one's almost-fiancée with the barrel of a forty-five caliber pistol staring at her face.

Before I had placed the pistol in Sandy-the-waitress's hand and aimed it at Vero, I'd pointed the thing at my own head and pulled the trigger. If something bad has happened, I would argue that the original intent was self-infliction of death, not murder.

No, I would not. Whatever I come across when I reach Cookie's is my responsibility.

I just passed the turn-off for Keaton. Seventeen more miles.

I'd wrapped Sandy's fingers around the gun very loosely. Does anybody out there know what happens when a gun goes off in a loose grip? Me, neither, but I sure hope the thing will jerk backwards and in so doing send the bullet way off target, like at least a foot higher than the human head at which it was initially aimed.

Fourteen more miles.

Let's say the pistol did go off and fire true. The bullet's moving in slow-motion. As I recall from a "Make Your Own Weather" article from an early-nineties issue of *Popular Science*, tornados can spin at up to 300 miles per hour. A bullet can travel way, way faster than that. The motion of the hellfire tornado was visible to my eyes. Assuming the pistol's bullet is in the same time dominion as the tornado, it would travel a shitheap faster than the tornado. But if a bullet travels faster than a tornado, and if I can see a tornado move, then I should have seen the bullet exit the gun.

But I didn't see any bullets exit the guns at the House of Pronghorn, which doesn't make sense. Except, it does. Before a bullet exits gun, the trigger mechanism has to do whatever a trigger mechanism does. This surely involves the motion of multiple levers and a firing pin, not to mention the initial combustion of gun powder in the bullet itself. This process could easily take several seconds.

I hadn't stuck around in the van after I'd aimed Cookie's pistol at my head. I'd pulled the trigger, shuddered, and left.

Twelve more miles.

If the gun fired after I placed it in Sandy's hand, and if the bullet is traveling straight, and if time in the Palace is the same as time under the hellfire storm, then there's a better-than-even chance that Vero has been seriously injured and a worse-than-none chance that she's headless.

Everything I know about ammunition, I learned from Dirty Harry—.38s will bounce off windshields, .44s will not. A .44 will take your head clean off. The gun I pointed at Vero was a .45. Dirty Harry didn't say anything about a .45, but I presume that if the extra .01 made it better than a .44, he'd have owned one. Which puts it in the realm of windshield bouncers. To conclude, Vero's just fine, assuming her face is as hard as a windshield.

Nine miles.

Before I'd left the Palace, I'd pulled the chair out from under Vero. Boy, was I angry. Maybe she's falling down faster than the bullet is flying toward her. Maybe that's highly unlikely.

Seven miles. Gotta get new shoes. These soles are shot. My feet are fine, but my knees are starting to get cranky.

There's no rationalizing this. I pulled a trigger and pointed a gun at a human. Even when there are no consequences, there are consequences.

This is what it means to be human. This is what it means to be a fucking *butterfly.* Flap yer wings today and tomorrow you're complicit in the destruction of New Orleans.

Listen, Narwhal, even though you're all alone, you do not exist in a vacuum. And even if you did, there's still a thing called morality. Back in the days, I used to impose my morality on basketball teams. Recently, I've imposed my morality on a perverted trucker and drivers with cell phones. But my sense of morality apparently flies right out the window when I betray Vero's confidence and read her diary. And then, when I don't like what I learn from this diary that I have no business reading, I point a pistol.

What ludicrous hiccup of idiocy inspired me to point the pistol?

As a referee, I altered rules to fit my moods. I did this because it was the only way to guarantee that the correct team won. I've been doing the same thing on a much larger scale ever since I became the only moving human on earth. It's my duty. I'm the adjudicator.

No, I'm not. I'm a lousy cheater.

Vero doesn't care for penguins, never has. As she tells it, one day, when she was a sophomore in high school, she was visiting her Auntia in St. Louis and a PBS penguin documentary came on the TV. During a pause for fundraising, Vero shouted to her Auntia. Auntia was in the kitchen and Vero shouted, "*¡Tía! ¡Tía! ¡Los pinguinos son más lindo que el pelo del bebé!*" For reasons that Vero was unable to adequately explain in her recollection, this statement caused Auntia to laugh so hard that wine came out of her nostrils. As a joke, when Vero's next birthday rolled around, Auntia mailed Vero a stuffed penguin doll.

Vero's big sisters saw the penguin perched on her nightstand and decided, as a joke, that her Christmas gift that year would be a penguin poster that they'd seen at the poster store at the mall. 'Twas an image of two penguins walking down a beach, flipper in flipper. At the bottom of the poster, a single word: *Friendship.*

"From there," Vero told me, "word got out that I was a penguin lover. It must have been a relief for my friends. Why do something thoughtful for me when you can buy a shitty bobblehead penguin or an ice-cube tray decorated with penguins or a Pittsburgh hockey jersey and wrap it in penguin wrapping paper? I have whole a closet full of penguin shit."

Aloud, I laughed. Inside, I was jealous; no one has ever given *me* a penguin.

On the glorious day, all those months ago, when Vero moved out of her place and into mine, I was with her as she opened the closet in the empty, echoing bedroom in her soon-to-be-former apartment and I found myself gazing upon at least a thousand dollars' worth of ironic penguin gifts. It was almost dreamlike, actually, a grotesque exhibit of what it means to wish to be thought of as thoughtful.

Vero said, "Stare while you can, boyfriend." She then reached into her beehive hair and pulled out a tube of something called UltraGlue, which she proceeded to squeeze all along the door frame. She tossed the empty glue tube onto the closet floor and said, “Lean with me.”

She pressed the closet door closed and the two of us rested our shoulders against it until the glue dried.

At this point, the dream may have ended.

Vero, I will not allow your affair with The Blad to become your new penguin, nor will I allow it to become my butterfly. Which is to say, in layman’s terms, I will neither allow your affair to create a new definition of who I think you are, nor will I allow it to cause a hurricane. I forgive you, sweetheart. Please have a head when I see you next.

I’ve made visual contact with the grain elevators of Holliday. And, look, here’s my Mack truck with its watermelon fetishist and trailer full of wheat. I jog past without stopping, but I do glance back. The magazine photos I’d placed in the windshield have fallen down.

I’ve been incredibly wrong. Time is moving, gang. It’s just moving really, really slow.

As I enter town, I reach up and slap the *Welcome to Holliday* sign. I salute skyward in the general direction of the one-legged seagull, who, if anything, has flown even higher, now a prick of white, nearly invisible.

After my twenty-five mile dash, I’m wheezing, my chest is heaving, my legs have no bones, and my eyebrows are dusted with grains of sweat salt.

My feet bring me to the Palace Diner’s parking lot and to the front door. I lean my shoulder against the door for a moment, then I pull it open and enter.

Nobody is moving, but everything has moved. Veronica is sitting splay-legged on the floor with her right hand pressed against her forehead. Her face is intact, a swirl of fear and anger with a healthy dose of pain. Sandy is running toward Veronica, her arms outstretched.

Old Timer leans forward on his stool, gazing at the pistol, which Sandy has dropped on the floor.

The evidence strongly suggests that I’m too late.

A while ago, Vero and I were watching the local news and there was a story about one of the mass shootings that are so popular in the States these days. One of the witnesses, a young woman shivering in the cold, her face illuminated by the twirling lights of emergency vehicles, was asked by a reporter to describe what it had been like to witness such mayhem.

"It was unsurreal."

Until I found the tornado and discovered that time is moving, my frozen diorama had been a dreamscape where I could do whatever I wanted. It's not a dream anymore. It's chaos in slow motion, and it is most assuredly *unsurreal.*

With my over-jogged lungs still gasping for air, I creep to Vero where she's seated upon the floor. I squat before her. The tendons in her neck are taut, her fingers are white where they press against her forehead. This is a wartime magazine photo. *Innocent woman struck by crossfire, possibly.*

The wall behind her is clean. No splash of brain, no skull fragments. The back of Vero's head has no visible damage. I rub my hand against her hair all around her head. No sign of an exit wound. This leaves open the possibility that the bullet is still inside her skull.

Her right hand is still tight against her forehead. Underneath her hand, that's where I'll find the hole.

At this moment, I don't know if Vero is alive or dead. The only way to preserve the illusion that she *might* be alive would be for me to leave her hand where it is and get the hell out of here and never look back. We can all agree that that would take some serious courage, walking out in the midst of such a potent moment. We can also agree that courage requires only a gentle nudge upon the sternum before it teeters backward off the Cliff of Dignity and tumbles into the River of Shame.

It's Sandy-the-waitress's eyes that supply the nudge. She who has called me Hon, and who has brought us food, and who has been pouring coffee for Old Timer, and who doesn't know Vero from any other city twit passing thru town, and who is wearing the onion ring I'd intended for Vero's finger. Sandy, who does not have the luxury of pondering the meaning of *unsurreal,* is rushing to help a stranger in distress. If this country waitress can be bold enough to approach my gal after a phantom gunshot, then I can at least bear witness to the damage I've done.

I grip Vero's thumb and, atom by atom, I peel her palm away from her lovely forehead.

The skin beneath is perfectly intact. No hole, no bruise, no evidence of gunplay at all.

Please allow me a moment to curl up on the floor and weep with relief.

Thank you.

Why the hand on the forehead? Because she thinks I snuck out of the bathroom and yanked the chair out from under her and she can't see why I'd pull a bush-league prank like that, and so she's imitating a gesture she learned from her oft-exasperated *madre*, that's why.

I walk to where the pistol lays on the floor and I lift it up. It's one of those square-looking jobbers with a clip in the handle, as opposed to a revolver you'd see a cowboy employ. I sniff the barrel. It has the same gunpowdery aroma as the guns from the House of Pronghorn, which suggests that the gun *has* fired recently. But if it had been fired, it would have projected a bullet and ejected an empty shell. I check the floors, the walls, everywhere. No empty shells, no bullets.

And so therefore. Therefore, forget this forensic nonsense. Vero's alive, man! Bathe in the joy. I press my cheek against her chest. I pat her hair for several moments and then I walk to Sandy and slide the onion ring off her finger, with the intention of putting it on Vero's finger. But I stop. You can't put an engagement onion ring on someone's finger without *thon*'s consent. I place it on the table, next to one of Vero's uneaten French fries.

*

Having recently run a marathon, and now being embraced by the warm calmness that one encounters when one realizes that one has not murdered one's almost-fiancée, I was suddenly beset by exhaustion and dehydration and the desire to eat as much food as possible.

I devoured a bottle of water and then another. I reckoned I needed to get some calories in my belly before I took a nap, so I went to the kitchen. Cookie the chef was in the process of opening the door to see what all the commotion was about. I had to shove him out of the way before I could enter.

I pulled the basket out of the oil and attempted to eat a French fry. God almighty, they were hot. If I really want a French fry, I can eat one of Veronica's. Perhaps I will, someday. For the time being, my repast shall consist of hamburger buns upon which I smear grape jelly scooped from single serving plastic containers.

I went outside the diner and ate on the front step. I plowed thru half a dozen buns, eating another couple of bottles of water as well. I fell asleep halfway thru bun number seven, awoke with jelly on my forehead. To hell with the front step. I crawled sleepily into Cookie's van and passed out on his mattress.

I haven't spoken of my sleeping habits. When I'm on the road, I try to find a bed in a dark room and I lie down and then I wait. The mattress never properly squishes under my weight and, as a consequence, my back always hurts. I lie there, listening, but there's nothing to hear. I have only the sound of my breath and my heartbeat. The moments of sleepwait are an isolation chamber. You think that'd be dreamy, but it ain't. I'm *already* completely isolated. Sleepwait isolates me from my isolation. It's like going to jail and then getting sent to solitary confinement, and then being straitjacketed, weighted down, and tossed into a lake.

Deep breaths, count sheep, recite freshman French vocabulary, you know the shtick. Eventually, the anxiety gives way to the vacuum and I drift away.

Lately, occasionally, I'll dream. Same thing every time: I'm stuck in dream freeze—the one where I can't speak or move—and everyone else is buzzing around me in a blur. When the dream gets too intense,

I awake sweating, pulse out of control. That part's familiar to anyone who's had a nightmare. But coming to in the dark on an unfamiliar bed that doesn't squish, with no clock or any idea of how long I've been out—what a shit way to start the day.

Having said this, I slept like a fucking baby after running that marathon to discover to my eternal relief that I hadn't killed Vero.

PART TWO

Since there were no reference points, I had no idea whether my fall was fast or slow. Now that I think about it, there weren't even any proofs that I was really falling: perhaps I had always remained immobile in the same place, or I was moving in an upward direction; since there was no above or below these were only nominal questions and so I might just as well go on thinking I was falling, as I was naturally led to think.

— Italo Calvino,
Cosmicomics

I awoke upon the mattress in the back of Cookie's van, stretched my arms, yawned, had a brief moment of panic, remembered that Vero did *not* have a bullet in her head, and cheerfully vowed that this would be a great day. It was already a great day. I'd been fully awake for at least three minutes, and I hadn't thought about The Blad *once*. And now that I *was* thinking about him, the thoughts were borderline grateful. If I hadn't started on my quest to exact my revenge, and if I hadn't stood there on the cusp of the town of Last Chance and looked back to the hellfire storm, I may never have seen that glorious eruption of lightning that led me to the tornado that led me to the House of Pronghorn that led me to run my ankles off to save the woman I love.

As I was backing out of the van, just about to push the passenger door shut, I saw a shaft of sunlight streaming thru a small hole in the driver's side doorframe, just above the window. I climbed back in for a closer look. I poked my pinkie thru the hole. I sniffed several times and picked up a strong scent of burned gunpowder.

I jumped out of the van and examined the hole from the outside. Based on the tulip petals of splayed metal, this was an exit wound. I reentered the van and pawed thru the fast food wrappers and Rolling Stones CDs until I found an expelled shell with *.45* stamped into the back.

I contemplated this shell for several minutes before it came to me. You've already figured it out.

If you recall, when I had initially removed the gun from Cookie's glovebox, I had pointed it, the gun, at my head and pulled the trigger. The cry for help in an empty forest. Then I had released the gun to float. A short time later, after I'd left the van, the gun had silently fired a slow-motion bullet, which had pierced the frame of the van.

A day or two later, I had removed Cookie's pistol—which, upon reflection, was not in the same place where I'd left it, sort of upward and further back—and brought it to the restaurant and placed it in Sandy's hand, aimed at Veronica, totally harmless.

I enter the diner and say hello to everybody. I return Vero to her chair and adjust her into an approximation of the pose she'd held when Time-Out began, the soggy French fry approaching her mouth, her left eyelid halfway raised in the same goofy freeze-frame face from before. I pat the top of her beehive and say, "We can work thru this."

I arrange Sandy and Old Timer into their original positions, even down to molding a new tongue of coffee for Sandy to not-quite pour into Old Timer's cup.

I leave my onion engagement ring on the table, next to Vero's plate. The gun, I return to Cookie's glove box, after wiping it clean of fingerprints.

Here's what I've learned in the last two days.

1) Vero is safe.

2) Recent events (lightning, tornados, guns, etc.) strongly suggest that the world has not, as I previously believed, come to a complete stop. Rather, it's just moving incredibly slowly.

If I'm gonna to confirm my slow-but-not-stopped theory, I'm gonna need a telescope.

I wandered the dirt streets of Holliday until I came upon, glory on high, a school. It was tucked away behind an enormous farm building, but still, there's no reason why I hadn't been curious enough about this town to have found it earlier.

The school is fully integrated: kindergarten thru senior, everybody in one building. Flipping thru the composite photos in the hall next to the office, the average class size has historically been somewhere between seven and twelve kids, the average haircut is high and tight (male) or tall and wide (female). K-12, 130 kids, total. This is a small school. They play six-man football, won state in 1968 and 2002.

Let's contrast this to the experiences of young Narwhal Slotterfield. Over the course of thirteen years of education, not counting Referee classes, I had progressed from elementary to middle to high school, each with a new building with an entirely different staff, different set of rules, a different lunch lady, and a different opportunity to re-start my social life, which inevitably ended with me upside-down in a bathroom stall.

Back to the Holliday experience. Imagine spending your entire academic career trapped inside the same building. Same classmates, same teachers, same reputation following you around for thirteen years. My God, it'd be like living in a cult. People must drive each other crazy. And yet, you never hear of a mass murder in a rural school.

A school is a wonderful, wonderful resource. Holliday elementary/middle/high school includes shoes in lockers, shitloads of food in the cafeteria, textbooks covering all subjects, a surprisingly well-stocked library, and, best of all, a science room closet containing a dusty 140-power PlanetEye refractor telescope.

I set up the PlanetEye and its tripod outside the Palace and pointed it toward the sky in hopes of communing with my one-legged seagull. It's not easy to point a telescope straight up, but I shortened two of the tripod's legs and got the thing more or less vertical and stable.

Lying on my back, I twisted knobs and jigged the telescope until I found the white dot of the seagull. I zoomed in, focused. The seagull is not a seagull, turns out. Rather, it's an airplane, white with red stripes, dragging itself across the sky by a single propeller. Maybe a crop duster, although I'd always pictured crop dusters as biplanes. The plane was way the hell higher up in the air than a crop duster—or a seagull—had any business flying.

Also, the plane was upside down. I'm no expert in small aircraft, but that seemed out of the ordinary. I adjusted the telescope until the plane grew larger in the viewfinder. This brought me close enough to see thru the windshield and make out the faces of two men, both in a state of absolute delight, hair floating, mouths open in bellows of barnstorming joy. At least someone's getting their jollies. I did not begrudge them for not being a seagull.

I watched the plane for a long time. The telescope was eerily still, absent the typical jitters one encounters in long distance viewing, which gave the image a static feel, except for the fact that the propeller was spinning, slowly, like the tornado. I watched the prop make a full revolution and then several more. This gave me an idea. The seagull plane was moving too slowly for this idea, but the sky was full of passenger jets that'd be perfectly suitable.

I moved the telescope away from the little plane and sighted it upward at the leading end of one of the contrails that crossed the sky.

At this distance, the telescope wasn't powerful enough for me to pick up any faces thru the windows, but I could tell I was looking at a passenger jet, right side up, probably headed for Denver International.

I aimed the PlanetEye so the tail of the plane was at the far-left edge of the viewfinder. Then I went back into the school and ate a fist-sized hunk of government cheese and then came back and looked thru the scope again. In that time, probably six minutes, the plane had moved halfway across the viewfinder.

I gnawed cheese and pondered. If I could parse this correctly, I'd be able to figure out how fast time was moving. To hell with my hair. Measuring time in inches and months, that's a calendar. I wanted a clock. To the math room, quick.

Remember when I was desperate and depressed and running two-dozen miles to save Veronica's life? She's okay, I'm okay, save for some lingering soreness in my lower limbs, and now I have an inkling of what's going on around me. The world has slowed to the point where one second of world time consumes approximately one day of my reality. Which is to say, in the time it'd take for Vero to say "blueberry muffin," I've eaten, digested, and shat a blueberry muffin. I'll promise not to show my work, but I do feel compelled to give you a rough idea of how I came to this conclusion, just so you know I'm not joshing you.

From reading *Great Rivet Birds: A Pre-Young Adult Exploration of Manned Flight from the Wright Brothers to the Lockheed SR-71 Blackbird* in the school library, I ascertained the make of the jet plane (Boeing 747) and from there I determined the length of the plane (231 feet, or so). The cruising speed of a 747 is 550 mph. The telescope's view finder was six and a half times as wide as the plane was long, which means that the view finder at that depth could see a disc roughly 1500 feet in diameter. So when the plane travels from one end to the other

You get the point. The wild card here is my resting heartbeat of fifty-to-seventy beats per minute. That's a lot of room for bullshit. But the bottom line is that a Narwhal day equals somewhere between .5 and 1.5 Vero seconds. This explains everything that's happening. Not *why* everything's happening, of course, or how. But other than that, it explains everything. The tornado twists, the propeller spins, and the guns fire and fall just like they're supposed to, except way too fucking slowly.

Everyone is still alive!

A single day, that's all it takes for me to get over my own murderous idiocy. I learned my lesson, now let's move on. No more gunplay. No more snooping diaries. No more cruelty. Me and Robinson Crusoe and sweet Vero, we're gonna be okay, for I am irrepressible.

*

There was a time in my life when I was nearly repressed. Three years ago, spring 2006, I was a well-established basketball official in the lesser Denver area. At only thirty years old, I'd already had eleven years of experience and had been on crew for multiple high profile high school tournaments. I'd worked a few junior college games in Greeley and I'd even subbed for a couple of games at the University of Denver, an actual, if untalented, Division-I school. If I continued with my trajectory for a few more years, I'd be working college games exclusively, and then, who knows. Italian league? NBA?

By 2006, when I was on crew, games were better than if I wasn't. It wasn't anything you could point to in particular, but players, fans, and coaches walked away from my work with a sense that things had worked out for a reason. When I say players, fans, and coaches, I mean those on the winning side. The losers are always ready to string up the ref. But the difference between me and other refs was, if your team *won*, you felt really good about how it happened. The assholes got what was coming to them and the weak inherited the mirth. With three seconds on the clock, and a five-foot-three sophomore on the line for a one-and-one to win the game, I'd whistle lane violations until the nervous kid hit the two free throws required to bring glory to his school and family. When the gazelle gets away, everyone cheers—even, secretly, the lions.

The folks who oversaw my career picked up on the existential justice that followed me around. As I mentioned before, no one remotely suspected me of being on the up-and-up. But the up-and-up-ness didn't matter; my overseers judged me in the same light as you would a man who fakes a sore ankle in order to let his six-year-old son win a footrace.

And so, on the morning of March 8, 2006, I received a breathless call from Don Connelly, Head of the Office of Big 12 Athletics Oversight.

He: *Slotterfield.*

Me: *Whaddya got?*

He: *Big-12 Tournament. Round One. Are you ready to go?*

Me: *Point me in a direction, light the fuse. I do not require batteries.*

Don pointed me toward the Beer Sponsored Events Center at the Boulder campus of the University of Colorado. Both referees who'd been slated to work the game were stuck in an Omaha airport shrouded in fog and, due to a brutal combination of leg injuries, civil lawsuits, and a flu virus with an affinity for zebras, the entire available pool of qualified subs had been whittled to just one man, Ralph Bennett, a semi-retired legend with an affinity for jump balls and denatured alcohol. Which still left them one ref short.

Don Connelly said, "You're a few years away from this, kid, but I hear you have style. The game will be televised on ESPenis. Bright lights. Don't wither."

Knock this one out and I've made it, I'm part of the club. In the summertime, rather than blow my whistle at YMCA tournaments, I'll get to work the NBA summer league in Las Vegas. Fuck up and I'd never touch a Division-I court again.

I took a bite of my cereal. "When's tipoff?"

CU was the worst basketball team in the conference. They were taking on Texas Tech, the number five team in the conference. By all rights, the game should have been played in Texas, what with them having the superior regular season record. But it was apparently Boulder's turn to host the tourney, so they, the Buffs, got the benefit of the unearned home court advantage.

It wasn't the TV cameras that took me down, or the seven thousand fans, or the importance of the tournament. It was the awfulness of the CU Golden Buffaloes Men's Basketball squad. CU was one degree above horrible. Texas Tech was two degrees under breathtaking. From the opening tip-off, I knew exactly why Don Connelly had called me, referee shortage be damned. Clearly, one of CU's boosters had shoveled a wheelbarrow full of cash into a bank account in order to make sure the Golden Buffaloes prevailed. None of that money would make it to my pocket, of course. I was deceptive, but I was never corrupt. That's another reason why the poohbahs liked me; they got to retain one hundred percent of the contents of the paper bags.

We were midway thru the second quarter when I realized I'd bitten off more than I could digest. The Buffs were no match for the Texan Technophiles, no matter what I tried, and I tried everything, including calling a traveling violation on Tech's starting point guard for shuffling his feet before shooting a free throw.

The poor Buffs couldn't make a basket, much less dribble or pass. The halftime score was thirty-two to sixteen in favor of Tech. Without my help, it might have been fifty to zero. The only way I could have possibly gotten CU the win would have been to cover the Tech hoop with a plexiglass lid, and even then the Buffs would have had to actually make some baskets of their own. My partner, Redfaced Ralph, was no help. He shuffled from one side of the half court line to the other while I sprinted from baseline to baseline, trying to cover for him. He didn't blow his whistle once, which was fortunate because the effort may have led to a heart attack. Plus, he spent halftime speed-drinking a bottle of Everclear.

Texas Tech scored the first six points of the third quarter. I countered by calling them for fouls on seven straight possessions. It was ridiculous, way beyond my spacious comfort zone. I exist in the shadows, I dwell in the subconscious, and here I was farting aloud in church. The Golden Buffs missed every single one of these gifted foul shots.

The Tech players, coaches, and fans fucking hated me. There was a lot of airfare on the line. I'd never been glared at so violently. The players started lipping off and accidentally hip-checking me as we ran down court.

High schoolers and frat boys, you can threaten with a technical foul and they'll shape up. I, however, did not actually *issue* technicals, and the Texans soon picked up on that. They decided that if I was going to call them for phantom fouls, they might as well commit real fouls. They started clobbering the Colorado kids. Elbows in kidneys, knee-to-knee, knee-to-crotch. This wasn't a footrace between me and a little kid. It was a lion versus a baby bunny and I was trying to direct the events with a limp carrot.

In other words, I was no longer in control; I was in over my head; I was out of my league; the power dynamic had shifted radically. Upon recognizing this, I fucked that noise and started calling the game straight.

Once I stopped trying to help them win, CU put up a furious fourth quarter comeback and managed to lose by only nine points. One wonders what they could have accomplished without my meddling in the previous three quarters. At the game's conclusion, a stout man in a grey suit approached me. With a grim mouth, he informed me that his name was Don Connelly, of the Office of Big 12 Athletics Oversight, and that, after the little stunt I'd pulled, he would personally see to it that I'd never work a D-I game again.

For several days after, I avoided sports radio and the papers. I did not avoid the liquor store. I lounged in my recliner and drank and loathed myself. It was a week before I regained my soul. Nothing specific happened, I just gradually realized that there's no place for a man like me in the big time. Don was right. I never got a call to work a D-I game again, and I'm okay with that, for I am irrepressible.

Slowness of time is infinitely more manageable than the absence of time. It's the difference between being dead or being on life support, and *that*, even if your name is Kevorkian, is a significant difference.

Those weeks ago, when I first exited the bathroom in Cookie's Palace Diner, I'd been dropped alone into a universe of manikins. But now, with rotating tornados and spinning propellers, my manikins are once again humans. This is the difference between death and life support. In an absence of time, I'm alone. In a *slowness* of time, I can communicate with Vero. I simply need to be patient.

I have a plan. I acquired three music stands from the Holliday school music room. I placed one stand each directly in front of Sandy, Old Timer, and Vero, a couple of feet from their respective noses. I wrote "You have nothing to fear" on two sheets of paper and placed those upon Sandy's and Old Timer's stands, respectively. I thought about this. If you truly have nothing to fear, it shouldn't be necessary to say, "You have nothing to fear." The default setting in life should be nothing-to-fear.

I crumbled up the papers and stuffed them into a trashcan.

What, then, does one write? I had to be direct, convincing, and, most importantly, concise. I couldn't say, "Don't worry, fuckers. Time as you know it has slowed to a crawl and I accidentally almost shot the beautiful woman over there, who, as far as you're concerned, recently fell on the floor and then mysteriously reappeared in her seat. My name is Narwhal Slotterfield. Last you saw of me, I was entering the bathroom. I'm no longer in the bathroom. I will take care of you in your state of time-retardation, for I am a professional amateur basketball referee. Also, there's a tornado about thirty miles to the west."

I settled on, "I am not a ghost."

I placed the papers on Sandy's and Old Timer's music stands and set to figuring out what to say to Veronica. After eight million rewrites, I came up with:

Vero, this is Narwhal. Everything's okay. I love you.

Get the essential stuff out of the way. Now for some sort of explanation.

Odd things have happened in the last few seconds. I'll explain later.

Sometimes it's best to punt.

If you can read this, wink RIGHT NOW.

Without interaction, we're mmunicating. I want to CO-mmunicate.

Please wink IMMEDIATELY.

End with a touch of desperation to acknowledge that, although everything's okay, it's not normal.

It's a first step.

With the notes placed in the lines of sight of my three principals, I simply needed to wait. I figured it'd take Vero six seconds to read the note. I figured that, after she read it, she'd read it again, which meant another six seconds. A couple more seconds to process the content and then, assuming her first impulse was to trust the words I'd handwritten on a sheet of paper that had magically appeared on a music stand that had also magically appeared, another half-second to wink. Fifteen and a half seconds. At one second Vero-time to one day Narwhal-time, it'd be at least two weeks before I knew if I had communicated with my love.

I had to find something to do with myself for a fortnight and a day.

I'm back on Route 36, headed west. Don't worry, The Blad is not on my itinerary. My sole intention is to slay seconds, murder moments, commit chronocide, kill time while the people of the diner read my notes. My sunglasses are on, I'm wearing a farm cap plucked from the Palace's lost-and-found box, which contains nothing but farm caps. My specific plan, insofar as I have any plan, is to spend the next fifteen days retracing my truncated trip toward Denver. I want to see what's been happening in the world since I was last out in it.

First stop, watermelon fetishist. The Mack truck has now veered toward the ditch and the driver's mouth is wide open in a tobacco-spewing scream. Consider it from his perspective. Out of nowhere, all his dirty pictures appeared on his windshield and then fell on his lap. It is socially acceptable, under these circumstances, to scream and veer into a ditch.

I float-drag the driver out of the cab and press him safely onto the road several dozen feet behind the semi. I go thru his pockets and find two hundred and thirty-seven dollars and a greasy comb. I keep the money.

Since there aren't any cars coming, and because the driver is resting at a safe distance, I decide to let his semi continue toward its fate in the ditch. Nobody's gonna miss a load of wheat.

On to the first farmhouse I'd visited, the one with the grilled cheese sandwiches and the découpaged "Footprints." In my first visit, I'd eaten four sandwiches and hidden "Footprints" under a mattress. With the Missus now looking bewilderedly upon her empty serving tray, I assemble four more sammies from the white-bread-and-sliced-cheese fixin's and leave them on the griddle to fry. Supper has been restored.

I slide fifty of the trucker's dollars into the back pocket of my hostess's jeans, to go along with the three bucks I'd already given her.

"Footprints" will remain under the mattress.

*

Next, the car with the college flunky. The kid has spat out the half-joint I'd put in his mouth. It's on the floor between his feet. He's clearly trying to act calm in spite of the uncanny marijuana manifestation. In their front seats, Mom and Dad remain oblivious.

I pocket the joint and leave the merry family to their own dervishes.

I continue west, past the sign for Keaton, past the depressing buildings of Dorsey, to the edge of the hellfire storm, to the House of Pronghorn, of redbrick, pot roast, and guns. I bring all twenty-one guns back into the house and place them in their gun rack. I leave a rolled-up dollar bill in the barrel of each of the guns. That oughta cover the price of the ammo I'd accidentally sent skyward.

More walking. I count nine cell phones that I've placed perilously underneath the left rear wheel of nine different automobiles. Every one of those cell phones is now smashed to pieces, the cars several feet further along in their journey. The drivers all wear the same furrowed brow of confusion. I find this gratifying.

The pronghorns were a bit of a problem. The deeramid had collapsed and most of the animals were already bounding away. But, in falling, one of them had apparently fucked up its leg. As in, added an extra joint. The creature was in mid-writhe, like a sock being wrung out by invisible hands.

It were my invisible hands that done this. I swear by the beard of Jesus, if I'd've had any idea that my shenanigans would cripple a pretty thing like this.

I walked two miles to the nearest farmhouse and borrowed a ten-inch Everslice chef's knife and then walked the two miles back to the pronghorn.

Having put the critter into its misery, I was, per the Law of the West, obligated to put it out of its misery. My options were plenty: stab the heart, cut the throat, lock the animal in a car with the windows up on a hot summer day. In a synchronized world, any of these would do the job. But in my asynchronous state, any one of those acts could fail—miss the heart, slice the wrong artery, fail to turn off the a/c—and I wouldn't realize it for months.

*

I opted for the sure thing. The procedure was every bit as unsettling as you can imagine. It gave me a newfound disrespect for my hunting buddy at the House of Pronghorn. Sawing away, squatted on the dirt next to the pair of tumbleweed pompons, I gazed into the dying, dying, dying eyes of this blameless creature and got myself a slap of repressibility. I'd injured a thing and now I was killing it, all because it couldn't run fast enough to escape me.

When the deed was finished, I cleaned the gore off the knife by wiping it on my sweatpants. Then I balanced the animal's head back upon its neck so it would look more natural.

The setting sun glared at me. There are consequences aplenty, amigos.

I fished the half-joint out of my pocket and held it between my thumb and index finger, so my hand made an *okay* sign. If you've lost track of the journey of the joint: I got it from Axel Buster in the Palace Diner, then gave it to college-unbound Brock, and then I stole it back. If only I could light a match and actually smoke the thing.

I ate it and then I waited. Nothing happened, drug-wise or otherwise. If I wanted to get stoned, I'd need to eat more than half of a joint. Eventually, I put my head in my hands and curled up and wrinkled my chin and shivered next to the dead pronghorn until I fell asleep. When I awoke, the pronghorn's head had slipped a half-inch sideways off the neck and blood had begun to seep. Its eyes had closed, at least.

I once read an article about a scientist who, back in the day, during the French Revolution, caught the severed head of a nobleman just as the guillotine dropped, and then leaped into his horse-drawn buggy and rushed the head to his lab where he had prepped a live cow with hoses sticking out of its neck. As fast as possible, he attached the hoses to the stump of the dead head and started the cow's blood to flowing, whenupon our monstrous scientist shouted the name of this particular dead noble person and the head's eyes opened up and stared and even followed the scientist's finger around for a few moments.

Just before it turned grey and went still, the head's mouth formed the shapes of words. The scientist couldn't read the lips, but one gathers that the gist of it was, "Holy fucking *sacré bleu*, does my neck hurt."

Point being, I felt bad about the pronghorn.

Next stop, Jones Compound. Tiger, outhouse, kooks, pot plants. It was the plants that tugged me the hardest. I was past due for a moment of disassociation, a change in perspective, and, with a little luck, some uncontrollable giggling.

I put on my shades, lowered my cap, and shuffled along, half depressed about the pronghorn, half giddy about knowing that Vero was, at this very moment, reading my note. And the yonder weed, promising to show me a good time.

When I reached the compound, I went directly to the old post office full of pot plants. If half a joint won't get me high, I reckon half a plant will.

I'm no expert on marijuana, but I've certainly tried it before. As I mentioned previously, I'll take a whiff at a party if someone offers, or at an outdoor concert if a joint gets passed down my row, or first thing in the morning if I find a nugget stuck to the bottom of one of my socks.

The last time I got stoned was with Vero. We were settling in for a weekday night with must-see TV and she went to her bedroom and came back with a baggie of some Strawberry Elway Diesel that she'd acquired from a friend who had a medical marijuana license. We rolled the dope and smoked it and started watching that John Wayne movie where he pretends to be Genghis Khan. We laughed our faces off for twenty minutes and then passed out.

Laughing and passing out; that's precisely the effect I hope to enjoy today.

The plants are lined up, real neat. They're roughly knee high and plump with sticky, hairy buds, all aglitter with crystals so they look like someone soaked them in sugar water and let them dry. Say what you will about the Joneses, they've got at least one green digit between them.

I snap off a mouse-sized chunk of bud and hazard a nibble. This is what they call skunk weed, as in it literally smells like a skunk. For some reason people find this appealing. The weed's so sticky that most of it gets clogged in my rear molars as I chew. Ever the stalwart, I take another bite, and then another.

I shall chronicle the events as they undress. I'm sitting crosslegged in the middle of Route 36, reading a paperback I found on a dusty shelf in the old post office. The book is called *Jesus Wins a Grammy, Jimi Wins a War: Volume Sixty-Eight of the Chronicles of Christ.* Written by Artemus Miracle, published by Hellickson Press, 2004.

The book starts in 1967 when Jesus comes back to earth in the shape of a San Francisco hippie. If the book's cover is to be trusted, the Messiah's only concession fashion-wise to the passage of one thousand nine-hundred and thirty-four years since his death is the addition of a Hopi headband. That's Jesus for you.

By the third chapter, Jesus has formed a psychedelic band with a posse of sloppy, heathenistic, acid-eating homeless hippy drop-outs. The group calls themselves The Technicolor Phoenix Scrimshaw Revolt.

Holy shit, the weed is working. I leave the book on the road and take a gander at the world around me.

The sun dips into the horizon and the hellfire storm tugs it back up. I am a poet.

Blood cells
White no more
Yellow forever
Unchanging
Until you change.

I'm sitting in a room, directly across from a tiger. Maybe six real-time seconds have passed since my first visit, since I gave the tiger the jerky. The creature's face is plunged into the salty meat. I can practically see the cat purring with culinary lust. I stroke the lawn of fur on this mighty hunter. I am allergic to cats. I plunge my face into the fur and inhale. I am not allergic to tigers.

Shame on you, Jim Jones. How dare you confine a creature of infinite wisdom within an iron collar?

I must have a word with my host.

I went to the john to have a conversation with Jim and I ended up climbing down the rope ladder so I could meet Jane. I overcame my revulsion at entering an outhouse hole, embraced the pot-induced paranoia, and descended the wiggling ladder.

Lazies and genitalworms, children of all rages: at the bottom of the right hole in that two-hole outhouse there lies a mushroom farm. I don't know why Jane would choose this moment to climb down there, what with her hubby taking a dump in the adjacent hole, but it's clear that she's more interested in fungi than she is in dungi.

It's a clever setup. As I interpret it, they poo in one hole for a few months, and then switch to the other and wait for the previous hole's poo to compost into dirt, into which they then cultivate their mushrooms. This explains the plywood partition between Hole Number One and Hole Number Two. Sanitary reasons.

How did I miss all this? It's because, back before I understood the slow creep of time, I was all about Narwhal Slotterfield, Referee of the Universe. But my ego has since left the building, *ergo non*, and I can understand things without imposing myself upon that understanding.

To wit, the canvas shopping bag on Jane's shoulder is full of mushrooms, which she has recently harvested from a thriving colony at the edge of the mound of brown. And the mound of brown is not just poop, but a vegetable-strewn compost pit. These folks are hippies. Insane hippies, also known as preppers. Learning how to survive off the earth so they can build a gun tower and shoot down all who wish to appropriate their survivalistic goodies after civilization is destroyed by the coming global weather disaster that'll be caused by sunspots.

The weed I ate is really kicking in. Right now, at this moment, I'm totally cool with these wackos. We could be friends.

I extract a single mushroom from Jane's satchel, pat her on the shoulder, and climb out. I still find it odd that she's wearing a bikini top down there.

*

I feel much better about Jim and Jane. Don't get me wrong; they're freaky. It's just that they're more than just psychopaths. They're psychedelic psychopaths. Psychepsychos.

In the main living quarters, on the kitchen table, right next to *The Confederate States of Southern North America*, there's a well-loved copy of *Psilocybin: Magic Mushroom Grower's Guide: A Handbook for Psilocybin Enthusiasts.* Not to mention a copy of *The Humanure Handbook*, which, upon perusal, explains the motivation behind the unconventional outhouse/fungus farm.

Rounding out the library is a print-on-demand typo-ridden how-to tome called *Mellow Jello: Enhancing and Preserving the Psychedelic Experience*, written by a guy named Magic Randy. This softbound gem explains how to extract psilocybin from magic mushrooms via a "revolutionary steamheat prosess" and how to then convert the hallucinogenic component into a powder, which can be added to their "Propriatery Jellatin Preservation Recipe." The final product, many examples of which I found stacked into a pyramid inside Jim and Jane's refrigerator, is completely undistinguishable from those little ramekin cups full of Jello shots that you have to endure at parties hosted by overly ambitious hosts.

Not one to jump blindly into hallucinogenic drug desserts as concocted by tiger-owning neoconfederate preppers, I opt to begin the augmentation of my marijuana mind-journey with one of Jane's humble mushrooms. I know it isn't poisonous because I looked it up in Jim's copy of *The Magic Mushroom Grower's Guide*.

I gobble down the 'shroom, which tastes like something you'd scrape off a decaying body, and I return to my spot in the middle of the road and dive back into *Jesus Wins a Grammy, Jimi Wins a War: Volume Sixty-Eight of the Chronicles of Christ.*

Reading on drugs is wonderful. I'm led into the world of the living, of motion. Like, as I read this Jesus book, I enter it and walk amongst the people and, Oh, Aldous can you hear me now?

By chapter thirteen—this thing is a quick read—The Technicolor Phoenix Scrimshaw Revolt have overcome several moments of self-doubt, as well as one unplanned pregnancy, long enough to release their first single, "Peace in the Alley (Pax Divers Culpa)." A few pages later, the song shoots to number eight on the singles chart. Although the power trio's ensemble vocals are delivered with richly intonated competence, the real strength of the piece lies in the extraordinary evocations of Jesus's free-form wah-wah guitar solo, which takes up the latter third of the song.

The solo is so amazingly extraordinarily gut-wrenchingly powerful that upon hearing it, Jimi Hendrix, who was in London at the time riding high on the release of his debut album, decides to quit the music biz. Check it out, man, in the space of fifty-seven mind-boggling seconds, Jesus has said *everything* there could ever be said electric guitar-wise. Jimi abandons the sessions that would have been *Axis: Bold as Love* and returns to the States to re-enlist in the U.S. Army's 101st Screaming Eagles Airborne Division, from which he had been honorably discharged a few years earlier after pretending to suffer a back injury.

Upon re-entering the army, Jimi gets shipped directly to 'Nam. With a parachute on his back, an M16 in one hand, and an American flag in the other, he leads the United States to comprehensive victory.

The book concludes at the 1968 Grammy ceremony in which Hendrix is awarded the Congressional Medal of Honor and then The Technicolor Phoenix Scrimshaw Revolt are awarded the award for Best Rock Single. After accepting the trophy from LBJ, Jesus thanks his father and ascends to heaven.

I'd rate *Jesus Wins a Grammy, Jimi Wins a War: Volume Sixty-Eight of the Chronicles of Christ* up there with the finest novels I've ever read. Far better than *On the Road*, which, technically, I've only partially read, and very nearly as good as *The Road.*

Thank you, funk-flavored mushroom, for this gift. At the moment, my brain violins are playing that Steve Miller song about time ticking into the future.

The three-dimensionality of my vision is greatly enhanced. Distances are things, not just concepts. Look down. The painted lines on the highway are taller than the asphalt. Look around. The prairie grasses on either side of the road where I'm sitting cross-legged are waving in a wind that blows only in my mind. Each blade of grass is distinct. Gaze inward. The colors of the world.

I have to get something to eat.

I stole beef jerky from a tiger, Vero. I am faster than a tiger. Fastman. And I am brave. I will open the fridge. Done. I will upend two, three, four ramekins and slurp the cold Jello out with my tongue. Done. The sugar masks the decay. I hope there's no such thing as a lethal dose of mushrooms.

Outdoors, well off the road, I find a pair of rattlesnakes making love under a sagebrush. I lift them to the sky and shape them into two intertwining rings, each snake with its own tail stuffed into its mouth.

I call the work "Matrimonial Snakes Vomiting Their Own Bodies."

I will recline upon this warm, sandy earth. To my right is a yucca, to my left, a yucca. To my east is Veronica. Oh, Vero, what are you up to? What strange thoughts creep thru your slowed-down brain?

I close my eyes. I'm in your skull now, sweetheart. I'm a loinclothed Tarzan swinging amongst the stringy branches of dendrites and axons within the humid jungle of your cerebral cortex. Thru the tangle, a sluggish flash of lighting, like the one I saw in the Henry Fonda cloud at the cusp of Last Chance. It glows and jumps the gap between synapses and then fades. More flashes, all around.

I wriggle thru a web of dendrites toward a massive bundle of excitable synapses; wet purple mushrooms, bursting with orbic faeries that glow and retreat. I plunge my head into the midst of the mushrooms and am treated to a first-person trip within one of your memories.

Watching thru your eyes. You're walking next to me on a Colfax sidewalk, just a few blocks from the capitol building. It's a windy day, dry leaves rattle on the tree branches.

I remember this. It happened just a few weeks ago, on an afternoon. I turn to you and I say, "Would you describe me as swarthy?"

You say, "More like not quite white."

End of conversation, we keep walking.

Your hand reaches forth and rests on my shoulder. Your fingers brush my ear. I remember that moment, loving this person who would choose to touch my ear on a pointless promenade.

We pass by Jerry's Record Exchange and your eyes glance at the shop window and see themselves in the reflection. Your eyes are alive and moving, your face content with a casual, unquantifiable grace. But when you see yourself, your face makes a quick adjustment, like when you're reading a good book and someone walks into the room and says, "Catchin' flies?" And you realize that in your literary reverie you've become so content that your cheeks are drooping and your mouth has gone slack. You've lost your self, lost your ego, lost muscle control.

The spell is over, you bring your cheeks up, your lips flatten, you are dignified.

I bow to your bundles of thoughts and exit your mind.

Why have you forsaken me, cruel world? The universe is a squatting mule. I must tug its harness, tickle its ear, convince it to carry on with its march up the canyon.

Ye gods! I demand that you bestow upon me a genuine hallucinatory vision with the theme of: Will I ever again hear the voice of Veronica Vasquez?

And so it came to pass that from a varmint hole in the ground there did arise a harmony of light and sound. The harmony swirled about in a dizzying fashion and then coalesced into the hovering form of a shortish human female clad in white linen.

She floated before me, eyes closed. The color of her skin fluctuated like a cuttlefish. The flesh was dark like moist earth, and then it lost all color and resembled wet tissue paper and, even thru her robe, I could see her heart pump blood into her veins and I could see her muscles expand and contract with her breaths, and then her skin gained color until it went as black as a moonless sky and then faint stars, millions of miles away, twinkled. And then her skin went brown again and stayed that way, which didst please me because it was far less distracting.

Toes floating inches above the dirt, the human female spread her arms wide, very Christ-like, and took several more deep breaths. My respirations became synchronized with her respirations.

A sound emitted from her face. A low, quiet hum, resembling the noise a fluorescent light makes in a library. Her mouth opened wide and the sound grew louder and higher, a winter wind thru a chain link fence. Then the sound stopped altogether and I was overcome with coldness. I feared she would draw in her breath, and with it my soul.

She did not consume my soul. Instead, she opened her eyes, two glowing orbs that broadcast light and warmth and comfort all upon my being, and then, in a voice like a buttercup, the human female spake unto me.

Hear me, Narwhal Slotterfield. I bring to you a message of wonder and hope.

Once upon a time, millions of long miles from the sun, on a teeny sphere known as the former planet known as Pluto, a race of intelligent beings did evolve. It's awfully cold on Pluto; the sun is a teeny little pinprick, not much brighter than the rest of the stars. But still, a hardy bunch of critters evolved and survived by eating the iron flakes that were plentiful in their planetoid's soil due to the nature of its gravi-meteoroidal genesis. The critters, who called themselves Plutons, were not, as a rule, happy, it being so cold and dark all the time. They spent most of their lives underground, huddled together like frightened kittens.

Given their dreary environs, the Plutons wept constantly. Being cold as it was, their tears froze solid as soon as they slid out of their eyes. The frozen tears were so abundant that they accumulated into conical piles of shiny, glassy, teeny droplets that the Plutons periodically scooped out of their subterranean dwellings and deposited in great mounds upon the surface of their non-planet.

One day, it came to pass that a young and curious Pluton named Pinta said, in the language of her people, "I shall use our surplus of frozen tears to construct a spaceship." And so Pinta emerged from her family's underground den unto the unfathomably cold surface of Pluto. There, with the tiny sun flickering overhead, she took up a handful of tears and breathed upon them and molded them. She took up another handful and another and many more and built a vessel which glittered and shone like a crystal egg, or, if one wishes, the NCAA football championship trophy.

Pinta boarded the vessel, promised her family she would discover a warmer, happier world, and flew away toward the sun, hoping that she could find something for her people to do other than shiver and cry.

Pinta the Pluton flew past Uranus and Neptune and Jupiter and Saturn and Mars and dodged all the asteroids in the asteroid belt and then she saw Earth, all blue and green and cloudy. Goodness, she said, I'll stop there. So she did. This was one hundred and twenty centuries ago. Pinta landed in what is now North America, right smack in what is now known as Colorado. The land was lush and full of giant beasts: sloths that could pluck the antenna off your roof; mammoths the size of busses; lions the size of elephants; wolves the size of bears; and rats the size of cats. The animals, although enormous, were placid, and the soil was loose and moist and brimming with yummy iron deposits. Pinta praised her good fortune.

But two horrible things happened. First, the warm wind melted Pinta's spaceship, stranding her on the planet. This wasn't horrible, exactly, since she loved Earth.

Second, soon after Pinta's arrival, the planet stopped being warm and comfy. Clouds filled the skies, the plants shriveled up and died, the temperature nose-dived, rains turned to snow, and the entire situation went to shit. Pinta understood that her mere presence as an extraterrestrial had compromised the harmonious environmental balance of the entire planet. She was an infection. The only recourse was for her to leave immediately and hope things got better.

But she couldn't leave because her spaceship had melted. Alas, this troubled her greatly, for Pinta alone bore the weight of the sudden decline of this lovely planet. In her sadness, she cried thousands of tears, which froze in the newly blustery weather. And so, with those tears, she didst construct a new spaceship and verily did she prepare for her return to Pluto.

But first, she had to save the animals whom she'd doomed to a frigid death. She dug a cavern in the ground and cast upon it a preservative spell of Plutonic magnetism. She intended to fill the cavern with as many animals as she could find, thereby saving the creatures from the coming apocalypse.

Alas, when she beckoned the animals to enter the cavern, none would follow. The beasts stood in the fluttering barrage of snow and watched her, dumbly, and then they walked, slithered, flew, and rumbled away from her, rudely. It was as if they blamed her for destroying their planet, which was entirely valid, since she had. Nevertheless, the rejection was very painful for poor Pinta.

"My goodness," she exclaimed, "I wish to save them. But they do not trust me. Because I ruined their home. I have failed in every way imaginable."

Pinta stood before her space vessel, watching the retreat of the animals. After some time, she curled into a tight ball and wept in a piteous fashion.

In the distance, while Pinta shivered in her self-loathing, a saber-toothed tiger sprang from the bushes and pursued a slow-moving wooly mammoth who was at the very rear of the massive herd of enormous animals who were rudely abandoning Pinta. The terrified mammoth turned and ran back in the general direction of Pinta, who heard the commotion and sat up to take in this display of nature in action.

Pinta watched as the tiger nipped at the ankles of the slow-moving mammoth. She watched the mammoth's large belly sway back and forth. She watched the tiger leap onto the back of the mammoth and plunge its cartoonishly large teeth into the flesh of the mammoth's cartoonishly wooly pachydermis. Pinta watched as the panicked mammoth carried the tiger directly toward her.

Just before it reached Pinta, the mammoth collapsed to its front knees, sending up a burst of snow and dirt. The mammoth stared at Pinta with its mammoth eyes while the tiger's mouth tore out great tufts of bloodied hair.

Pinta raised herself to her full height and, in the language of her people, shouted, "Begone, ye great-toothed tiger! Begone!"

The tiger, with a mouth full of hairy flesh, looked upon Pinta and tilted its head.

And then, with a trumpeting roar, the wounded mammoth didst rise up on its hind legs and shake the tiger from its back. The tiger landed, dazed, upon the ground, whereupon the mammoth piledrived one hairy forefoot upon its back. Thus did the tiger die. Having dispatched her pursuer, the mammoth rose her tusks to the sky and waved her head triumphantly, flinging giant drops of her blood all about, sprinkling Pinta the Pluton. Then the mammoth wavered and dropped dead alongside the tiger.

In silence, Pinta stood and rubbed against the bony brow of the mammoth. She thought unto herself, I am the cause of this slaughter.

But alas, from the rearward area of the mammoth's belly, there came a noise. The noise was wet and gloopy, like a large custard sliding off a laminated table top.

With great care, Pinta crept to the rearward area of the dead mammoth's belly. There, she didst see a wondrous thing: from a large cavity, a small, wet mammoth didst emerge. It was breathing.

In death, the mammoth had given birth. Pinta scooped up the newborn creature, cute and drippy, and brought it to the deepest chamber of her underground cavern, where she placed it on a pedestal. She wiped the little critter dry and patted its furry head. Pinta wished the baby mammoth good luck and then she exited the cavern, sealed the entrance, and, seeing no point in returning to her frozen rock of a home world, boarded her ship and jetted out of the atmosphere and directly into the sun, where, as one would expect, she perished, albeit in very warm fashion.

Sadly, Pinta's self-immolation was altogether unnecessary. With Pluto being so far from the sun, Pinta had never experienced any season other than brutal cold. The idea that a planet with a twenty-three-degree offset axis would naturally cycle between warm and cold in its yearly seasonal rhythm was completely alien to her.

In short, she committed suicide because it was winter.

And then the female human closed her eyes, slid back into her varmint hole, and the world went dark.

Not to sound ungrateful, oh, mysterious, imaginary, linen-clad human female but your heart-rending environmental fable has absolutely nothing to do with my original question, which, if you recall, was: *Will I ever again hear the voice of Veronica Vasquez?*

But, as they say, ask for a story, you'll get a song. And Holy Lead Guitarist of The Technicolor Phoenix Scrimshaw Revolt, the tale of Pinta the Pluton just hit number one. If there's nothing else to be learned from the experience, it's that Jim and Jane Jones know how to jellify their fungi. But there's much else to be learned and I've learned it, I say.

The lady in the gown was saying, *Know your perspective, Nar. Sometimes it's not you, it's them, and sometimes it's not them, it's you.*

In the case of Pinta the Pluton, it was an innocent misunderstanding of an offset planetary axis. In my case, it's an unforgivable misunderstanding of the relative nature of time and motion.

To put it another way, I am a moron.

The world is not broken. *I* am broken. It's not the *world* that's moving *slow*; it's *me* that's moving *fast*. I must say, the sensation is thrilling.

Short intermission, as I indulge in a limerick.

There once was a man named Occam.
Known for the size of his cock-am.
He said with a smirk
As he wiped off his dirk
If they cannot be beaten, then shock 'em.

Seriously though, there once *was* a man named Occam. He's dead now. According to an article I read in good ol' *Omni*, at some point prior to his death he said, "When it comes to figuring out how the world works, the simplest explanation is usually the most correct explanation." Occam's keep-it-simple-stupid theorem became so popular that they eventually named a razor after him.

Let me ask one simple rhetorical cosmological question. Who's more likely to be responsible for the sluggish state of matter? Me, the simple human mammal? Or EVERYTHING ELSE IN THE UNIVERSE? It's me, of course.

When I'd exited the bathroom in Cookie's Palace for that first time, I had been, via some as yet undetermined mysterious machination of time and matter, shifted into state of ultra-overdrive, of hypertemporality. I'm Flash, Mercury, Carl Lewis, the only difference being that Flash, Mercury, and Carl could slow down when they wanted. I'm stuck running at a million miles an hour.

I lay on my back and stare at the clouds. Once they stop moving, I'll know that my sobriety has re-asserted itself.

It's time to go home, and I don't mean Denver. Home is Vero. I don't have a clue how long I was in my chemically enhanced state, and that's exactly why I should get myself back on the road. Vero could be winking at this very moment.

I spent many miles of my eastward march by pondering my life as the fastest man in the world. I can walk fifteen miles in less than one second. I can alter lives, bring down governments, heal the sick, disarm nuclear bombs. Hell, I could change a car tire in less time than it takes a normal human to blink. Somebody hire me for a pit crew, pronto.

Vero once told me a story that's applicable to my current state of mind. I'll let her recite it. Setting: winter 1981, somewhere in North Denver. Pretend you can hear her lovely voice, with its clipped Latina vowels and droll question marks at the end of each sentence.

"We had a great big hill, Forney's Hill, in our neighborhood and my family was poor so we had an old wooden sled with metal rails that you guide with your feet. It was at least five feet long. All the other kids had flexi-toboggans or those discs that looked like giant plastic woks. The thing is, even though it was an antique, our sled was super-fast, and it was big enough to fit all four of us, me and my three sisters. I was only four, so I was too little to drive the thing. I usually sat right behind whichever of my sisters was in front.

"One day on the hill, this other four-year-old, Bonnie Consuelo, accused me of being too stupid to race against her and her sisters on their toboggan, which was just a sheet of blue plastic that sounded like thunder if they shook it hard enough. My oldest sister said to Bonnie, 'Stick it, Bonita. Veronica will kick your butts.'

"My sisters put me at the front of the sled and they climbed on behind and we sat at the top of the hill next to the Consuelo sisters in their toboggan. Stanley Zwygardt, a little kid in a coat made out of shag carpet, stood between us, ready to signal the start of the race. Sarah Jentsch was at the bottom of the hill, ready to call the winner.

"Stanley dropped his arms and *dlooop!* the Consuelos went right down the hill.

"I immediately freaked out, swerved, and flipped our sled on its side, dumping me and my sisters. I'd never driven a fucking sled before. My sisters didn't panic. They picked me up, put the sled back on its rails, and we all jumped back on. As we pushed off again, my second sister, Cecilia, leaned forward to whisper to my ear, 'Bust her shit up.'

"The Consuelos were halfway down the hill at this point, but our shitty old super sled was fast. As we caught up with them, Big Mouth Bonnie turned her head and opened her big mouth to shout some shit back at us sisters. In the process, she lost control and the toboggan flexed and dumped all four Consuelo sisters to tumble pell-smell down the hill. I steered us past one sister, then another, but they were all over the place. I couldn't miss 'em all. One of my sled-rails slid directly over the left calf of Bonnie Consuelo. The sled continued with minimal loss of velocity and we crossed the finish line moments before the Consuelos' empty toboggan did. Sarah Jentsch did not declare us the winners, though, because she was screaming about the crimson stain that was expanding around Bonnie Consuelo's leg.

"My sisters and I were never allowed to ride Forney's Hill again. Also, Bonnie's entire leg ended up getting amputated.

"The whole thing was an accident, obviously. Still, I felt like an asshole when Bonnie would limp into school with her crutches. I can't describe my shame. Her sisters refused to speak to me. My sisters told me to buck up. But I couldn't.

"The truth is, everybody should have been glad I ran over Bonnie's leg, because it saved her life. When the doctors went in to clean out the wound, they found she had some kind of leg cancer; the really serious kind that would have killed her in just a few months. The only way to stop it was to remove her whole leg, so they did.

"I'm not taking credit for saving her or anything, but I sure as hell shouldn't have been blamed for the whole deal. But we were just dumb kids and none of us had ever heard of cancer."

*

Allegorically speaking, Vero, I'm the cancer, but not in a malicious way. More like, nobody will know I'm here until someone gets run over by a sled.

I arrive in Holliday without further incident or epiphany. But boy am I excited to see Vero.

I enter Cookie's Palace Diner. Nobody is looking at their signs. Instead, Vero, Sandy, and Old Timer are looking at each other, their mouths forming words that expose their upper incisors. One suspects that they're saying some variation on, "Just what in the tarnation/hell/fuck is going on here?"

I am delighted. My signs have worked. They generated a genuine reaction from genuine humans!

Let's parse this diorama for usable data. Vero, Sandy, and Old Timer are clearly in states of bewilderment. Both Sandy and Old Timer have a touch of the V-shape to their eyebrows and a hint of a squint, which suggests either suspicion or anger. Old Timer is raising his right hand, as if poised to point a finger. And, look, Sandy's chest is thrust forward, emphasizing—I can't help but add—her shapely bosom, and her hands are at hip-level, palms-up in the international sign for "What the shit?" The success of this gesture is impressive given that she's holding a coffee pot in her right hand and, get this, not a drop has spilled. She's really a whiz with that thing. I wouldn't rule out the possibility that she is prepared to use it as a weapon.

Most significantly, Sandy and Old Timer are looking directly at Vero. Why not? Vero's the wildcard in this scene. One minute, it's coffee and gossip. The next moment, the string-bean guy heads to the bathroom and Sandy finds herself pointing a gun at this city chick who has scooted her chair out from underneath herself and is falling to the floor.

Then, a few seconds later, it's as if none of this had happened. Everyone's right back where they were, except they aren't. Because what happened, happened.

Consider Sandy's thought process, starting with the sign I placed before her. "I am not a ghost." Who the hell pulls a stunt like that? It had to be the string-bean who installed them, surely. By the way, I hate it when people call me a string-bean, but it's true. I'm six-eight and thin as a rail. Sorry I haven't mentioned my weight earlier, I didn't want you to form an undue impression of me since string-beans are always portrayed as the dim-witted arachnoidal object of pity. If you don't believe me, watch a coming-of-age movie.

It's an elaborate plan to fuck with us, thinks Sandy. City people are always fucking with country people. Maybe it's one of those Group-Mobs that I've seen on the internet where one minute you're enjoying Styrofoam Chinese at the food court and the next minute all the so-called civilians who are similarly enjoying their own lunches begin to leap about in a choreographed interpretation of the Alan Parsons hit, "Games People Play."

Sandy has a point. Group-Mobs are amusing when viewed from the privacy of your home computer, but let's look at it from the perspective of the victim. And yes, the innocent eater of Styrofoam Chinese is a victim. When *thon*'s food court compatriots begin their exhibition, the poor fucker's entire concept of civil society is temporarily inverted.

"All these people," thinks *thon*, "have planned this thing out and no one thought to invite me." This spurs regressive thoughts of third-grade outcastery: solitary stroganoff at the far corner of the cafeteria, games such as "don't stand in line next to the extremely tall kid."

The Alan Parsons hit continues for several verses and one interminable harmonized guitar solo, which these Group-Mobbers interpret by leaping about like extras from the Sandy Duncan production of Peter Pan, which I have never seen, until the song awkwardly fades out and all the participants erupt in self-applause.

With plastic chopsticks, our innocent eater attempts to bring a morsel of shrimp to *thon*'s mouth. *Thon* looks at the half-cold morsel of food, lathered in corn-starch and high-fructose corn syrup and lets it plop back into the Styrofoam dish.

In a word, no one likes to be pranked.

Switch focus to my darling Vero. She is struggling with internal conflict. Her dominant facial expression is *What is going on here*, underlayed by a strong serving of physical pain, a consequence of falling on her ass a moment ago, one presumes. If anyone's been pranked, it's her. Her chair disappears, she bangs her coccyx, and then the waitress drops a pistol on the floor and starts trying to help her.

And then, *zwoop!* we hit reset and everyone has a brief moment to feel bewildered before three music stands appear out of figuratively nowhere and then, while Vero is in the midst of reading the crypto-note on her stand, the waitress and the old guy start up with the accusatory *What the fucks.*

> *Vero, this is Narwhal. Everything's okay. I love you. Some odd things have happened in the last few seconds. I'll explain later. If you can read this, wink RIGHT NOW. Please wink IMMEDIATELY.*

In retrospect, I should have included a message of similar length on the signs I placed in front of Sandy and Old Timer, both of whom would have read *I am not a ghost* in a glance and immediately dismissed it as bullshit. Meanwhile, I've saddled Vero with an entire paragraph, one that includes a specific instruction to wink.

Let's examine those eyes of hers. There's definitely some moisture. Pain, fear, you name it. She has every reason to cry and each of those reasons is the fault of the shortsightedness of Narwhal Slotterfield. I did this to her. In the sprint to the finish line of the Asshole Stakes, the horse known as Veronica's Dalliance With The Blad has slipped several lengths behind The Time The Corrupt Referee Started Freaking Everybody Out.

Horse-race analogy inspired by George Jones.

Vero's face is pointed at the note on the music stand, but her eyes are facing Sandy and Old Timer. Vero is looking at them because their rising voices compel her to do so. She really just wants them to shut their mouths so she can read.

I put my hands on Vero's table and place my face directly before hers. Do I appear as a ghostly blur? Does the breeze from my hyper-speed blow back her hair? Is my every movement accompanied by a sonic boom? Questions best reserved for later, or better, one of those conventions attended by people who wear handmade alien costumes.

Closer now, let's examine the skin around her eyes. People typically wink with their non-dominant eye. Being left-handed, Vero will likely wink with her right eye.

The mechanics of a wink are not as straightforward as one assumes. It's not a simple matter of an eyelid dropping down and then flipping back up, accompanied by a brief flash and a resonating *ting*. Unless one is an expert winker—Vero is not—the entire winking side of one's face scrunches up, accompanied by a slight sneer of the lip.

I see in Vero's face a tightening of the skin below her right eye. There's a touch of a crease between her right nostril and the corner of her mouth. I do believe she's about to wink.

I'm concerned that Sandy and Old Timer will interrupt Vero's potential wink with their shouting and finger-pointing. In my pre-accelerated state of mind, I would have solved this problem by dragging them out of the room, you know, so Vero could interact with me unencumbered.

In my post-hallucinogenically-enlightened state of mind, I am no longer comfortable with capriciously manipulating the bodies of people—or things—unless absolutely necessary. Consider it a Personal Prime Directive: *Because my actions, even the most benign, can potentially lead to unforeseen, unintentional, and unpleasant consequences, I will do everything I can to not fuck with people who live in the normal time-stream.*

I'll leave it to the Star Trek fanatics to determine if, when it comes to Prime Directives, I'm a Kirk or if I'm a Janeway.

My best course of action is to find a comfortable place to sit and watch things unfold.

It takes forever for things to unfold. I've been watching Vero's face for thousands of heartbeats, leaning in close, fooling myself to think some part of her has moved. I can't tell if she's winking. I've got to re-think this. I will memorize her face, then leave, and then come back. Hopefully, I'll be able to tell if anything has changed.

With the intention of figuring out how long I had been away from Vero during my round-trip journey to the magic mushrooms, I revisited Holliday High. There, I found a slide rule, read the instructions, went out to my telescope, got down on my back, and peeked up. The 747 had moved several degrees away from the viewfinder. Shit. Outside the viewfinder, it couldn't tell me anything; it would be like trying to read a thermometer after the mercury had exploded out of the glass; all you know is that it got hot; or, in this case, all I knew was that a chunk of time had passed. Silly me, I should have reduced the magnification before I'd headed out so the plane didn't take up as much room in the viewfinder. Instead, I was stuck measuring a flea with a yardstick. Or maybe the opposite, a skyscraper with an inchworm. Whatever. In order to sort this out, I'd need a sextant or a protractor or, preferably, a geometry tutor.

Screw this. Reading a thousand magazine articles at the dinner table does not make one a scientist. Holding a slide rule doesn't make one a mathematician. And fuck it all anyway. Keeping an obsessive lock on the passage of time no longer matters to me in my post-hallucinogenically-enlightened mood. The hypertemporal Narwhal is compelled only to keep track of himself.

I shifted the telescope toward the daredevils in the Cessna formerly known as a seagull. The plane was slightly less upside down, with the nose now pointing a little more down and the tail a little more up. The daredevils appeared to be coming out of a loop-de-loop. The pilot and co-pilot retained their expressions of delight. Go get 'em boys. I'll be down here, waiting for my gal to wink.

My hair is still growing. I can keep track of time thataway, if necessary, which it won't be. What's so important about keeping track of time? I subscribe to the theory that clocks were invented solely so people could keep track of their TV schedules.

I returned to the Palace and sat across from Vero. I waited for her to wink and I counted the hairs in her eyebrows. Eventually, I became tired. I couldn't allow myself to go to sleep. I'm pretty sure I'm sleeping at least twelve hours a pop. Over the course of twelve hours, Vero could complete her wink and return her face to both-eyes-open. If that happens, I'll have to ask her to wink again and then I'll have to wait again.

I ate two cans of caffeinated cola and kept on staring. Patience, young jackass. A watched sex pot…

The caffeine wore off. To perk up, I took a quick half-mile hike to the fetishist's semi. The wayward truck was in mid-careen. The front wheels had crested the shoulder and were hovering in air above the ditch, just prior to their big slambooie. It wouldn't be but a few more hours before the fireworks.

Behind the action, my trucker buddy was sitting bolt upright on the road where I'd left him, his jaw slack. I wish I could help you, guy, but I'm not strong enough to move that steering wheel. As seekers of serenity, you and I must also accept the things we can't *un*change. At least we can look forward to an explosion.

I sat with the driver for several minutes. When it became unreasonable to stay awake, I sleep-walked back to Holliday.

I entered Cookie's Palace Diner, hoping one thing, expecting another. I got my wish, which gives me hope. Vero's eyes have migrated away from Sandy and Old Timer and they've settled back on my sign. The corners of her mouth have shifted into the suggestion of a wry smile. And her right eye is distinctly, halfway closed.

I refrained from hugging her. Instead, I shouted into my ear bones, "That's my Vero!"

This is the happiest day of my accelerated life. We can communicate. Even better, Vero trusts me. Under extraordinary and trying circumstances, with two intimidating strangers raising their voices at her, Vero read a note that appeared out of nowhere and followed my instructions.

Veronica and I can't continue this conversation in the middle of the nonsense in here. Cookie is about to come out of the kitchen and he's probably going to join Sandy and Old Timer in accusing Vero and her pee-pee boyfriend, me, of conspiring to freak them out. But my Personal Prime Directive demands that I don't interfere. But I've already interfered. Therefore, ipso facto, common sense suggests that although I can't uninterfere, I can at least minimize the degree to which I have interferenced.

To that end, rather than drag the Hollidayans out of their diner, which was my first inclination, I shall instead remove Vero. Before I do that, it'll only be polite of me to warn everyone, and that includes Vero.

I've placed signs in front of Sandy, Old Timer, and Cookie:

Sorry about the commotion. Please be respectful to the woman at the table over there. She's not responsible for any of this. I've taken her elsewhere. Please go about your business and pretend you never saw us.

yrs sincerely,
Narwhal S.

Vero's turn. I *could* haul her away right now, and screw the note. It's not like I'm afraid of injuring her; I've moved people around without harming them; that's not the issue. But I am concerned about giving her a heart attack. If she finds herself *instantly in a different place*, it'll surely freak her shit out. And then how long would it take for me to convince her that everything's totally cool?

I'll write something short, something she can read quickly and which will still prepare her, even if only a little bit, for what's about to happen.

Hang on. I'm taking you out of here. It'll happen quick.
Love, Nar.

I'll give her two seconds, two of my days, to read this one. After that, whether she's ready or not, it's goodbye to Cookie's Palace Diner.

I went outside and sat upon the diner's front step, absorbing the orange light from the unsettling setting sun. The thing about this sun is, it's not shining or glowing, it's *on*. It, and the blackening blue sky to the east are so motionless they don't even seem three-dimensional.

You know how it sometimes happens that you look up on a summer day and you *know* that the sun is closer to you than the blue sky is, even though you can't *really* tell, and in fact, you don't even know exactly what the blue sky is other than some vaguely washed out version of outer space? But still you know that the sun is separate from the sky, and within the sky?

That illusion of depth is gone. It's all a single, distant two-dimensional projection. Since the air doesn't move, there are no mirages or heat waves on the horizon. There *are* waves of focus and distorted ripples around the corona of the sun, but the waves don't *wave* and the ripples don't *ripple*. It's more like flawed stained glass.

To the west, though, the sky is closer, with the bubbling clouds of the hellfire storm, which is itself worthy of at least two paragraphs of well-considered synonyms for *looming, brooding*, and *beckoning*. I've seen those clouds from many different angles and I know that they're three-dimensional and that they contain rain and hail. I know that underneath the cloud that looks like a young Henry Fonda—but only when viewed from the west side—there's an actual tornado, capable of picking up actual rabbits. And, lookee there. Up sizzles another slow blossom of lightning. It takes my breath away, again. And it's a reminder that, although I may be neck deep in the *Twilight Zone*, I'm not yet over my head.

What do I do for the next two days? I can't just sit here on this front stoop of the diner. Why, I oughta take a trip to that town, Keaton, whose Route 36 sign I've passed four times in my comings and goings.

I made it there before lunch. Keaton is two miles south of the highway. It's perched upon a nameless paved road which doesn't even show up on my map, and which leads to a town that, per my road map, might as well be a fly spot. In the real, non-map version of the world, Keaton is an actual place.

On Route 36, all the towns are laid out in a linear fashion, the highway splitting them each down the center, with buildings flanking either side, and maybe a few dirt roads to count as surface streets. No stop lights, no stop signs. Any street signs are hand-made, with names like "Liberty Lane" and "Old Gusman Road."

Keaton is like two of those Route 36 towns superimposed upon each other in the shape of a cross. Or, to discourage the symbol-hunters amongst you, in the shape of a plus-sign. Or, to be less vague, Keaton has two distinct streets, the nameless north-south paved road intersected by a nameless east-west dirt road. There's even a four-way stop.

I suspect that the towns on Route 36 initially survived on traffic tourism until such time as the interstates were constructed and siphoned off all the motel/gas/diner business. You can tell that Keaton, being as it is off the browbeaten path, has never suckled from the bosom of the transient automobilist and, as such, it's learned to make do on its own. Someone could actually live here without traveling thirty miles for basic necessities.

The town has two whiteboard churches (Methodist and Foursquare), a bank, a meat locker, a mechanic's shop, a Co-op with towering grain elevators, a gas station, a hardware store, a grocery, and a couple dozen residences, few of which I suspect will survive the hell-storm once it blows in.

The houses aren't all pretty, but they're livable, inviting. The yards contain kitschy sculptures made out of old tractor parts formed into things that look like rusted robot cowboys, rusted miniature windmills, and rusted tractors. The fences around the houses are maintained, but, again, not entirely prettily. Some have been patched with barnwood, some are neatly tied together with scraps of baling wire. It's almost cheery here.

The Keaton Cooperative Grocery is a gem of the Great Plains. You don't know how badly you miss soymilk until you come across a half-gallon carton in a country store. It's a miracle they stock the stuff, here in the land of milk and beasts-that-secrete-milk. As evidence of how little it takes for me to consider anything a gem of the Great Plains, the Keaton Cooperative Grocery is basically a glorified convenience store, down to the Swisher Sweets behind the counter. Except convenience stores don't normally carry soymilk. I guess even yokels can suffer from lactose intolerance.

I peel apart a carton of soymilk and drink until my belly swells over the elastic of my sweat pants.

There's only one person working tonight. She's slender with long, straight, brown hair streaked with grey. I'd put her at roughly fifty-five years old. Her arms have the sinewy, tawny look of an old person who spends a lot of time outside, lifting rocks, digging holes.

The plastic nametag pinned to her blouse reads *HELLO MY NAME IS: I Don't Discuss the Weather*. She's leaning against the counter, staring at a tabloid article about a child raised by wolves. According to the sign on the window, the store closes at eight o'clock. Just another half-hour and you're free to go.

I'm instantly fond of I Don't Discuss the Weather. Please don't tell Vero, with her beehive, but I prefer straight hair on humans. Every other woman I've seen in these parts seems compelled to turn her hair into a highlighted, multi-leveled, gravity-loathing, exhibit of sexual potency. The style is 1988 by way of 2009, arranged in a fashion that says, "I don't care what y'all city folk do. We're sassy, we're country, and we're proud."

For the record, the men I've encountered are all wearing caps, most of which advertise seed companies, tractor factories, irrigation facilities, and a mystifyingly popular shoe manufacturer.

I don't wish to sound judgmental. The hats and the hair must serve their respective purposes, otherwise nobody'd bother with them, right?

Still, I lean straight, hair-wise. Straight hair declares nothing, demands nothing, thus preventing and preempting stereotypicism. This presumes, of course, that the hair was straight to begin with. A black person with straight hair says the opposite.

Let's tidy this up. I often find myself admiring people who allow their hair to grow in a natural fashion in spite of what fashion mores unnaturally demand.

I Don't Discuss the Weather's billfold is stashed under the counter. According to her driver's license, her name is Charlene Morning and she lives here in Keaton. Also in the billfold are twenty-three dollars in cash and an old, beat-up Topps ABA rookie card for a small forward named Kitch Riles.

Well, now.

You are not alone in not knowing who in the tarnation Kitch Riles is. He played less than half of one season in the American Basketball Association, a league which, for reasons that make zero sense to me, has retreated into the dustbin of mystery. Heroic figures of the ABA include Ray Eiffel, Bobby Flowers, Doctor J, and Moses Malone. There were plenty more, many of whom migrated to the NBA, where they kicked ass after the ABA went teats-up in 1976.

Bear in mind, I never got to see an ABA game. The league dissolved a few months before I was allegedly born. But I know my history. The ABA gave us the three-point basket, afros, on-court inebriation, and some of the most idiotic owners in the history of human athletic exhibition. As in, let's create a league without any money and then try to get the NBA to buy us out, even though no one comes to our games.

Kitch Riles was a Colorado kid who played half a season with the Kentucky Colonels in 1975, the final season of the ABA's nine-year existence. Riles scored fifty points in his last game, on New Year's Eve in Denver, and then he completely disappeared.

I know this mainly because of a single paragraph written about Riles in *Loose Balls*, the one decent history ever written about the ABA. That paragraph also states that Riles was an obnoxious, thrill-seeking hillbilly with possible links to a ring of Peruvian narcotic distributors. The drug charges were never proved.

If this seems like arcane knowledge, please understand that I love basketball; the game is not simply a job to me. When played well, the collective improvisation displayed on a hardwood court is as impressive as anything accomplished by anything short of a late fifties hard bop quintet. Even then, Max Roach never had to worry about someone stealing his sticks in the middle of one of Sonny's solos.

My belly sagging with soy milk, I lay down on the floor next to a shelf of kiddie cereal and I held the Kitch Riles ABA rookie card in front of my nose. The card had acquired a permanent curl from living in Charlene's wallet. Even so, it was probably worth twenty dollars.

Kitch is pictured in black and white in a defensive stance, one hand up, one hand down. Not the most dynamic of photos, but those were the times. He's wearing his Kentucky Colonels uniform with number thirty-one on his chest. Since it was his rookie card, and since Kitch had yet to accumulate any stats as a professional basketball player, the back of the card indicates only that he averaged 16.2 points and 9.6 rebounds in his single season with the Southern Colorado State College Warblers. And this dandy of a paragraph:

With only a year of junior college ball under his belt, the dynamic "Cowboy" Kitch Riles has made the leap into ABA where he's sure to turn heads. Hometown: Dorsey, Colorado. Quote: "I'm in it to win it!"

I *knew* there was something about Dorsey. Shit. I'm ten miles from the boyhood home of the most underreported sports enigma of the modern era. And I'm less than twenty feet from a woman who I presume was sweet on Kitch. I bet they went to prom together. I bet Charlene has a box full of Kitch Riles memorabilia under her bed. Maybe she even knows how he died.

I chewed a celery stick, leaning against the counter opposite Charlene, wondering what manner of tales she could tell about young Kitch. After I finished my snack, I returned the Kitch card to the billfold and put the billfold back under the counter.

*

I'm going to go outside now and I'm going to find Charlene's house. I must see how this straight-haired falsifier of nametags lives, I must find the hypothetical box of sports memorabilia under her hypothetical bed.

The houses in Keaton don't actually have street addresses. It's the kind of place you just write "Farmer Jones, Keaton" on the envelope and the postman delivers your letter. Fortunately for me, each mailbox includes a small wooden sign with the resident's name routed into it. I imagine some old tinkerer-type made them as a favor for everyone.

A walk down the paved street quickly yields a box with *C. Morning* dangling below. It's half a block from the store. Sweet commute. The house is surrounded by a white picket fence, freshly painted. The flagstone path to the front door is bordered with irises. The lawn consists of rocks and cacti and not a single weed. A hand-crafted crafty six-foot-tall two-dimensional plywood daisy is staked in the dirt next to the front door. Before entering the house, I circle around back. C. Morning's vegetable garden is enjoying the last full bloom of the summer. Fat tomatoes, carrots, the whole twenty-seven feet.

I pass thru the garden and enter the house via the back door. It's a perfectly normal place, which disappoints me. I was hoping for some flair, a saltwater fish tank, at least. Instead, it's a country home with doilies on the tables and, in the kitchen, an art deco sink painted white so many times it looks like it's been slathered in mayonnaise. It appears that Charlene lives alone. No photos anywhere, much less a family portrait.

Into the living room. I'm pleased to see that her TV is a ten-inch cathode-ray-tube antique. She owns an old record player with a dusty copy of *America's Greatest Hits* on the turntable. The latest edition of the *Strattford Messenger* is folded upon the coffee table.

Into the bedroom. The bed is covered with a grandma quilt sewn into a Fibonacci sunflower, bursting in colors that match the approaching sunset in the window beyond. No art on the walls. The nightstand has a bottle of lotion on it. Charlene's closet contains country blouses, quality shoes, cowboy boots, moon boots.

This is all nice, but I'm looking for a box of Kitch Riles clues, ephemera, memorabilia, whatnot. Under the bed, pronto.

Just as I predicted, I found it, maybe. The box is an old wooden army ammo crate roughly the size of a cocker spaniel's coffin. I drag it out to the middle of the rug. It's shaggy with dust bunnies and fastened shut with a shiny padlock.

Stupid padlock. Now I'm gonna have to go thru all of Charlene's nooks and crannies in search of a key, with all the guilt and shame that'll come with disobeying my Personal Prime Directive.

Did you see that? I am developing a conscience. Imagine the Narwhal Slotterfield of just a few Vero-seconds ago. I'd have torn into that box. I'd have made that padlock suffer. But I'm a decent human being and I don't break stuff.

I've never, ever, in my entire life coveted a thing because it had been touched by an athlete. But this is different. Maybe there's a Bobby Flowers card in there, from before cocaine destroyed his career. Or a deflated ABA ball. God, a jersey with actual sweat stains! Love letters from Kitch! Lurid Polaroids that confirm the nature of his mysterious disappearance!

It makes my ears tickle.

I looked all over Charlene's house and I couldn't find that damnable key. And, you know, I'm not sure I could even make a key work. Padlocks are complex mechanisms. If I can't pedal a bicycle, then who says a key will turn a padlock.

You want me to bust the box open. But look what happened after I read Vero's diary. In case you don't remember, I almost blew her head off. No, sir. No can do, at least not yet. I'm not gonna mess things up for anyone anymore, not least C. Morning, who is leaning on the counter in yonder store, waiting to get off work.

I slid the box back under the bed and left C. Morning's house and headed back to Holliday. I'll come back, Keaton, don't you worry.

On the way back to Holliday, a half mile out, I pass my ditch-bound semi for—what is it now—the fourth time? The sixth time? The front portion of the tractor portion of the tractor-trailer has collided with the ditch, crushing itself flat.

Our driver remains seated in the middle of the road, jaw even more slack than it was last time I saw him. I hope he appreciates the fact that he isn't in the truck, as otherwise he'd be highly perforated.

The truck's underslung fuel tanks remain intact, but I doubt they will remain so for much longer. I watch for several heartbeats. A sharp streak creeps up the center of the windshield and then spreads until the safety glass is decorated with spiderwebbed traces. It's hypnotic. I could watch this for days, but I won't.

To Cookie's Palace Diner.

Things have progressed. Old Timer's face has assumed the stern look of a patriot whose yellow ribbon magnet has gone missing from the tailgate of his pickup. He has knocked over his music stand, presumably without taking the time to digest the letter I'd so carefully composed. He's reaching toward the back of his britches where—lookee!—a small pistol is wedged into his big butt crack. Christ almighty. What's with these people? I'm going to have to start frisking them before I start freaking them out.

Old Timer's eyes are focused squarely on Cookie, who has now completely emerged from the kitchen. Cookie, it should be noted, is carrying a meat cleaver. His expression suggests that he'd happily remove the hand of whoever is responsible for all this goddamned nonsense. For reasons that I can't entirely suss out, this expression is directed toward Old Timer. Perhaps they have a history of distrust.

Sandy may or may not have attempted to read her note, but the emerging conflict between Cookie and Old Timer has proven to be too much of a distraction for her to focus on some silly words on a magical sheet of paper. Instead, we find her with palms raised, aimed, respectively, at the two men. Her face is begging the participants to engage in a moment of self-reflection. As in, "Cool it, you dopes."

Bless her soul, Vero is the most lovely human on earth. She's in her chair, as upright as a yoga instructor. Further contributing to the yoga-look, her mouth is in the self-satisfied smirk of one who knows something that everybody else doesn't. Completing the picture, her eyes—her lovely brown eyes—are closed in a state of gentle contemplation.

She has read my note, she has understood my note, and she's ready to get the hell out of here.

With great care, I lift Vero into the air and flatten her into a horizontally-floating magician's assistant pose. With her arranged thusly, it's a cinch to drag her feet-first thru the air.

I pillage one final bottle of water from the Palace's fridge and bid the occupants adios, but not before I pluck the gun from Old Timer's crack and remove the cleaver from Cookie's fist. I bring both weapons to the kitchen and guide them into the vat of French-fry oil, pressing them to the bottom with a metal spatula.

The worst that'll happen now is that someone will poke someone else in the sternum and then Sandy will tell everybody to shut the hell up and eat some pie. And what the hell happened to all the pie? Where's the fucking pie? If somebody doesn't reveal the location of seven slices of cherry, two of rhubarb, and five of pecan, eyes are going to roll.

Aw, hell, Sandy. After all you've done for me, I can't leave you like this.

I scrawl a note on one of her tickets.

It was me. I took the pie. You can have my car. Here's the keys.
Your tip is in your right shoe.

I leave my keys on the counter. Then I pull off Sandy's shoe and place six flattened twenties on the insole and put the shoe back on her foot and that spells the end of my relationship with Cookie's Palace Diner.

Fry on, my friends.

I glided Vero out the front door of the diner and left her floating next to my car while I made one last visit to Holliday elementary/middle/high school. Just a sweep to see if there was anything I could use for the trip. Well, really, I was looking for a specific article of clothing. I went to the boy's locker room, and therein found the customary storage closet full of shoulder pads and helmets and badminton racquets, none of which I cared about. The thing I did care about was hanging on a coat hanger that was hanging from the plumbing that ran along the ceiling of the closet. 'Twas a black-and-white-striped referee's shirt. I ran my fingers over the cotton-poly blend, loving its silky looseness. Blessed be the gods of garmentry, the shirt was an XXL.

Narwhal is a zebra.

Before I left Holliday altogether, I took one last look at the daredevil Cessna thru the telescope. The plane was now pointed straight at the earth, still way the hell up in the sky, the occupants still having the time of their lives.

Fly on, my one-legged seagull.

I begin the trek to Keaton, my hands pressing gently upon Vero's shoulders, she on her back, feet-first floating in front of me.

A half-mile out of town, we pass the semi. The truck has begun to jackknife and the trailer is spilling wheat out from under the canvas. The front end has plowed three feet into the ditch's soil, with the cab compressing into a flat bulldog face with tears of glass popping out of its windshield. One of the truck's chrome underslung fuel tanks has begun to buckle. I float Vero behind the truck and leave her hovering next to the driver, who is just now starting to grasp the implausibility of his situation.

I stand next to the cab of the truck. Over the course of several heartbeats, the rightmost fuel tank expands like a blistering balloon, and then bulges and glows and stretches until cracks appear in the seams. The cracks stretch wider and wider, peeling outward until they split. Freed to the open air, the vapor and diesel glow and billow and blossom and eventually evolve into a flaming cloud, expanding until it's a sun the size of a whale's brain, complete with folded sulci traced in carbon black. It's hot. I step back. Time creeps and the fireball grows, donutting around itself like an atomic explosion. Filigrees of black smoke twine around spheroidal balls of ghostly convections. It's really amazing.

So long, Mack.

Vero and I resume our journey. I look back once, after a mile. The fireball continues to grow. I can't tell from this distance, but the fire may very well be spreading. I hadn't considered the dry weeds in the ditch. Hell. You can't put 'em all out.

43

We're in Keaton, at Charlene's house, in the backyard. A robin is perched on a white fence picket. I've placed Vero in a wicker chair. I can already tell that these new environs are a massive improvement over the diner.

A mile before we reached Keaton, my right knee started making a clunking noise. It's not painful, but it is unnatural. One suspects a chunk of cartilage has come loose. I'm going eat a half-gallon of water and fall asleep.

I awoke in Charlene's bed, atop her Fibonacci grandma quilt, with the evening sunlight casting the walls a homey tinge of orange. Shoes on, stretch, and then up and out to the backyard to say hello to my true love. She was still seated as I'd left her, but now her eyes were opened wide, her mouth gaping in a state of complete joy.

Do you know how it feels to be trusted completely? Vero closes her eyes in a tiny diner full of hostiles and opens them a moment later to find herself in an Edenic country garden. An Edenic country garden is precisely the type of place Vero and I would make fun of under normal circumstances. But she gets it, she gets that something strange is going on. She's ready for anything, even though she can't possibly have a *clue*.

Still, I can't expect Vero to tolerate this forever. It's time I explained what's happening, in as few words as possible.

Please read quickly.

I love you.

I am healthy. I am well. I don't know why, but I am in a different time stream from yours. I'm moving too quickly for you to see me.

Using the pencil to your right, please answer the questions below:

Are you comfortable? ☐ *Y or* ☐ *N*
Do you trust me? ☐ *Y or* ☐ *N*

It's not exactly an explanation, but it'll have to do. I placed the note and a pencil on a TV tray and placed the tray in front of where Vero was sitting. I also plucked a daisy from the garden and set it in an antique green soda bottle I found on the windowsill in front of Charlene's sink, and put that on the TV tray.

I still want to get into that box that's under Charlene's bed, and I still want to do so without smashing it open. Since the key to the lock is not in Charlene's house, then I suspect it's on Charlene's person. To the Keaton Cooperative grocery store, ye bloodthirsty possémen.

People wear tight clothing out here. Given the blistering heat, I do not understand why. Fashion is a powerful subtractor of common sense.

On the plus side, with the tightness of her jeans, I didn't have to actually stick my hands into Charlene's pants' pockets in order to determine their contents. I rubbed my thumb over the pocket area and found no bas relief to indicate any contents at all.

This was after I'd checked her wallet again and found nothing of interest other than the Kitch Riles ABA rookie card, which I again stared at for several moments.

Purse and pockets out of the running, I reached for the silver chain that was looped around her neck. The plumb of the chain dangled into her blouse, disappearing into the crevasse of her boobs. I had been tempted all along, but decorum insisted that I save it for last. I carefully tugged the chain upward, aware of the fact that it was rubbing on skin that one should never disturb without the permission of the owner, and extracted the weight on the end.

The weight was a key.

The contents of the box are spread before me on Charlene's kitchen table. Newspaper clippings, stacked more or less in sequential order. They start on January 8, 1976. Cue the frantic music and the spinning newspaper montage:

LOCAL HOOPSTER GOES MISSING
Strattford Messenger, Jan 8, 1976

NO SIGN OF MISSING RILES
Denver Post, Jan 9, 1976

FOUL PLAY IN BASKETBALL DISAPPEARANCE?
Rocky Mountain News, Jan 10, 1976

COLONELS DEDICATE REST OF SEASON TO ABSENT KITCH
Louisville Courier-Journal, Jan 12, 1976

RILES' BROTHER MISSING AS WELL
Strattford Messenger, Jan 15, 1976

I should point out that each article includes photos of the brothers, the same two photos every time, as supplied by the Dorton High School yearbook staff. First, the older brother, John Riles. His is a senior picture, the classic me-and-my-horse pose endemic to kids who have horses: horse in a stall, John standing next to it, wearing a bolo tie, staring into space, ready to get this shit over with so he can get back to milking the cows.

Kitch Riles, in-game wearing his Dorton Rangers high school basketball uniform. It's a good picture, better than the one on his rookie card. It's a close-up of him tearing a rebound off the edge of the rim. His arms are thin and strong. Even in the yellowing, pixelated newsprint, you can see the wicked glee in his eyes, the sweat flying off his nose.

We now return to our headlines.

COACH: "KITCH NEVER HAD DRUG PROBLEM"
Rocky Mountain News, Jan 16, 1976

NEW LEAD IN RILES CASE: HE WENT HOME
Denver Post, Jan 24, 1976

CONFLICT BETWEEN BROTHERS
MAY HAVE LED TO VIOLENCE
Rocky Mountain News, Jan 25, 1976

RILES INVESTIGATION EXPANDS TO PERU
Denver Post, Jan 27, 1976

ALL-STAR GAME HONORS MISSING MAVERICK
Louisville Courier-Journal, Jan 28, 1976

POLICE CLEAR SOUTH AMERICANS IN RILES DISAPPEARANCE
Rocky Mountain News, Jan 31, 1976

LOCALS HELP FEDS SEARCH FOR RILES BOYS: NO LUCK
Strattford Messenger, Feb 12, 1976

KITCH'S LOVER GRANTED PERMISSION TO RETURN TO FRANCE
Rocky Mountain News, Feb 14, 1976

KITCH-LESS COLONELS BOUNCED FROM PLAYOFFS
Louisville Courier-Journal, Apr 29, 1976

LOOKING BACK: SO MUCH POTENTIAL, SO MUCH SORROW
Strattford Messenger, April 30, 1976

CLUELESS COPS CALL OFF KITCH CASE
Denver Post, August 15, 1976

You get the gist. From the articles themselves, I gather that, on the morning of January 1, 1976, Kitch Riles drove a rented Corvette from Denver to the home of his brother, John, who lived six miles north and west of Dorsey, and then the brothers disappeared.

Then, a whole new headline, a whole new subject, a whole new twist:

MYSTERY BABY AT COURTHOUSE
Strattford Messenger, Sept 9, 1976

Our story thereupon veers hard left. On September third, 1976, a newborn child was deposited at the doorstep of the Strattford County courthouse. The long of it consumes several consecutive weeks of front-page headlines in the *Strattford Messenger*. The short of it is: a teeny, cute, possibly premature infant boy shows up at the courthouse, no parents come forward, and, after much debate, the kid is sent to an adoption agency in Denver.

If our plot were water, someone has just stirred into it a cup of cornstarch.

At the bottom of the secret box, under the newspaper clippings, there's a stone spear point. Like an old Indian thing, shiny and black, about five inches long. And under the spear point is an actual piece of sports memorabilia. It's no dirty jersey or anything, but it is a ticket stub from the final game Kitch Riles ever played: McNichols Arena, December 31, 1975, Kentucky Colonels vs. the Denver Nuggets. That's the one where Kitch scored fifty points and his team still lost.

I bring the clippings out to the garden and set up a second wicker chair and a second TV tray opposite from Vero. Her gaze has settled on my hand-written note.

I read every word of the stories again, as slowly as possible. In simple terms, here's what happened: On January first, 1976, Kitch and John go bye-bye. They are never found. Eight months later, a baby arrives on the scene and is anonymously donated to the Strattford County Courthouse.

And *it just so happens* that Charlene "I Don't Discuss The Weather" Morning, who, thirty-three years later, still keeps a Kitch Riles trading card in her billfold and retains the ticket stub from his final game, has obsessively collected articles about both stories.

There is no mystery here. Evidence points in all three directions to a triangular love affair. Let's speculate: As a kid, Charlene fell for Kitch Riles, but when he left town to play basketball she switched to his older brother, John. A few months later, Kitch comes home after a monster basketball game, sees Charlene in bed with John, goes nutty. There's a battle on the plains, both brothers die, and are eaten by wild animals.

Alternate scenario: Kitch comes home, climbs into bed with his old lover, Charlene, and is discovered by John, who goes nutty. The final scene—battle, fratricide, wild animals—remains unchanged.

Let's continue with the speculation: I am adopted. This is not speculative. However, my actual birth date is unknown. It's believed to be around September 1, 1976. Kitch Riles disappeared on January 1, 1976, which is precisely eight months before I was born. If Kitch and John killed each other over an unsanctioned act of sexual congress with Charlene, then it's quite possible that the possibly premature baby Charlene dropped off at the courthouse was a direct consequence of that congress.

How do I know that Charlene was the anonymous baby-dropper? I do not. But everything I'm imagining right now leads directly to that conclusion. Charlene becomes pregnant with a Riles child. She keeps her pregnancy secret from her neighbors. I'm not sure how you do that, but let's say she hides the pregnancy somehow and gives birth in her own bathtub. After she cuts the umbilical cord, she weeps over the baby, terrified of sharing her secret with the world. Be it oppressive parents, judgmental townsfolk, poverty, or guilt about her role in the deaths of the Riles boys, she decides that the baby will be better off in the hands of complete strangers than in her own. So, one night, she drives the fifty miles to Strattford, the closest town with a courthouse, and gives the baby away.

Moving on. Kitch Riles was tall. I am tall. Kitch Riles played basketball. I officiate basketball.

Further, Kitch and John have similar noses. Sort of Roman, round and pointed, and broad and flat. I go into Charlene's bathroom and look in the mirror. After several moments of shifting angles and cross-eyed focus, I concede that there is, indeed, perhaps, a close resemblance of the familial kind.

Ladies and gentlemen of the jury, the facts lead to only one conclusion.

Dramatic pause, whilst the gallery holds their respective breaths.

I have brought my girlfriend to my mother's house.

Tacked to the wall opposite Charlene's toilet is a 1974 map of Strattford County. The map is big enough that a four-year-old human would be able to sleep comfortably upon it, assuming the map were augmented by sheets, pillows, and a mattress. The map itself is a black and white reproduction of an assessor's grid, including every parcel of land in Strattford County with the names of the landowners written in each rectangle.

Perhaps you think it's odd that Charlene hung this map in her bathroom, where, multiple times a day, she must sit and stare at grids of townships and sections and topographic whorls. But it's *not* odd. Charlene is wise. What better way to spend your toilet time than by pondering the county you inhabit?

Since 1974, when the map was produced, Charlene has crossed out several of the names that were originally printed on the land parcels and she has penciled new ones in. Some of the parcels have changed hands five times in the last thirty-five years. Consider, for example, one stamp-sized square at the bottom left corner of the county: ~~*Maus*~~, ~~*Katze*~~, ~~*Wolff*~~, ~~*Jager*~~, *Engels*. Other parcels haven't changed at all, which suggests they've been under the same ownership for the last three-and-a-half decades. Amongst those parcels are a handful attributed to *Vernon Riles.* The land in question is just a couple of miles north of the House of Pronghorn.

Remember that abandoned homestead I passed thru after my near-death adventure with the hellfire tornado? The picturesque one that was filled with reverberations of dread? Remember? It, too, was just a couple of miles north of the House of Pronghorn.

I know from Charlene's newspaper clippings that Vernon Riles is the father of John and Kitch Riles. Which means, if my wild suppositions are correct, that Vernon Riles is my grandfather. One wonders what the hell is going on.

*

Not long ago, the world was utterly still and my sole ambition was to go to Denver and give a man named The Blad an alpha-male ass whupping. Now, the world is moving (slowly), I'm moving (quickly), and I have two (count 'em) purposes: to communicate with Vero, and to establish the veracity of my wild ancestral claims.

Like a shook-up snow globe, my sense of purpose is settling and I'm starting to see the little plastic gingerbread house within. Who might be living in that little plastic house? I don't know, and I'll most likely abandon this snow globe metaphor before I ever find out.

Bloodthirsty possémen! Join me as we march to Township Four South, Range Forty-eight West and heretothere meet our maker, or, at the very least, frolic amongst the remnants of his childhood home.

First, though, let's visit Charlene's backyard to say goodbye to Vero. Her index finger is now only inches away from my note, her eyes are squinted in concentration. I reach toward her hair, wishing to adjust her beehive, which has begun to lean Pisa-like after our hasty journey from Holliday. I restrain myself. Let the woman read.

I kiss Vero on the forehead, shoulder my backpack, and head up the street. On the way out of Keaton, I stop by the grocery store, where I slip the key chain back over Charlene's neck and let it drop between her bosoms.

Hello, potential mother. My eyes are grey; yours are brown. My hair is brown; yours is brown-with-grey. You've got a button nose, not unlike that of Anne Murray. Mine is difficult to define, not unlike that of Elvis. I'm six-eight. The top of your head barely comes up to the bottom of my sternum. I'm swarthy. You're the color of a lifelong tan. And although we both have slender fingers, neither of us owns a piano.

Okay, now let's go knock on the door to my gingerbread house.

This is definitely the bucolic ranch of dread that I passed thru after my run-in with the tornado. There's the collapsed barn, the sand blasted house, the broken windmill. It's the same patch of land marked *Vernon Riles* on Charlene's bathroom map.

Lingering, as it is, directly beneath the dark sky of hellfire storm and illuminated, as it were, by the hazy red sun on the west horizon, the whole ranch is coated with a film of decay. This is not a friendly type of decay, like you might find when you lift up a paving stone and discover some roly-polies eating an earthworm. This decay is more like what you'd see when you hold an untreated case of frostbite under an infrared lamp. As I describe the scene, imagine every piece of barn wood, every shard of broken glass, every molecule on this homestead as limned in the red-grey haze of the hellfire sun.

When I had originally passed thru this place, after the tornado nearly ate me, I had been in an understandable rush to get out from under the storm and so I missed a few things. Item A: next to the old barn, there's an old telephone pole with dead wires hanging off it and a circle of bird shit forming a halo around the base. Attached to the pole is a warped, peeling chunk of plywood that's been jigsawed into an approximation of a backboard. Approximately ten feet below the backboard, half buried in the sand, is the iron basketball hoop itself, rusted and decorated with yet more bird shit, and with a yucca plant growing thru the center.

Surely, this is the Old Country Hoop into which young Kitch Riles tossed an Old Country Basketball day after day, night after night, as the snow fell and as the crows called.

I imagine back to that dismal first day of 1976, with John and Kitch Riles playing one final game of basketball to settle their differences vis-à-vis their respective relationships with Charlene. After much back and forth, and amidst escalating rhetoric, Kitch ends the game by dunking the ball so hard that it tears the hoop off the pole. And here it lays, still.

The fact that vandals have never stolen the hoop suggests that this here Land of the Dead Brothers was deemed haunted by the locals and assiduously avoided. Either that or the locals never appreciated the significance of an honest-to-gosh relic from the twilight of the ABA.

To the barn. With the roof collapsed, it's hard to get around inside, but I weave thru the labyrinth of cracked grey wood and dusty shingles to find some old livestock stalls, one of which contains the skull of an actual cow. There's a worn workbench scattered with rusted tools: hammers and horseshoes and whatnot. On the dirt floor, next to a mouse nest assembled from the leaked stuffing of a rotted saddle hanging on the wall above, there's a giant stainless steel syringe with a glass—whaddyacallit?—cylinder. The needle is as long as a pencil. Maybe after Kitch won the one-on-one game, the Riles boys decided to kill each other in a suicide pact that involved cow tranquilizers.

I enter the farmhouse. There are holes in the plaster walls revealing lath, there are mouse turds everywhere, carpet rotted, light fixtures smashed, chunks of their frosted glass on the floor below. There's also a strong suggestion of recent human habitation. A portion of the roof has caved in and the hole has been covered with a blue plastic tarp that still has its creases from its time on the shelf in the hardware store. On the living room floor are two giant cans that, per their labels, once contained tapioca pudding.

There's a door so I open it. It brings me to a bedroom with a dirty mattress on the floor. Upon the mattress, two dirty kids are beating the everloving shit out of each other. They're maybe six and nine. The boy, younger, is on bottom, the sister, older, is on top with one hand around the boy's throat and the other hand cocked and ready. Shirts are torn, slobber drips, blood gathers on teeth. It's a full-on inter-sibling battle.

As to the source of their mutual rancor, it is doubtless the upended bag of antique coins that has been spilled at the foot of the mattress. Ignoring the children's frightful display of rage, I squat to examine the coins.

I'm no numismatist, but I recognize money when I see it. Tarnished silver dollars from the way-back days, buffalo nickels, wheat-head pennies, fifty-cent pieces, all manner of obscure currency. How and why these things ended up in the possession of two children in a condemnable house is beyond me.

All right, I'll give it a shot. If I were the type to believe in the supernatural—and given my predicament, it's odd that I still don't—I'd be inclined to suggest that this scene is the ghostly manifestation of the souls of the Riles boys, created by a trickster demon solely for my bewilderment. But I don't believe in the supernatural and I don't care to dig into yet another dysfunctional family, my own being my primary concern, so I'll pretend that these children are none of my business.

Ahoy, what do we have here, carved into the chipped paint of the molding in the far corner of the room?

Kitch tested Excal.

What's "Excal"? Why was Kitch testing it? I neither know nor care. All I care about is the "Kitch" part. This is, without question, the childhood home of Kitch and John Riles.

One of those brothers is my father. Kitch, most likely, seeing as we're both tall, and because he's cool and carves things in molding. I squat and run my finger over the crooked graffiti. Imagine growing up here. Tossing a ball thru the Old Country Hoop, beheading the Thanksgiving turkey, wearing boots and neckerchiefs and multi-gallon hats.

I go thru the rest of the house. I look at my nose in the cracked bathroom mirror, I poke my head into the crawlspace, I pull open the crusty old oven door. I fail to find any documentation of my parentage. I do find, on the back of a shelf in one of the bedroom closets, a dusty pair of binoculars. It's a nice set, of an early fifties vintage. The lenses are intact, the focus mechanism still works.

Avoiding chunks of glass and fly carcasses, I put my elbows on the windowsill and point the binocs northward. I make out the slowly spinning pipe of the tornado thru the drops of rain and hail.

I hang the binoculars around my neck, claim my rightful ownership. I don't feel guilty for taking them. While you may doubt it, I'm almost certain that I'm the son of one of the Riles boys. Shit, I *am* a Riles boy. Technically, everything here is part of my inheritance.

Speaking of which, fuck it, I'm taking those antique coins. I return to the master bedroom, where the two kids are still beating the everloving shit out of one another, and push the coins one by one into their cloth bag. There are fifty-five of them. Based on the fact that they're all more than a hundred years old, I figure they're probably valuable to someone somewhere, which means I should do something stupid with them.

Those fisticuffing kids are driving me crazy. I can't possibly leave them posed like that. I'm a referee, after all. I may be an unconventional cuss, but I never hesitate to stop a fight.

I haul the kids outdoors to the red-grey dread. I bring the girl to the west side of the barn and fold her into a cross-legged Indian-sit, so she's facing the glow of the setting sun. The boy, I haul to the opposite side of the barn, where I place him flat on his back so he's facing the bottom of the hell-fire storm. The change of scenery ought to terrify at least one of them into civility.

I don't know what the hell else I can accomplish here. I've ended a fight, acquired coins and binoculars, and confirmed that Kitch Riles lived in this house.

There's no reason to rush back to Keaton, as I'm sure Vero hasn't finished reading my note. How about another visit to the tornado?

I walk into the cool air of the downpour, binocs over my neck, coins in my backpack. Since I'd last been under these clouds, enough rain had struck the ground to render it properly wet. Prisms of raindrops are suspended in the air, the grass hunches over in the invisible wind, and, in the background, the tornado continues its stately spiral.

I march straight to it, my own personal vortex. The tornado has completely devoured the stand of trees and is now progressing up the far side of the bowl-valley. As it creeps along the landscape like a morning shadow across a bedroom floor, the limbs from the mutilated trees poke out like straw in a stray cat's fur.

When I'm close enough to feel the faint vacuum tug of wind on my arm hair, I stop. I look up, up, up and see the molecules of water vapor collide and burst. Faintly, at the very tiptop of the tornado, little snakelike strings of lightning creep in and out of existence. You could fly all the way to Mars and never see anything like this.

And way, way up there, what's that? I bring the binocs to my eyes and focus. Yes, it's little Fiver the rabbit, his rodent jaws opened wide in terror. I'm rooting for you, kid.

I remove my backpack and extract the bag of coins. I slide one of the less tarnished silver dollars into my pocket and then bring the rest of the coins to the front of the tornado. I stand as close as I dare and then empty the bag so the coins float in mid-air right in the path of destruction.

I step back and watch and wait for minutes or hours until the coins begin to draw toward the tornado, first one, then another, slowly rotating, accelerating, then being swallowed into the column and up to the great jukebox in the sky, where all currencies are accepted.

I return to the wake-side of the tornado and sit on a patch of soft grass and eat from a box of granola cereal and chew from a carton of soymilk I've brought with me. The ground is sloped here, like a natural theater in the round, with the tornado climbing up the staircase on the opposite side. I sit with my feet pointing toward the bottom of the valley where the splintered, twisted stumps of the mutilated trees raise their shards to the clouds above.

I nap on the soft grass. When I awake there are actual water drops on my clothes. My naps are pretty long, I think. Long enough for rain to accumulate.

I stretch, focus the binoculars to the very top of the tornado and then let my eyes slide down. Deep within, about twenty feet off the ground, I see the glint of coins.

On the walk back to Keaton, my left knee begins to hurt. This is in addition to the clunking noises in my right knee. At approximately thirty-three years old, I'm no longer a kid. I gotta take it easy in this thick air. I walk slowly. Eventually I enter Keaton and pass the gate into Charlene's backyard.

To my great surprise, Vero has finished my letter. How long was I gone? Three days, maybe four. Five, tops. A week? Whatever.

Happily, she's answered yes to both of my questions:

Are you comfortable? ☑ *Y or* ☐ *N*
Do you trust me? ☑ *Y or* ☐ *N*

Delightfully, there's been time for her to draw a smiley face:

Aw, Vero. Look at you, leaned back in Charlene's wicker chair with that pencil casually tucked behind your ear. How many humans would be so calm, so cool, so funny when faced with a hypertemporal boyfriend?

Even when I'm not traveling a hundred thousand times the speed of time, I'm a difficult person to be around. I'm a hypercritical, hypocritical, unmotivated, entitled, socially-disengaged ass of a man. It's a miracle you've chosen to remain in my orbit for these past several months, Vero.

The thing with The Blad, that was my fault. Every time we go out, I complain. The food's too hot, the service isn't too hot, the ethnic music playing on the speakers is too modern, the chairs are too high relative to the table. I'm difficult. No wonder you went out for sour cream on the side.

But it's *me* you brought to St. Louis for your aunt's funeral, not The Blad. You did your dalliance, yes, and decided that in spite of my mountain of flaws, when life gets shitty, you still want to hang out with me.

Eat it, The Blad. I fucking win. You can pound yer Rocky Mountain pisswater with Lord Elway all day long. Vero likes *me*.

I completely overestimated how long it'd take for Vero to read that note, which suggests that my time-keeping methods are far less accurate than I thought. I could refine my methods, I suppose. I could go back to Holliday and stare at the old 747 thru the old telescope, or I could drop pennies from a ladder and calculate their acceleration due to gravity. But I find that I don't care. Screw time. Ever since I've been here, all I've thought about is time and I'm weary of it.

And so, I will no longer be a slave to the clock. My days are mine and Vero's hours are hers. I don't relate to Vero's temporal experience any more than she could relate to a hummingbird's. That'd be like worrying about how many molecules of air I inhale with every breath. I don't even want to be *aware* that I'm breathing. I just want it to happen.

We were downtown one warm day, Vero and I. We'd gone to the art museum and were just enjoying the city. I pointed to the sun as it dangled over the Rockies and said, "That's you. You're my sun. I orbit you."

Vero's cheeks went rosy and then she said, "If I'm the sun, then you're the Earth, Narwhal, and we live in a pre-Copernican solar system."

End of story.

In Charlene Morning's backyard, I touch my girlfriend's hair. I'll be the Earth, Vero, if you'll be my sun.

Let me share a conversation Vero and I had the morning after she'd spent the night at my place for the very first time. It was a Sunday, we were both puffy-faced, an early spring rain was pitter-pattering against the window of my little garden-level apartment, and I was buttering toast.

Vero said, "Eighty-two percent of suicides occur on grey days."

I said, "There are two ways to spell *grey*."

She said, "I went to college for a while, at Boulder. Did I tell you that? My freshman year, by the time spring break rolled around, I was sick of the place. I was one of, like, three *chicas* on the whole campus. Everybody else was either white or on an athletic scholarship. And *everybody* was obsessed with skiing and snowboarding. When they weren't skiing or snowboarding, like on the two days a week they actually had classes, they'd ditch school and get baked and watch snowboard videos."

I said, "I prefer the version with the *e* rather than the *a*—g-r-e-y."

"It was nothing but stoned conversations about counterfeit season passes and three-sixty dragon-flip face-boomers. I wanted to burn the mountains to the ground. Even worse, the weather sucked. That year, 1997, was cold all winter and grey all spring. I hated it. So for spring break, I decided to find some warm sand and lie down on it."

I said, "On the other hand, when you pronounce it with an *a*, your mouth is compelled to smile. *Gray.*"

"I didn't have any money, though, so I couldn't go to that stupid Island of Drunken Assholes that everyone loves down in Texas."

I said, "With the *e*, the word practically oozes out of your lower jaw. *Grey.*"

"I had a total of nine days to find a beach and then get back to Boulder. I loaded my suitcase, stood on the shoulder of a south-bound highway, and smiled pretty."

I said, "*Grey. Gray.* The difference is subtle, but remarkable."

"Four days later, I stepped out of a station wagon in some town in New Mexico. The south part. I can't remember the name of the place. I leapt out the car and got blasted with hot. Like, a-hundred-and-five degrees hot. I was standing in front of a diner in a strip-mall and in front of the diner was an actual palm tree growing out of a squared off box of sand. The sun was bright enough that it made the sand look white. I was wearing a bikini top beneath my t-shirt and I took off my t-shirt and lay down in the sand until the manager of the diner came out and told me I was scaring away customers."

I said, "The English generally use the *e* version and Americans employ the *a* version. Which makes sense when you consider the relative outward demeanors of the two countries."

"Then I got up, crossed the street and hitched home. I had spent probably ten minutes total on the warm sand. I got back to campus just in time for classes, but I didn't bother going. I didn't care for college."

I wrote Vero another note, a short one.

If you'll be my sun, I'll be your sand.

I entered Charlene's bathroom to look for something to help with my sore knees. A few hundred milligrams of any old over-the-counter anti-inflammatory would do me fine. The soreness had become a constant, but it wasn't anything that would have kept me out of a game. Stay on top of the pain, lay off the marathons for a while, and I'd be fine.

Good ol' Charlene, she had a family-sized bottle of aspirin in her medicine cabinet, between the tweezers and the Q-tips. Behind the aspirin was a prescription bottle of hydrocodone. The label said to take them for back spasms. Charlene's back must have made a full recovery; the bottle was still half full and the pills had passed their expiration date six years ago.

Here's where I have to be smart.

I've seen what happens when you start with the scrips. Careers in officiating can last thirty, forty years, well beyond anything an actual basketball player could manage. You can't do that unless you listen to the old guys. They show you how to shuffle down the court without pounding your joints, where to stand so you can see as much action with as little motion as possible, how to gracefully dodge careening balls, and how to flamboyantly employ your hand signals as a means of stretching your upper body. I sometimes call offensive fouls as an excuse to put my hand behind my neck and stretch my upper back.

But when you hit your fifties, as happened to most of my colleagues several decades ago, not even the hands on hips and full pelvic thrust of a blocking call will offer relief from the accumulation of ache and strains. Which is why virtually all of my colleagues have a secret pocket in their duffel bags where they store their plastic baggies full of multicolored pills.

It always starts with an ankle sprain; the doctor suggests a few Meloxicam or Sulindac or Naproxen or any of the other easy relievers that sound like they were named after the Grand Commander of an alien warrior species. That lasts a year or two and then somebody, usually another colleague, offers *thon* something a little stronger. Next thing you know these old fuckers are gobbling down opioids and ADHD meds like teenage rockabilly musicians. We're talking five pregame pseudoephedrine, a halftime cocktail of Oxies and Ritalin, and a postgame handful of Ambien.

Typical conversation:

"You know any doctors?"

"No, but I got a guy."

"Put me in touch?"

"He's not taking customers."

"Come on, man. I'm low on frog liver extract."

"No prob. I got more frog liver than I need. Gives me acid reflux."

"Talk trade? I got a surplus of bennies and a mason jar filled with Mexican Viagra."

"Deal."

With some of these guys, I think the drugs are the only reason they stick around.

More substance-abuse commentary: Somebody on the Number Twelve bus once said to another body on that bus that he had seen photos of Chris Farley's corpse. I was sitting in the seat directly in front of those buddies. My stop, two blocks away from the garden-level apartment Vero and I shared, arrived before I could finish eavesdropping on their conversation. But I'd heard enough. Dead celebrity, tragic, internet.

When I got home, I made Vero turn on her computer and we sought and found the photos my busmates had been discussing.

Chris Farley was a comedian, he was fat, he was messed up on drugs, he was desperate to get well, he was a genius who died shirtless on the floor of his brother's condo. The prostitute he'd spent the evening with had thrown a handful of dollar bills in his face when he was convulsing and foam was coming out of his mouth and he was begging her to stay and help him. Then she took photos, then he died. Technically, the pictures Vero and I looked at weren't of Farley's corpse. They were of him turning into a corpse.

After we saw the pictures, we ate some ramen in silence.

Vero said, after a while, "The prostitutes always get fucked. Chris Farley. Entwistle. Hendrix. Sam Cooke. It's always the man who does the coke, eats the pills, approaches the hotel desk drunk and horny, screaming about who stole his fucking pants. It's always the man who dies and, after it's all over, everyone blames the poor prostitute for not taking the idiot to the hospital in time."

I said, "Chris Farley was not an idiot. More of a tragic figure."

Vero said, "I didn't mean idiot, exactly. How about *sap*?"

"It's said by those who've seen them that the police photos of Elvis' death scene are some of the most horrific images ever taken."

Vero said, "My point was more about the prostitutes."

I said, "They get the short end of the stick."

"Correct. Whores are paid to do things that sad, lonely, pathetic men can't get anyone to do for them for free. And yet it's the whores who get called the moral scoundrels. No wonder they always leave the scene without calling for help."

I said, "I think the term is sex-workers. And Hendrix was with a girlfriend when he died."

"Are you listening to me?"

I said, "Yes. A non-mutual love affair can only work if at least one person pretends it's not real."

Vero shrugged. "Close enough."

I said, "We're real, Vero."

She fell out of her chair and pretended to convulse.

If anyone ever had an excuse to jump into the unsanitary pit of scrip addiction, it was me. Sore knees, isolation, no job, no alarm clocks, product available behind every bathroom mirror. All I had going for me was the driving force of irrepressibility. And that, kids, is why I didn't eat any of Charlie's hydrocodone. Because the first thing to go when I start on the painkillers will be my astonishing ability to keep on. If I lose my drive, I'll turn into a slobbering turd, licking pills off the necks of Lauren Bacall look-alikes.

I dry-swallowed four aspirin and returned the bottle to the medicine cabinet. The cabinet was old wood, chipped pink paint. The door itself was awfully thick, a fact that I attributed to ancient methods of cabinetry. But to what could I attribute the little hook latch at the top of the inside of the awfully thick door. Apparently, this was one of those old-fashioned medicine cabinet doors that included a secret compartment. I unhooked the latch.

Contents: The nub of a No. 2 pencil and an old notebook.

I extracted the notebook from the compartment and held it carefully. It was a spiral, like a kid would bring to his first day of fourth grade in 1978. The cover was red, decorated with a print of an Indian. The edges of the paper inside were sun-browned and stained with finger schmutz.

With hands aquiver, I brought the notebook out to the garden and sat across from Vero, whose eyes had not yet alighted upon my latest note.

If the newspaper articles under Charlene's bed had been a cryptic tabloid tell-all, this notebook was her authorized autobiography, not so much a diary as it was a captain's log written in the form of experimental prosody.

Excerpts:

June 24, 1974: Hot. No rain. Job boring.

October 31, 1974: Bradley went to the football game with me. Dinner at the café.

January 3, 1975: Blizzard. Lost power for nine hours. Ate ravioli out of the can.

Oct 23, 1975: Blizzard (another?!?). Lost power (again?!?). Spent night in store to stay warm.

For someone whose nametag declares that she doesn't talk about the weather, Charlene sure likes to talk about the weather.

A month later, we have our first Riles sighting. In a departure from her daily haiku, Charlene commits an entire paragraph to John, the older brother:

Nov 22, 1975: Sunny. Johnny Riles brought a poodle to the store. Kitch gave it to him for his birthday. I think Johnny likes me. He's so nervous. He's always under Kitch's shadow. Has a real nice way of walking. He's a cowboy who doesn't act like a jerk. Too bad I'm taken.

Then …

Nov 27, 1975: THANKSGIVING! Snow is melting. The whole family was here, plus Bradley. Fun until family left me alone with Bradley. Maybe Johnny's right about him.

Dec 12, 1975: No weather. Bradley cheated on me.

Dec 13, 1975: Mid-forties. Skipped work b/c of the cheating asshole. Johnny stopped by. We went to Strattford for a movie. I got drunk. He wouldn't give me a cigarette. I didn't invite him in. Not sure if that was a mistake. Am sure Bradley was. Little prick with a tiny p—.

Dec 15, 1975: Another warm one. In a couple of days, I'm going out with Johnny. Not a date. Maybe a date.

Dec 17, 1975: Windy in the A.M. Calm in the P.M. Bradley called to apologize. I canceled the date with Johnny. He was upset. Bradley arrived late, we talked later. Love was made. He's a human.

Dec 25, 1975: Snowing. Fucking fuck Bradley. He got a girl pregnant. We're over. Johnny stopped by. We drank rum and necked a little. He left to feed his cattle. Planned to come back but he got stuck in the storm. I'm drunk. Warm.

Dec 26, 1975: Melting. Johnny didn't actually get stuck. He drove into the ditch because he was drunk. I visited him today. He wants to get off the whiskey. I'm not to visit him for five days. And then we're going to Denver to see Kitch play against the Nuggets!

Dec 31, 1975: Unseasonably warm. Heading out to Johnny's. After the game, we'll probably stay overnight in a Denver hotel. I think he's a virgin!

Jan 1, 1976: Snowing. Oh god. Please be okay.

Jan 4, 1976: Cold. He's gone. Kitch did this.

Jan 8, 1976: Cold. In our last phone call, Johnny said to drive north of his house in case something happened. I did but I didn't know where to go. The sheriff doesn't know his ass from his ankle.

Jan 15, 1976: Cold. Oh, Johnny. I crossed the river in my car. There are no roads out there. The prairie beats my car up. No signs of humanity.

Jan 22, 1976: Cold. No sign of Johnny. Police don't have a clue.

Jan 29, 1976: Cold. I don't know where to look. I wander around north of his house, watch the clouds, sit, cry.

Feb 12, 1976: Cold. Missed a week. Hope is gone. Bradley called. Told him to fuck off.

Feb 19, 1976: Cold. I found Johnny's truck. It's in a bowl valley, all burned up. Told Chester. He came out and poked around. No sign of anyone, no bodies inside. He left the truck where it was.

Feb 26, 1976: Cold. Sheriff Chester says Kitch probably took Johnny out north and killed him. Or Johnny killed Kitch. And then whoever did the killing killed himself and they both got ate by coyotes. The sheriff finally hauled the truck away.

Mar 4, 1976: Thawing. Wind. When I can, I go to the valley and sit and think. There's nothing there but thinking. I hate Kitch.

This continues for six more months. Every week, she drives north of the Riles Place, to a bowl-shaped valley, to meditate on the disappearance of Johnny. I suspect that this is the same valley where I saw the tornado.

On September 2nd, big news:

Windy. Drove to the valley. Walked around. Heard a sound.

Looked under a sagebrush. I found a baby wrapped in a lady's nightgown. His eyes are barely open. He's my miracle with a tuft of hair. He's my little unicorn in the deserted ocean.

Beneath this entry is an actual pencil sketch of a unicorn. Stiff-legged, but otherwise pretty good.

Followed three days later by:

He won't stop crying. People will hear. He's tiny. I can't do this.

Sept 6, 1976: I left him at the courthouse, with his name pinned to his blanket. It was like cutting off my own head.

And then there's a drawing of a grim-faced narwhal, complete with a tuft of hair on its round head.

That's the last entry.

The jury is in. I am the mysterious baby. Why not? Charlene Morning found me under the sagebrush and left me on the courthouse steps.

It also appears, to my disappointment, that Charlene Morning is *not* my biological mother. That is, unless she went the duration of a gestation without realizing she was pregnant and then accidentally gave birth to me on one of her weekly trips to the Valley of the Riles.

Once again, I am motherless. It's about as heartbreaking as one would expect when one is me. Still, even if she isn't my mom, Charlene saved me from being raised by coyotes and so I'm grateful to her.

Charlene adored John Riles, that's fer sure. Of the two Riles boys, I'm now hoping he's my father. Kitch, in spite of the fact that he's a basketball hero, is starting to sound like a real pain in the ass.

Wake, eyes open, another dreamless sleep. I'm on Charlene's bed, and I'm confused and lonely.

To review: I'm moving extremely fast, I found my mom, I lost my mom, one of the Riles boys is clearly responsible for the shape of my nose, Vero's eyes are locking onto my latest love note, I'm sore-kneed, and I strongly suspect that I was discovered as an infant lying under a sagebrush in the middle of a prairie grassland. Adventure! Mystery! I should be totally jazzed right now. I'm not.

Listen, I am amazingly resilient, but I do have limits. Read the previous paragraph again. Now tell me I *shouldn't* be confused, lonely, overwhelmed. The dangling threads, the conjecture vis-à-vis parenthood, and, well, this whole shit-mess of stuff that I've been trying to explain to you just now, it's like there's a pit bull trapped inside my ribcage.

The situation demands some deep thought. In an effort to find equilibrium, here in the garden behind Charlene Morning's house, I shall fold my stiffening legs into the lotus position and summon my spirit animal. Oh, eternal narwhal of the oceanic dream, where does your wisdom lead me?

Many breaths later, I am graced with neither a spirit animal, nor even with a linen-clad hallucinatory woman, nor with anything *close* to contentment. Nay, I am graced only with a desire to abandon everything before me, to leave Vero in this backyard garden, and to once more walk west on Route 36.

That's preposterous. You can't just run away.

And yet, what would it hurt to get out of here for a while? Everything that's happening excruciatingly slowly now will continue to happen excruciatingly slowly until I get back. I don't care about time anymore, remember?

I'm still in lotus position, by the way, and my hips hurt. More deep breaths.

*

A memory.

In my early twenties, I occasionally smoked pot with a girl who had recently dumped me, but who I figured would undump me if she inhaled enough weed to forget that I was an idiot. This is the girl who gave me my unread copy of *On the Road.* I know I said I wouldn't mention her again, but.

Shortly after she'd given me the Kerouac book, this being the interim between the time she dumped me and the time I *realized* that she'd dumped me, I still made regular visits to her place to smoke pot, as I've just mentioned. On this occasion, the two of us were high as kites, playing canasta on the floor of her Capitol Hill apartment when her roommate, Tina, returned home from her job at the soda fountain. It was winter and dark.

As Tina the Roommate was unwrapping herself from her scarf, my ex-girlfriend said, "I'm gonna get some pizza."

Tina said, "Cool."

I said, "Cool."

My ex-girlfriend grabbed her coat and grabbed her hat and off she went.

I was sitting on a beanbag with a deck of cards spread over the floor in front of me. A Bauhaus CD played low on the stereo. Tina lounged upon the couch, eating Fig Newtons and writing in the little notebook that she carried to coffee shops in hopes that a boy would ask her if she was a poet.

I ignored Tina and focused instead on waiting for the ex- to return with some 'za. The CD finished and Tina swapped it out for some early Genesis, the Peter Gabriel era. Tina had orange hair. She loved prog rock and Wiccan recipes.

Ten minutes in, I'm having an auralgasm, which is what happens when you've smoked enough weed to actually enjoy early Genesis, when the music sends you flying like a dove over an ocean filled with Day-Glo dolphins.

In the midst of this auralgasm, Tina saw me squirming around, rubbing my belly and whatnot, and she said, "She's not coming back."

Up to this point, I hadn't registered that Tina was a person. She'd always been My Girlfriend's Roommate, an obstacle, someone to be polite to when, the morning after a sleepover, I needed the bathroom before we all headed to our jobs. This was shortly before I became a basketball official. I believe I was working at a map store at the time.

I asked Tina to clarify the meaning of "coming back."

She said, "Both. She's not coming back with pizza, nor will she ever come back to a conjugal relationship with you."

I said, "What do you know?"

She rolled her eyes behind her huge lenses. "I know she's ready to date other people. I *am* her—"

"Is she dating other people at this moment?"

"She went to a movie. By herself. I'm her roommate. She tells me things. She doesn't like your goatee."

I had a goatee at the time.

Tina said, "Your facial hair is a mask you hide behind. Just like you hide behind your sarcasm."

"Did she tell you that, too?"

"Your sarcasm told me."

Tina made some markings in her notebook.

"You appear to be taking notes on this conversation."

"That's what poets do."

"Define *poet*."

"Shall I read some of my work?"

I said, "Only if you do so silently."

Tina said, "Poetry should be heard, not read." She stood up with the grace of one who has recently begun attending yoga classes and went to her room. I expected her to return clad in bondage gear with a black plastic leotard and nipple holes. You never know with these poetic types.

The Genesis CD ended and I put on the Crash Test Dummies, because I hated them.

When Tina returned, I was mostly relieved to see was still wearing her black jeans and white T-shirt. Also, she was smoking a joint, which she generously shared with me.

She sat cross-legged on the couch, opened her notebook, and began to read. Her voice was smooth, languid at times, with occasional hints at the slam syllabic ejaculations that had recently become The Thing Young Poets Do. Her work centered on a common theme: puppies trapped inside her chest, lonely little beings that needed to climb out but she couldn't dare let them out because they were too bloody and small to live in this world.

Tina's poems were her puppies, you know, and she let them out for me, and they were bloody, gruesome, desperate things.

After she'd finished several pieces, to which I listened with a rapt expression on my face, she said, "I've never read to anyone before."

I said, "Your pronunciation is spot-on."

She said, "You're strange, Narwhal. There's something." She tapped her cheekbone. "Something *obscured* about you."

I said, "I'm hiding behind my facial hair."

Tina tilted her head at me, skeptical. Her orange bangs were asymmetrical, sort of sloping to one side. She said, "You're a funnyman."

"Thanks."

"Do you know how to be anything else?"

Just three days ago, during the conversation in which she had dumped me, my ex-girlfriend had asked me that very same question. At the time, I had taken it as a compliment. Hearing it from Tina suggested two things:

1) I had been the subject of deep, inter-roommate conversations.

2) You know, maybe it hadn't been a compliment, maybe I *was* a pathological wisecracker, and maybe that was a problem.

It's virtually impossible to ease gracefully out of a conversation of this sort, especially when you are cross-eyed stoned. There's no defense against this type of psychotherapeutic prodding, and to go on the offensive would only lead to accusations of denial, projection, Oedipal issues.

Pugilistically speaking, it was time for me to take a dive.

I said, "You're absolutely right. I am a scared little puppy." I said this with the same inflection one would employ in saying, "You're right. There *is* a tiger staring at us thru the blades of grass." Done correctly, this inflection can be very convincing, and I did it correctly.

Tina was on the couch, I was seated on the beanbag facing her. She leaned forward, her back straight, and kissed me on the forehead. Then she returned to her upright position and said, "Honesty is soap for the soul."

She gave me a come-hither look.

Screw it. I joined her on the couch and pretty soon we had our shirts off, hands pawing at flesh, kisses on shoulders.

Tina's jeans were tight and not particularly flattering to her belly, which flowed over the top like a floppy chef's hat. I had developed a beer belly of my own at that stage and had my own spillover problems. I ran my fingernails over her back, scraping off tiny scabs, those little pinhead ones you get from a mild case of post-post-adolescent back-acne. Her breath picked up.

I said, "Perhaps we should remove our trousers."

She ran a finger along my ear lobe, "No can do."

I said, "Okie dokie." Although shedding clothes had a definite, deviant appeal, I was completely open to keeping things just as we were, she and me stoned on the couch, the Crash Test Dummies singing about birthmarks, our bellies stretched fat by the puppies within.

She said, "I can't take off my pants."

I said, "That's fine." It really was fine. This could have ended at any moment, or we could continue as we were. I didn't mind.

She said, "Three words."

"Three words what?"

"I can't take off my pants because of three words." She nipped her teeth at the tip of my nose.

I said, "I am uncertain of how to proceed."

Tina said, "Don't be. There's a good reason why I can't remove my pants. And that reason can be explained in three words. That's all."

Be the scared puppy, Narwhal. Be sincere. Must. Resist. Humor.

I said, "Are the three words, 'Jumanji, Jumanji, Jumanji'?"

She tilted her head and said, "I can't tell you, Narwhal. Not now."

Screw the scared puppy. I needed to know the three words. I looked at her with my big adopted eyes, waited a beat.

"How about now?"

My wit was working. She looked at me with her big poetic eyes. A broad, naughty smile crept out of her mouth. She said, "Promise not to—"

Whereupon my ex-girlfriend returned, burdened by a cardboard pizza box. What's a person to do? What are *three* people to do? Not being a porn flick, it did not conclude with the lot of us squirming around on the kitchen floor. Rather, my ex-girlfriend brought the pizza directly to her bedroom and slammed the door as I rather hastily found my shirt and Tina found hers. Tina excused herself to the bathroom and I made a quick exit.

I never went back to that apartment, never saw my ex-girlfriend again, never saw Tina again, never finished *On the Road.* In the years since, I have replayed the scene in my head, focusing primarily on what may have happened if my ex- had arrived with the pizza just a few minutes later, long enough for Tina to say those three words that had required her to keep her jeans on.

I can only speculate what those words were. Candidates include: "Herpes simplex virus." "Incomplete sex change." "Embarrassing Nazi tattoo."

As a childhood fan of all things Narnian, particularly the goat-legged Mr. Tumnus, I lean toward "I'm a faun."

It was shortly after the pizza incident that I enrolled in a training course with the Denver Basketball Officials Association. I never again wanted to be in a room full of fucked up people where nobody knew the rules.

I unfold my lotus legs. I know what I must do. In order to evict that goddamned pit bull from my gut, I must find answers, solid, factual answers to the question of my conception. Not all of those answers will be found on the Colorado prairie. I must walk west. I will venture on a *vision quest* and I will return to Vero as a man of wisdom.

Before I depart, I add some text to my letter to Vero. It now reads:

I'll be your sand if you'll be my sun.
I'm going to Denver.
Back in a few minutes.

I could have come up with something better, but my head's all over the place, what with this new adventure upon which I am about to sally frothily.

I will walk straight to Denver. I'll bypass the tornado and the Riles Place and the Jim and Jane Jones Cult of the Jellified Mushroom and any other roadside distractions. I'll go to Denver and gather myself and then I'll come back to Charlene's backyard garden and see how Vero's doing, and then I'll solve the mystery of my parentage, and, finally, I'll figure out how to reset my clock so Vero and I can hold hands again.

My hair is an inch and a half long.

PART THREE

And there in the blue air I saw for the first time, in hints and mighty visitation, far off, the great snowy-tops of the Rocky Mountains. I took a deep breath.

— Jack Kerouac,
On the Road

Clunk, step, rattle, step, clunk, step, rattle. As my crumbling knees carried me all one-hundred and thirty miles to Denver, the rest of my body began to ache as well. Shoulders, elbows, neck, back, wrists, ankles, hips—name a joint, it hurt. The thick air that had made me stronger was now shaping me into an arthritic spider.

Wake up, stretch. After lunch, stretch. Pre-slumber, stretch. No running. Maximum of ten aspirin per day.

I stopped for neither semi, nor tornado, nor pronghorn, nor lunatic compound. My purpose was pure. I made my shambling pilgrimage thru the oceanic grassland, and the Rocky Mountains rewarded me by slowly climbing themselves up from the horizon.

I shambled until downtown Denver pressed out of the skirts of the mountains. The buildings grew like shoots from a garden of glass and steel and concrete until they were fully extended, ready for Jack to ascend and give the giant a dose of fee-fi-fo-fummery.

The lights were lit in the skyscrapers, which loomed as starry silhouettes against the orange and blue pre-crepuscular sky, each floor containing more light bulbs than any three of the towns I'd passed on my way there. The time was now nearly seven-thirty on September first, 2009; seven minutes had passed since I'd gone hypertemporal. Dusk was well on its way. Try to picture this: although the sun was higher in the sky the further west I went, the mountains—and therefore the western horizon—also grew higher. Consequently, as I approached the mountains, twilight accelerated.

Given the duskiness of the city, my first stop was a hardware store where I found a display of LED flashlights in which several models were in the blessed state of *on.* Ignoring the empty glares of dozens of patrons and the vacant stares of orange-aproned employees, I liberated a headlamp from the display. I put it on my head and strode out of the store confident that the batteries would last me the rest of my hypertemporal life, and optimistic that a little light would render the shady portions of Denver a shade less intimidating.

Dressed in my zebra shirt, a pair of sweats, and black shoes, I walked south to Martin Luther King Junior Boulevard and started my westward march into the city proper. MLK, like most MLKs, was four lanes wide, flanked by brick houses, corner shops, churches, liquor stores, and the occasional park. The folks on the sidewalks tended to be of a darker hue than I. The cars on the road itself tended to be driven by folks of a wealthier hue.

The scene was a wax museum, a zombie town, a manikin display, a diorama.

I haven't mentioned this before, because I hadn't noticed it before, but the people of the plains seem generally happy. If not happy, then at least bemused. If not bemused, then at least aware of their surroundings. In Denver, first off, there are people everywhere. It's disconcerting to have to dodge a pedestrian every ten feet. Second off, everyone is frowning, focusing on some tiny spot directly in front of their faces. Usually that tiny spot is a telephone whose screen consists of pidgin language conversations conducted in alternating green and grey cartoon bubbles. The few individuals not staring at phones are staring at absolutely nothing, which is where people look when they don't want to look like they're looking at anything. There's nothing worse than two corporeal persons admitting that they know the other exists.

I sat on a curb for a moment, rubbing my knees, which had recently begun crunching like somebody breaking up handfuls of dry spaghetti. I rotated my shoulders, *clunk* and *pop*.

Remember when I found that bottle of expired hydrocodone in Charlene Morning's medicine cabinet? And how I said I wouldn't ever take pills because I feared they would compromise my irrepressibility? Let the record show that I made that statement prior to walking to Denver. Let the record show that after walking to Denver I was profoundly sore, like, arthritically, practically cripplingly, sore.

I found a supermarket, the kind with a pharmacy. I exited the supermarket with several bottles of controlled substances in my backpack.

Fifteen minutes later, with two Vicodin in my belly, the joint pain had retreated, although the crunching continued. I will not overdo this, I promise.

Next stop, food. I chose a Chinese restaurant in a strip mall. I slid a plate of drunken noodles out from under the nose of the restaurant's sole diner, a balding black man, and gobbled it clean. Screw my Personal Prime Directive. When the zebra's in the city, anything goes.

Speaking of anything going, you know how you sometimes drive by a strip club in the middle of the day and see rusty hatchbacks in the parking lot and you think, "I wonder what's going on in there?" But you won't go in for the sole reason that you're afraid that someone might recognize *your* rusty hatchback in that parking lot and, at some unanticipated future encounter, accuse you of being pathetic?

Lucky for me, I no longer *have* a car. (You're welcome, Sandy.)

Also, bear in mind that, thanks to my incredible self-control, I hadn't seen nudity in months. And Vero did cheat on me. Even though I'd come to terms with this, I reckoned that I had sufficient karma-credit to justify a quick visit to a titty-bar. Plus, I was on a *vision quest*.

And so, without trepidation, I crossed the street, opened the door, and entered a place called Jiggles.

As I may have mentioned, a human looks goofy when *thon*'s motion is rendered static. Our eyelids, mouths, and everything else are intended to be viewed in a state of perpetual transformation. A mouth doesn't switch instantly from a neutral position to a smile. There's a transition that happens so quickly we don't see it. Unlike, say, herky-jerky songbirds, humans exist in a state of, as dear Heraclites would say, flux. In my hypertemporal state, the flux is fucked. All I see are the transition points. It's a connect-the-dots picture and I don't have a pencil.

My point, before I started trying to speak Greek, was that those transition points are never flattering. And if you *really* want to see unflattering transition points, disrobe a human and pay *thon* to dance. The very name of the club, Jiggles, suggests motion. Remove the motion and you end up with body parts that look like they've been pressed against a cold windowpane. Squished, stretched, distended, lumpy, and *extremely* unsexy.

Even more unsexy were the patrons, with their faces frozen in lust, their back-slapping idiocy, the spittle launching out of their mouths. I removed all the cash from all the wallets of all the creepy back-slappers and distributed it to the dancers, giving extra consideration to the less-pretty women, the ones who didn't have any money in their panties.

As I stuffed the cash in G-strings, I was struck by the warmth of the women's skin. I confess, curiosity compelled me to cup the breast of one dancer who was standing sufficiently still as to retain an iota of dignity. It was like fondling the body of the recently deceased. I withdrew my hand, ashamed, and also a teeny bit aroused.

You'll be relieved to learn that the shame outstripped the arousal. It'd take a lot of work to make myself feel comfortable groping one of these warm manikins. I am not willing to put in the effort to overcome that taboo. The world can rest easy knowing I haven't been pawing and petting my way into its G-string, except to load it with dollar bills.

Which brings up a question that you've been dying to ask. What's old Narwhal doing to address his, you know, perfectly natural human desires? I'll say this just once: when desires arise, I satisfy them in the traditional method employed by lonely folks of all ages and creeds, and in a responsible, tidy fashion.

As an apology for fondling the innocent dancer, I stuffed an extra handful of twenty-dollar bills into the waistband of her panties.

So long, Jiggles. It was weird for me, too.

If this were a zombie story, this is where I would return to my childhood home only to discover the corpse of one adopted parent devouring the corpse of the other adopted parent. This would convince me that there's no point in dwelling in the past. Buck up, load the shotgun, and splatter some brains.

My case not being zombie-related, I had much less to worry about. Unfortunately, there's something worse than seeing your father bite a chunk out of your mom's thorax: You could come across them in the act of intercourse on the living room floor, which is precisely the scene I'm not going to describe for you.

Of all the houses I've been into and all the privacy I've intruded, why is it that my parents are the only people I've found in a state of copulation?

Knowing that I'm adopted does not make it easier.

Me and the parents always got along well considering they acquired me when I was five and I had already gone thru several foster homes. I wasn't a loner or a bad kid or anything; I just never connected with anybody. My whole life, it was just me, although sometimes it was me and my teddy bear or me and my bike or me and my hula hoop. Never me and a friend.

Young Narwhal didn't interact with other humans, not in a loving way. Nor did I ever suffer from any actual ambitions, not as a little kid, not as a high schooler. I lacked stick-to-it-ive-ness. I spent my youth hidden behind a wall of sarcasm, and, briefly, behind a goatee. What do you expect from someone who was (apparently) found under a sagebrush.

I've got nothing bad to say about Mom and Dad Slotterfield, except that they were always more like roommates than parents. As long as I did my share of the dishes and replaced the toilet paper when the roll got empty, we got along. They gave me toys for Christmas. I made them construction-paper cards for Mother's Day and Father's Day.

They were semi-autistic, I think. I will offer no evidence to back up that statement other than to say they weren't big into hugging, or discipline, or pets. And they were both super dorky college professors. Nothing they said or did even remotely suggested that they were capable of something so intimate as a good *boinking.* I always considered my adoption to be a concession to the limited nature of their sexual relationship.

Once upon a time. I have a pet story. I once had a cat. I adored it. I called it Orion. Let's skip to the end. Like all pet stories, this one ends with someone digging a hole in the backyard.

This hole, I dug deep. I remember shoveling soil and worms out over my shoulder until the grave was significantly deeper than I was tall, and I was always tall for my age. I was probably eight years old.

With my feet buried under the soft dirt, I wiped my brow and looked up toward the circle of darkening sky above me, the crumbly walls around me. I'd gotten myself in too deep. I had lacked the prescience to tie a rope around the leg of the trampoline and let it dangle into the hole as a means of escape. In my defense, I hadn't anticipated that I'd dig nine feet into the ground. It's a miracle I didn't run into the sewage line.

Once I realized my predicament, me being stuck in a grave, I remained still for several dozen minutes, every now and then meekly calling for help. As dinnertime grew nearer, my calls grew louder, until I was actually shouting. My cries were answered some time later when my parents, both of them, appeared and leaned over the opening of the hole and reached their arms to me and pulled me out.

There were comforting pats on the head and then, together, we wrapped Orion in tin foil and lowered him to his new home on a rope of yarn, which I released into the hole to fall upon the foil like a beige scribble.

I'm fairly certain that if my parents hadn't have pulled me out I'd still be digging that hole.

You know what? Fuck off. I didn't go to that house so I could commune with my parents. I especially didn't go to that house to commune with *you* about my parents. I went to that house in search of documentation. Specifically, I wanted records of my discovery, adoption, that sort of thing. And, no, this doesn't qualify as a violation of my Personal Prime Directive. This is my childhood home, my life. I can do what I want.

I walked down the hall and entered the study, well out of sight from the coital horror of the living room. The study contained a grey, industrial, three-drawer filing cabinet. It was the kind of filing cabinet with a little metal frame on the face of each drawer, where you could slide a piece of paper for a label. Top drawer, *Mr. Slotterfield.* Middle drawer, *Mrs. Slotterfield.* Bottom drawer, *Narwhal Slotterfield.*

The *Narwhal Slotterfield* drawer of my permaparents' filing cabinet was filled with magazines: *Popular Science, Mechanics Illustrated*, and good ol' *Omni.* The mags were splotted with dried spaghetti sauce, hamburger grease, and various other types of dinner-related organic material. At the top of the stack was the October 1994 issue of *Omni.* The front cover promised articles about UFOs and God. But nowhere in that magazine, nor in the drawer, was there a single word about adoption agencies or county courthouses or anything that would tell me that I was the son of a Riles.

I closed the *Narwhal* drawer and moved to the ones labeled *Mr.* and *Mrs.* Mom's drawer was filled with meteorites. Dad's drawer was completely empty.

I checked drawers in the desk, looked under beds, poked around in closets, searched the entire house. Guess what I found? Nothing. Because this is 2009 and who needs paper anymore? Everything's been scanned, saved, backed up on stacks of hard drives. My secret origins were beyond my reach.

I crossed back thru the living room, left Ma and Pa in their sticky embrace, and headed toward my next destination, the humble home of Vero and me. This trip was not going so good, so far.

On the way, I made a quick side trip to a neighborhood shoe store, where I picked up a pair of officially-sanctioned referee sneakers, black and springy. I left my old shoes balanced on the head of the kid at the cash register.

On to Capitol Hill, Greek Town, good old 14th and Fillmore, just across the street from the Waldorf School and the Seventh-Day Adventist church. My garden-level apartment had a hint of celebrity to it. The previous occupant had been a man named Cordon Pruitt, whom you may remember because I mentioned him earlier. He wrote a bizarre exercise manual called *The Funnercise Handbook* and then froze to death in his living room and *then* some lunatic carved his heart out of his chest.

Fortunately, the gore had been thoroughly removed before I took occupancy. It was a cozy place. After Vero moved in, it only got cozier, although curious kids still sometimes peeked in the windows in hopes of seeing a ghost.

I went thru the place, wearing my absconded headlamp, sneaking around like a cat burglar. Shitty chair, shitty TV. A half-empty can of beer in the fridge, an unpaid gas bill on the arm of the sofa, the smell of Vero's shampoo. Just a dumb apartment with some dumb stuff inside. Clue-wise, it offered nothing. Sentiment-wise, it only reminded me of what a loser I'd always been. I sat in my recliner in front of my TV. I climbed onto our bed and closed my eyes and pretended to sleep. Then I opened my eyes and pretended to wake up, in the off chance that this would trick the universe into shifting me back in my proper gear. It didn't work. I missed Vero, that's all.

Before I split, I stuffed a few pairs of underwear into my backpack. As well as, fuck it, my unread copy of *On the Road.*

One more stop and I could head home. "Home" being in the town of Keaton, in the backyard garden where I'd left Veronica Vasquez.

I walked Colfax Avenue toward downtown. Colfax is one of Denver's great Hey-Zones. As in, every third person you encounter shouts, "Hey! Hey! Can I get you anything?" or "Hey! You got a dollar?" Also as in every time you try to cross a crosswalk, a car attempts to drive over you, so you shout, "Hey! Asshole!" and the driver shouts back, "Hey! Faggot!"

Twenty-nine blocks of Colfax and two more Vicodin brought me to the gold-domed capitol building, where I veered left and made the final three blocks to the Denver Art Museum, all modern angles and polyhedrons, as is the way of any architecturally-relevant art museum in the twenty-first century.

Turns out the museum closes at five-o'clock on Tuesdays, putting me two-and-a-half hours late for any kind of dignified entrance. I walked around the outside of the building until I found a service door whose rubber wedge prop hadn't been properly kicked out by the last person to take a smoke break. Once inside, I followed *EXIT* signs backwards until I reached the public exhibits.

There's a woman named Linda in the Denver Art Museum. She's been there forever. She's a hyper-realistic sculpture, sleeping on her side, a white cloth draped over her pelvic privates. There's actual human hair in the follicles on her arms. I've always loved Linda. Everyone has always loved Linda.

Now and again, the curators move her to a new room. You never know where you'll find her. When you do come upon her, every time, you shit your pants because some sexy, crazy lady with an out-of-date hairdo has stripped naked and passed out on one of the viewing benches. And then you say, "Aw, Linda, you got me again."

After a great deal of searching, I found her in an exhibit of contemporary hairpieces. She didn't startle me at all this time; sculpture Linda looked just like all the actual people all over Denver. Or all the actual people looked like sculpture Linda. I had been living within a still life for the last several weeks. Artistic renderings of it seemed redundant.

In my cloudy, Vicodizzened state of mind, I slid Linda off her pedestal and floated her to the men's restroom and pressed her so she lay on the floor of the handicapped stall with her feet poking out from under the door. That oughta scare the shit out of the next person who comes in here, and what better place for that?

With that, any remaining shred of my Personal Prime Directive floated away, at least with respect to art museums. Whistling without sound, I followed empty halls and climbed dead escalators until I reached the abstract art exhibit. There, I flipped a Jackson Pollock upside down. Moving out of the abstractions, I switched labels on numerous impressionist pond paintings. I placed a roll of toilet paper on a pedestal that was meant for a Grecian urn, I put a Grecian urn over the head of a bronze Fredrick Remington horse. I found a black marker in a drawer at the information desk and used it, the black marker, to write "DADA" on the backsides of a whole wall of cubist paintings. I was having fun!

In the room full of big, old, symbol-strewn European works, I signed my name in the bottom right corners of several Madonna-with-baby paintings. And then I came upon a picture, nearly as tall as me, of this old, naked angel guy sitting on a blue silk cape. Upon the angel guy's lap was a super pissed-off young naked angel baby. The naked angel baby was super pissed-off because the old man angel was chopping off the baby wings with a pair of old-timey scissors.

The picture was called *Time Clipping Cupid's Wings*. I stared at it a for a while, then decided I'd had enough of symbol-strewn European works and set out in search of the dark soul of the Denver Art Museum.

As everyone in Denver knows, the art museum was born in 1897. Its first location was the Holly Woods Mansion on Logan Street. By 1905, the collection had outgrown the mansion. This was shortly after the conclusion of the Great Standing Plague and so fewer people were dropping dead in the streets, and those who hadn't dropped dead were in need of some sort of spiritual uplift. In a win-win, the forward thinkers of the Holly Woods Foundation relocated the museum to the morgue that had originally popped up on 14th and Acoma at the beginning of the plague and was now, with the end of the plague, empty.

Although the building has been altered several times in the intervening century, 14th and Acoma remains the current address of the Denver Art Museum. It's rumored that, in a variation of the technique employed by Mayan temple builders, each new iteration of the museum has been built atop the previous one. Further, it's rumored that at the center of the art museum, one can still find vestigial evidence of the plague morgue.

I crept the lower halls of the museum, the places prohibited to the public. With my headlamp showing the way, I explored storerooms containing the junior varsity squad of human creative expression: archived collections of potsherds, shelved boxes containing fragments of mummified cats, and room after room filled with landscape paintings of the American West. Stuff you can't throw away, but which nobody cares to look at.

I crept deeper and deeper into the museum's guts. Down a dark hall, down a musty stairwell, to an ancient wooden door. The door was unlocked. I pressed it open, revealing a dark chamber. I aimed my headlamp. The chamber's walls were solid rock. I had found the morgue.

It had a nice vibe. The room was furnished with lounge chairs, circa 1972, upholstered in orange. Also present: paper coffee cups, a microwave.

This was a break room, maybe a secondary break room. Duct-taped to the walls were flyers for local bands, as well as a series of publicity photos of Lucha Libre wrestlers. This wasn't the place where the salaried employees hung out. Too dank. This was, like, a breakroom for the kids, the interns, the janitors, the fun crew.

In the center of this, like, breakroom was a long table of deep-grained wood. The edges were worn down and black with schmutz. The table was large enough to have easily accommodated several plague-dead human corpses.

Upon this table, in the absence of plague-dead human corpses, were two-dozen oversized glass jars. I leaned toward one of the jars. It was the size of one of those giant pickle jars you'd buy at a wholesale store for resale at the concession stand at the basketball game. The jar contained a squirrel floating in transparent liquid. The rounded glass distorted the image and reflected the glow of my headlamp in such a way as to grossly reinforce the Frankensteinian feel of the dead animal, all teeth and fur and glowering eyes. Written on the lid of the jar with a black marker was, *What happens when I submerge a squirrel in water? 06/21/08.*

The jar next to it contained another squirrel, this one considerably less solid. Small fragments of skin and fur were suspended in the water. On top of the jar, *What happens when I submerge a squirrel in water? 03/21/08.*

There were twenty-two more squirrels in twenty-two more jars, each one dated three months earlier than the last, each squirrel in a greater state of decay: fur at the bottom of the jar, skin dissolved, bones floating like wax in a lava lamp. At the far end of this incredibly long table, the oldest jar, dated September 21, 2002, contained nothing but grey liquid. I picked it up and shook it and it remained grey. No sediment, just a grey liquid that had once been a squirrel.

When does a squirrel stop being a squirrel and start being grey water? Somewhere around jar nineteen, I'd say.

A dot-matrix sign was pinned to the back of the wooden door: *What decays in this room, stays in this room.* At the bottom of the sign: *If you come across a freshly dead squirrel please let Hillary know,* and, *I promise not to blab about this to the general public*, followed by several signatures.

Huzzah, young ambitious museum employees. You've turned this

Room of the Dead into a hangout and a home for your own private installation. I find your jars of dead squirrels to be more moving than all the impressionist ponds in all the museums in all the world.

I left the museum and headed downtown to hike the 16th Street Mall. The Mall is a pedestrian-friendly valley of consumption that bisects Denver's cluster of skyscrapers. The concrete chess tables are occupied twenty-four hours per day, buskers sing their Jack Johnson songs, tweaker kids slouch upon concrete benches, ready to sell you drugs, tourists lug shopping bags filled with whatever tourists purchase when they're in Denver.

On a hot summer evening like this one, people of all ages and skin tones lounge upon benches like basking seals, dressed in tank tops, flip flops, and, in the case of white males, cargo shorts. Apparently, all white Denver males between the ages of twenty and fifty are required to wear cargo shorts festooned with the requisite six-to-eight pockets, four-to-six of which contain absolutely nothing. I know. I checked.

There was so much I could do here, but, you know, I didn't want to do anything here. I tried. I entered a dimly lit restaurant, nibbled sushi, chewed some wine. In a valet parking lot, I stood on the hood of a three-hundred-thousand-dollar Italian sports car. Maybe the Rockies were playing baseball. Imagine the chaos I could create in Beer Sponsored Field.

Good, now I don't have to go.

Denver was dim, there were too many vacant eyes attached to too many people, there was too much shit for sale, too many buildings blocking my view of the horizon.

The plains, though. The plains have this subtractive quality that forces you to *notice*. Remove the mountains, notice the sky. Remove the sidewalks, notice the dirt. Remove the people, notice the beetles. Beauty via absence. I missed that beauty.

Once upon a time, Vero took me to this little art museum on Capitol Hill. As we were walking around admiring the paintings, we entered an empty room. No art, just four white walls, a white floor, and a white ceiling.

As I turned around to exit the empty cube, Vero grabbed me by the sleeve. "Check it out."

"There's nothing to check out, darling."

She shook her head at silly Narwhal. "We're in a drop of milk."

The plains are not blank walls. They're decorated with bugs, a million varieties of wild grass, pronghorn, snakes, windmills, strange reptilian footprints. Hawks and eagles perch on telephone poles.

Choose any portion of land there and focus on the half-dozen dusty beetles caught motionless in their clamberings thru the sand and over broken grass stems.

If you want to appreciate the little things, you have to squat down and look at them. Unfortunately most people only squat if they're taking a shit.

I'm building up to a revelation. You can skip the next few paragraphs if you'd prefer to get on with the walking and moving and exploring.

There's a reason why the final two minutes of a basketball game are the most entertaining.

In those last moments of the game, time literally *and* figuratively slows down. By "literally," I mean the clock *stops* for time-outs and strategic fouls. By "figuratively," I'm talking about the way in which a last-second shot takes forever to decide whether it should slip thru the hoop or to clang off the rim and bounce out of bounds. As we concentrate on these fateful caroms, the accumulated drama of the game's preceding moments expands into a gazillion potentials while simultaneously zeroing in on a single inevitable conclusion: one team will exit the gym in a good mood, the other will be pissed at the refs.

There are people who don't understand this: Without the preceding portion of the game, the final two minutes have no meaning. These are the people who skip to the end of the book. Or, more likely, don't bother reading.

Back to the beetles, from which I have regretfully drifted. Any asshole can look at a mountain and write a poem about its majesty. It takes a real sophisticate to appreciate the beauty of the wind-schlepped plains. This is modern, minimalist art, grey grass filled with tiny creatures that move about with no apparent purpose. Screw museums, screw Denver.

My work here was done. I had discovered no useful data at my childhood home, I'd found no comfort at my garden-level apartment. On the bright side, I had defaced some art and discovered a bizarre chamber within the heart of the Art Museum. And I'd acquired a pair of officially-sanctioned referee shoes and a nifty headlamp. And I had acquired respect for the planar landscape and weird people of eastern Colorado. So, not a total waste. Not at all. Now, back to Keaton.

With one quick detour.

After hiking south and east for most of a day, I arrived at Dove Valley, home to the Denver Broncos' multi-trillion-dollar training ground for the administration of head trauma. I paused before the monolithic concrete sign that read *Denver Broncos Football Club.* Beyond the sign lurked a four-story glass-walled office building of the sort that requires a security pass.

Assuming he was working late, which I had no reason to believe was the case, The Blad would be where, exactly? First, I'd have to break in, then I'd have to find a directory of employees and then I'd have to hope he was in his office, then confront him and

I'm such a worry wart. The Blad was in the parking lot, opening the door to his German automobile. I recognized him from a hundred yards away. With his broad chest, tufts of hair balancing on his balding round head, and bowed legs, he was simultaneously a symbol of male virility and human decay. Jar three or four in the journey to grey water.

I stood before my nemesis, he in his black business suit, me in my referee shirt and sweat pants. I said to him, "Football has neither the grace nor the fluidity of basketball." He responded with the condescending silence so popular amongst alpha males.

I knew virtually nothing about The Blad. I knew he had declined to smoke weed at that party where I'd met him. I knew he enjoyed telling people how much he enjoyed telling cheerleaders how to be sexy. Based on Vero's diary, I knew he'd received at least one DUI. And I knew that Vero had once dated him.

Vero was a human of great taste. There *had* to be something decent about The Blad, otherwise she wouldn't have chosen him as her means of cuckolding me. But what that decent something was, I couldn't tell by glaring at him in a parking lot. I could only judge him based on the available data, and that data suggested that The Blad was a dick and he deserved to be punished.

Catch yer breath, Nar. Subsume the call for aggressive masculine projection and be honest with yerself. Vero didn't *choose* The Blad, she *rejected* you. Once you've sawn thru the trunk, you can't blame the tree for falling on you.

The tree in this metaphor represents the mutual sense of comfort that initially brought Vero and me together. The saw represents my tendency to be a curmudgeonly butt. And The Blad is represented by the previously unmentioned poisonous mushroom that's poking out of the dead leaves on the forest floor. Vero's no dummy, you know. She saw the mushroom, took a nibble, it made her sick, and so she spit it out. Remember what she wrote in her diary:

Türns oüt The Blad's an annoying, sports-obsessed, he-man jackass.

Yeah, baby.

Maybe I didn't actually cut down the Tree of Comfort after all. Maybe I just ran head first into it and knocked myself out.

I peeled The Blad's fingers away from the handle of his briefcase. I floated it in front of me and opened it up. Inside was a laptop and a half-empty plastic bottle of diet cola. Dude drinks diet cola. What a lame-o. I left the briefcase and its contents adrift.

I addressed him. "It's only by the grace of me that you aren't tied to the back of one of those semis over there." I pointed to I-25 in the near distance. "Keep that in mind next time you try to seduce one of your ex-girlfriends."

As parting shots go, it wasn't worthy of a Hollywood movie or anything, but I didn't have anything else to say to the guy. I turned away and started east.

Then I went back and punched him in the jaw. Fuck you, The Blad.

I walked the highway, Vero-bound. As I progressed out from the shadow of the mountains, the setting sun gradually climbed itself over the Rockies, the skyscrapers sank back into the horizon, and eventually the panoptical gaze of the city was replaced by the horizontal indifference of the flatlands.

In spite of its brief reprise, the sun was going down, no question. Every eastward step took me farther away from it and, at the same time, it was sinking ever so slowly into the horizon.

My walk was accompanied by the silent crunch of my knees, padded into painlessness by my decadent opiates, of which I was growing fond, but not, I swear, dependent.

I strode along, stopping at the occasional house for food, a nap on the front lawn. I passed the Jim and Jane Jones Mushroom Ranch, no desire for further hallucinations or story-telling shamanistas.

When I reached the spot where I'd constructed the fatal pronghorn pyramid, I stood in the ditch, looking over the barbed wire fence at the dead pronghorn where it lay on its side in the grass.

I stepped over the fence and approached the corpse. The head had rolled away from the body and settled to equilibrium on the ground, eyes once again open. I patted the animal on its still-wet nose. I apologized for placing it atop the deeramid and for its subsequent leg injury and decapitation. I assured it that soon the bugs and birds and coyotes would come to devour it, and so it would, in death, contribute to the great circle of life. I hoped I wasn't coming across as patronizing.

Ah, what's that sound? Could it be the whirring of gears in the mind of Narwhal Slotterfield, soldier of justice, wearer of the zebra skin shirt? It surely is, and it's yet another brilliant plan. As penance for my horrific acts vis-à-vis the pronghorn, I must allow the slain animal to contribute to my own life. Which is to say, I needed to eat it, or some of it. Thereby, and only thereby, would I honor the animal's sacrifice.

I squatted next to the corpse and used my Everslice knife to—

You know what? To share the details would only further exploit the animal. In summary, I consumed a teeny, raw portion of this beast whom I had accidently slain by pretending *thon* was a cheerleader. The meat was juicy and warm, so I consumed a slightly larger portion of the beast. It was delicious. I made a meal of the pronghorn and it made me feel better.

I was not worried about illness. I had no reason to believe that a hypertemporal zebra could catch a bug from raw pronghorn flesh.

I bowed to the corpse and then made my way back to the highway and continued toward Vero.

As I entered the Abila city limits—a mere thirty-six miles west of Keaton—my stomach went nuts. Turns out, I had been horribly wrong to believe that a hypertemporal zebra was immune to diseases carried by raw pronghorn flesh.

A yellow volcano erupted from my mouth. Rather than splashing on the highway in front of my sneakers, the expurgated material piled up into a ball right in front of my face. I staggered backward and then fell on the ground, where the volcano re-routed itself to another, lower orifice.

If you had stripped me naked and impaled me sideways on a flagpole, the subsequent and simultaneous semi-liquid secretions would have propelled me around like a pinwheel. As it was, I lay on the asphalt and felt horrible.

At the conclusion of the first wave of this agony, I forced myself upright and stumble-walked further into Abila to a house where a shirtless Mexican man was watering his lawn with his thumb over the end of a garden hose. I shook out of my sweat pants and then scooped up some of his hose water and tried to tidy myself. To the latter end, I scooted my ass across the wet lawn like an itchy dog. Then I lay prostrate on the grass for a few moments, and then I crawled into the man's house and lay on the living room carpet and waited to die. What followed were several wake/sleep cycles full of shits, pukes, shakes, and knots in my guts. I spent endless heartbeats on the floor, curled up in the fetal position, wondering why I'd thought it was a good idea to eat raw meat.

After some long time, the agony receded into mere misery, which was far more manageable. I crawled off the floor and found a pair of loose-fitting, and altogether too-short, khaki pants in the bedroom. I pulled them on, tidied up my zebra shirt by plucking off the larger chunks of poorly masticated pronghorn meat, and carefully exited the house and walked bowlegged to the Abila Grocery just down the road. I took a two-liter bottle of ginger ale out of the cooler and brought it back to the house. On my way in, I stopped to look in the owner's billfold and learned that his name was Anthony Juarez.

Sorry, Anthony, for the mess on the lawn.

I went back to Anthony's living room and took bites of ginger ale and swallowed three Vicodin. As I lay there on the corduroy couch, it became clear just how far I had fallen. Bad joints, bad knees. My skin was starting to chafe against the thick air. Food poisoning. I had no doctor, no clue what to do if something really bad happened, no internet to give me horrible advice.

Just think of the things that can kill me: pronghorn flesh, thick air, old age, stupidity. If I die in this state, my body will become completely still and I will decay a hundred thousand times faster than time itself. I'll be grey water before you know it.

As I convalesced, I acquainted myself with my host. There was a plaque above his dresser: *Tony Juarez—1998 MOST IMPROVED PLAYER Northeast Junior College Plainsmen Men's Basketball.* I wondered if I worked any of his games.

A framed newspaper article commemorated the fifth year of an annual Thanksgiving food drive he'd put together in Sterling. Nice guy, this Anthony. Sealing the deal, he owned a well-thumbed copy of *The Road* by Cormac McCarthy.

Which reminded me of the book I'd taken from the shelf at Vero's and my apartment. And so, friends, that is how, as I recovered from my run-in with raw meat, I, for the first time in my life, read the entirety of *On the Road*.

I'm sorry, Jack. Turns out I was an asshole. Upon revisiting the book, it's clear that my original judgment of your Beatness had been clouded by my breakup with the ancient ex-girlfriend.

Here's my revised judgment: *On the Road* is not a complex read, like, oh, some of that Faulkner shit, but it's detailed. Like a mosaic that resembles absolutely nothing from afar but whose individual tiles are stunning. This is the opposite of how mosaics normally work. It's the opposite of how novels normally work. And what better way to read an opposite novel than by sitting on Anthony Juarez's couch on a long September evening while recovering from food poisoning.

So go on, Kerouac, you pill-popping madman, run fast, go nowhere, and blurt your news to the world. You are, if nothing else, one irrepressible motherfucker.

And, by God, the book contains not a single flashback.

Not long after I finished digesting *On the Road*, the pronghorn's revenge exited my body and my stomach agreed to start digesting food again. Yesterday, I was able to eat an entire pear.

Yesterday, my ass. I don't even know how long a day is. I wake, I wander, I sleep. Who knows how many weeks have passed since I left Vero alone in Charlene's backyard? My hair knows. It's three inches long.

Without further fucking around, I cleaned up my messes as best I could and then I said goodbye to Abila and to Anthony Juarez.

I walked east, past cars I'd passed five times before, paying them no mind. Not long ago, I'd run twenty-four miles because I thought I'd shot Vero in the head. That was the old days, when running felt good. Now, my body felt like a rusted robot and I still had thirty miles to cover. My shoulders hurt. My ribs ached. The skin on my nose was flakey. The skin on my ears was flakey. I'm nothing but dandruff and crumbling bones. I itch, I walk, I stumble. I'm not a robot. I'm a zombie. Just a minute. Reach into pocket, extract pills, eat water.

I'm a relaxed zombie.

I keep thinking about those jars of grey squirrel water in the art museum. How do you turn grey water back into a squirrel?

I dragged my corpse under the hellfire storm. The tornado remained north of me, invisible thru the grey gloom of the rain and hail, I did not revisit it. I walked eastward, closer and closer to Charlene Morning's backyard and I paid heed to neither the grinding of my bones nor the gradual softening of my skull.

I went to Denver and came back more or less alive. The trip taught me absolutely nothing about my origins. But I did learn:

That my permaparents like to screw on the living room floor.

That the grooviest exhibit in the Denver Art Museum is hidden in an employee breakroom located in a former morgue.

That, within the proper context, *On the Road* is a brilliant piece of work.

That it feels good to punch The Blad.

That it's unsafe to eat raw meat.

That opiates, taken in moderation, can effectively ease physical pain.

That Denver is no longer my home.

None of my limbs have fallen off. My heart is still beating. I am home, here in Charlene Morning's backyard in Keaton, Colorado. Sitting across from me is Vero. She has leaned back in her wicker chair, hands behind her head, eyes closed. She's grinning toward the darkening sky. This darling human with her beehive hair and her shiny white teeth, she's waiting for me.

On the TV tray before her is a piece of paper that reads:

Welcome home.

Good ol' Vero.

I desperately need some sleep, but before I go inside and climb on top of Charlene's bed, I fetch a new sheet of paper and write three words and place it carefully upon Vero's TV tray. I tilt her head forward so she can see what I wrote:

Please marry me.

When I awake, the world has grown decidedly darker. My long September evening is nearly over. All that remains above the horizon is an orange yarmulke of sun. I feel like I've slept for days, and that may well be the case. I stretch my stiff limbs and take my morning medicine and visit Vero in the backyard. Her hands are palm-down on the TV tray, resting on either side of my proposal of marriage. She regards the note with squinted eyes. Her mouth is either smiling or it's just in that shape a mouth makes when one squints. Whatever the case, she's processing information.

I go to the grocery. Charlene remains at the counter, continues to stare at her tabloid article about the kid raised by wolves. The coincidental nature of this story is not lost on me.

I collect sandwich fixings and exit to the parking lot where I assemble them and eat while looking at the Keaton State Bank, which is across the street. I ought to go in there someday. Banks are *filled* with money.

Down the road, at the Co-op, the encroaching darkness triggers the dusk-to-dawn lights atop the skyscraping grain elevators. The lights flicker and shine. I can't turn on a light, but apparently a sunset can.

I return to Charlene's garden and spend the rest of my day watching Vero weigh my proposal. By the time I'm ready for bed, she's taken a breath and her mouth has relaxed a little.

I sleep then wake and walk to the store and eat another sandwich and look at the bank and then watch Vero some more. Her eyes have moved away from my proposal and to the pencil next to her left hand, which suggests that she's ready to give me an answer.

I want to put the pencil in her fingers, guide her hand to the paper, and scribble *yes* a thousand times. I will not do this.

My joints are recovering from the journey to Denver. My soreness has dropped from an eight to a four. Nevertheless, I remain on my six Vicodin-per-day diet. It makes me feel good. I'm not slurring my words.

In the grocery for more sandwich fixin's, I pause in front of the back-to-school display with its nubby scissors and glue sticks and plastic backpacks. I pick out a notebook and some crayons and return to the garden and sit across from Vero. If I'm going to stare at her, I might as well use this as an opportunity for self-improvement. I shake several crayons out of the sixty-four-color box, stretch my hands. I was eight years old the last time I touched a crayon. I hated the texture of the paper they wrap around those things. Still do.

My first attempts to capture Vero's essence are lumpy cartoons with giant hands and masculine features. I revert to stick figures. I draw dozens every day, waiting for Vero to answer my proposal of marriage. Soon, I've captured the delicate *S* of her dorsal curve and the opposing angles of her hips and shoulders. I focus on the oval of her face, on her hands. I fit five or six sketches on each sheet of paper and then flip it over and add five or six more to the reverse side. A hundred sketches a day. I wear down one crayon after another. I do studies of her eyes, the convex irises, the red flesh in the corners where the upper and lower eyelids meet. When a notebook runs out of pages, I place it on Charlene's kitchen counter and then go to the store for another. When the crayons are all worn down, I switch to colored pencils, which I sharpen with my Everslice knife.

The colored pencils introduce new opportunities for nuance. I give Vero bones, then muscles, then skin. I draw her in the nude, remembering her ribs and her belly button and her breasts and the scar on her back from some childhood bicycle adventure.

I give her clothes. I draw her in the outfit she's wearing. Which I realize I have not yet described: black tank top, a pair of mid-thigh cut-offs, flip flops. Perfect attire for a hot car. I draw her in a prom dress, as a clown, as Wonder Woman. I crosshatch, I shade.

I begin a ritual. After every meal, I sit in the same spot and make a small, credit-card-sized sketch of Vero in the upper right corner of the latest page of the notebook. I create a flipbook. Since the pages don't exactly flip, I use the fingers of my right hand to deftly fan each image flat as my left thumb slides to the next. Motion! Watch the lady breathe. She leans forward and one of her feet slides behind the other. Each movement by her hand is preceded by a tug of a tendon in her forearm. I flip the pages so many times the corners turn black from finger smudge.

Vero writes a letter, *R*, then *e*, then *m*. *Rem.*

Remorse? Remain? Remove? Remora? I can't watch this. I can't stop. Days later, the word grows into *Remember.* "Remember" is exactly what Spock said to Dr. McCoy just before he, Spock, sacrificed his life for the crew of the Enterprise in *Star Trek II: The Wrath of Khan.*

The world is my still life. I learn shading, perspective, foreshortening. I learn when to stop working on a sketch and call it finished. There's only so much detail a mind can care about. I expand my subject matter. Leaves of tomato plants, knots on fence pickets, the family of starlings that's picking bugs out of the rain gutter.

I see qualities in Vero's face I've never noticed before. Her mouth moves slightly as she slides the pencil across the paper. She looks to her left when she's between words. My little Mona Lisa.

A full sentence, finally, with a question mark:

Remember
the
perfect
game?

I have no idea what she's talking about.

"Perfect game?" How can you do this to me, Veronica Vasquez? I shake my fists at the sky, the eastern hemisphere of which is now beginning to light up with stars that don't twinkle.

I examine Vero's face, serene, cast orange in the dying sun. I can't make anything of it. She's either happy with herself for coming up with a tactful manner of declining my proposal or she's calmly processing the joy of her betrothal to the seventeen-thousand-mile-an-hour man. Or she's stretching her neck.

Vero's left hand brings the pencil back to the paper. She's not yet done writing.

*

Days and days go by. Her hand moves, her lips press tight. I know this look. She's suppressing a smile. There's a second sentence:

Remember
what
I
said
when
you
told
me
about
it.

Vero's fingers finally release the pencil.

This is her answer to my proposal. *Remember the perfect game? Remember what I said when you told me about it.*

Nope, but I hope you said yes.

I've worked a lot of games. A lot of them were terrific, but I can't remember any of them being *perfect.* There was the octuple overtime extravaganza between Manual High and Denver East. There was the donkey basketball game between several ex-Denver Broncos and the coaching staff of Heritage High school wherein the donkeys won. I got to work a three-on-three tournament in Park Hill in which a sophomore Chauncey Billups literally leapt over a stunned freshman for a dunk. I rewarded young Mr. Billups—future MVP of the 2004 NBA Finals—with a whistle for air-walking. I did a Cherry Creek vs. Overland game in which both teams were so obnoxious that by the end of the first quarter I'd fouled out everyone but three players on each team.

Each of these games is amongst my most treasured memories, but none of these games was perfect.

I won't prolong this any more than necessary, but I will prolong it for a bit, because I'm completely flummoxed. I reflect on my life from my earliest memory (slapping my wet hands against a rock) to right now (staring at a woman with a beehive on her head). I attempt to reconstruct my existence, my profession, this allegedly perfect game.

It's a yes or no question, Vero. Will you or won't you?

One considers the approaching conclusion to this tale and one wonders what good can come of it. Scenarios are limited to two:

I will remain in this state until I die—lonely, clueless, unredeemed, whereupon my corpse will turn to bones before Vero's sparkling eyes.

I will awake one morning, having miraculously returned to normal speed. Veronica and I will be wed in a ceremony officiated by the pilot of the plane I mistook for a one-legged seagull.

The first scenario seems far more likely. Miserable, arthritic, opioidal death with my arms around Vero's ankles.

*

I climb upon the roof of Charlene Morning's house and sketch the final rays of the sun as they drown into the edge of the earth. The drowning takes a good long while, like two days. The sunset itself happens too slowly to be considered dramatic, but the green flash was a nice surprise. As the last rosy finger of the sun went sub-horizontal, a green glow swelled like a bubbly borealis. This happened quickly, like in less than ten heartbeats. It grew larger and larger, and as it did so, it grew fuzzy around the edges and less and less vivid, until, it smeared into half the sky and finally dissolved into nothing.

It'll be happy, my ending.

Here's how the game went.

Once, shortly after Vero and I first met, we made plans to convene at a local tavern. I arrived a little late to the rendezvous. This was a Saturday afternoon. I was a little late because the tournament I'd been working went a little late.

The tournament was kiddie basketball. Little kids, pre-school with Nerf balls and plastic three-foot hoops. I took the gig because it paid fifty dollars and I only had to do three games, each of which lasted, like, fifteen minutes.

The kids chased around like kittens, never dribbled, shot at the wrong basket, and cried and cheered and whined and laughed constantly. The parents and coaches, I didn't even notice them. Just these little farts having a blast, learning about the most important sport on earth.

Without question, the kids were horrible basketball players. But being bad at something is not the same as being bad.

Listen, nobody gives a duck's wet ass about your millionth step. It's your teetering-toddler first steps that get the applause, and those are the most incompetent steps you're ever going to take. But they're your first, so that makes them special.

I fell in love with every single one of those little booger-dripping ballers, so much so that I voluntarily worked six more games. By the time the tournament ended, I was near tears. I remember hugging the fathers of a little girl who spent the entire game crawling on all fours pretending to be a puppy. The two dads did not reciprocate my love. In fact, I think I made them uncomfortable. I suspect they mentioned this to whomever hires the officials for these things, as I was never invited back.

But the thing is, I didn't blow my whistle once that day. A no-whistle game is a perfect game. It's a game that has no use for a referee.

*

I used to believe that, in the struggle between the immovable object and the unstoppable force, the immovable object would always win. Imagine the Statue of Liberty as the immovable object. This imaginary Statue of Liberty is imbued with the ability to not ever be moved by anything.

In the role of unstoppable force, I introduce the Incredible Hulk. Although our goliath in purple pants pounds mercilessly on the SOL, the statue neither bends nor breaks, for it is truly immovable. The Hulk, who draws his power from anger, grows more and more angry at the immovable object and he pounds her in the nose with his cinderblock fists. He clobbers the statue so hard the noise sends a flock of seagulls flying out of a park in Brooklyn. But Liberty doesn't move. Eventually, the Hulk grows so angry he suffers an aneurysm and his head explodes.

Lesson: One exerts a great deal of effort when one tries to move an immovable object, and that effort can lead to death. But it takes no effort to not move. It's *easy* not to move. You simply *don't move*. So go ahead, Hulk, punch that statue until your brain explodes. The SOL doesn't give a flying fig.

Now consider. What if the unstoppable force *isn't* a simple-minded gamma beast fueled by pure rage? What if the unstoppable force is an idealized version of Narwhal Slotterfield? I'd throw a couple of punches at Lady Liberty and then, upon concluding that she's immovable, I'd move on to a more productive activity, like telling Vero I love her.

Greater point: there's no point in me trying to tell the world what to do. The world doesn't listen and it doesn't care for my opinion anyway. And there's no purpose in me imposing my morality on a bunch of cute kids who want to shout and giggle and triple dribble. I just need to stand around in a zebra shirt and watch.

Screw unstoppable, my force is irrepressible.

I'm pretty sure what I actually said when I met Vero in that bar was, "I just reffed nine perfect games."

She would have made some sort of frequently cited womanly gesture, perhaps pushing a locket of hair behind her ear or pursing her lips, and then said, "Holy flarping shit. That sounds awesome!"

Vero Vasquez is my fiancée. I am her fiancé. Holy flarping shit. That sounds awesome.

We could call it quits right here.

The betrothal I intended to propose back when I was in the bathroom of Cookie's Palace Diner has been accepted. Time can now re-align itself and Vero and I will make love and have baby teeth. Reader, if you want to walk away with a satisfied hum in your heart, walk away now. Because this is not the end of my trials. My trials do not end.

Night has settled. The sun is a faint afterglow, soon to be even fainter. This isn't just some silly old Arctic winter I'm facing, with six months of darkness. Jesus Horatio Christ, no. It's going to be D-A-R-K here for… Let's think about this.

Due to the serious logistical issues posed by the night ahead, I have temporarily suspended my boycott of time-related—and demonstrably inaccurate—math problems.

One of Vero's hours is roughly one *year* for me, plus or minus six months. A night in early September lasts roughly twelve hours, normal time. Which means that, in hypertemporal terms, every acre of Eastern North America, from the Rocky Mountain peaks of the Continental Divide all the way to the New York Island, will be sunless for the next twelve years of my life, plus or minus six years. That's the amount of time that transpired between the death of JFK and Nixon's farewell speech, plus or minus the Johnson administration.

This darkness is going to be problematic. And *this*, my friend, is *solution*matic: Vero and I shall venture west. We'll abandon the Great Plains and we'll walk to the land of California, where the sun is shining and Lauren Bacall's home is open to all visitors. We will cross the Rockies, we will cross the deserts, we will see the land of plenty.

Before we go anywhere, I compose one more note for my darling.

Cool! Wanna get hitched in California?

It doesn't pack the emotional punch I would have preferred, but I need to keep it short. I am unwilling to twiddle my thumbs in the dark for a month while Vero plows thru a whole paragraph of exposition.

She does need to *see* what I've written, though, and that's become increasingly impossible since the sun went down. I enter Charlene's house and flip all the light switches to *on* but nothing happens. Why can't I turn on a fucking light?

I dangle my headlamp from the branch of an overhanging tree and arrange it to shine directly on my note. Until such time as Vero has finished reading it, I'll have to navigate the streets of Keaton by streetlights and starlight. I shoulda taken two of these headlamps when I had the chance.

While Vero reads, I prepare for our journey. A few of the houses in Keaton contain human occupants and those occupants have turned on their lights, which work even though when *I* flip a switch it does, as I may have mentioned, nothing.

I ransack these homes for shoes and sweatpants. I scrub my zebra shirt clean against the concrete of Charlene's front walk. I enter the grocery and load my backpack with granola bars and I say hello to Charlene. She has begun to turn to a different page in her tabloid. The woman has a serious ability to not give a shit about things. I really wish I could have met her.

The quest to California, I figure, will take us two hundred days, maybe a year if I pace myself. That's less than ten minutes in Vero's world. I'm about to walk (halfway) across America. Someone sponsor me, please. All donations will be used to purchase teeny crutches for one-legged seagulls.

You know, it occurs to me that, by the time we get to Cali, the sun will be setting there as well. No prob. I'll stow us away on a westbound cruise ship. We'll follow the sun and get ourselves a free honeymoon in the deal.

I double check my supply of painkillers, which, due to my growing tolerance, is starting to wane, but I'm not concerned, since there are a million pharmacies between here and the Golden State, and I bring my loaded backpack to Charlene's place where I sleep and then I wake and I fix a peanut butter and jelly sandwich. Then I wait. We can't leave until Vero reads my note and gives me a thumbs-up or a wink or something.

During this interim, when I'm not sketching Vero, I pass my time on Charlene's bed, eating, resting, digesting my pills. The less I move, the better I feel. My joints continue to improve, my skin stops flaking off. The Vicodin doesn't make me groggy anymore, but it continues to help with the pain. Disregarding the single, inconvenient, side-effect—this being a perpetual case of lethargic bowel syndrome—these little white ovaloids of indifference are pure magic.

Over several more days, I fill yet another notebook with time-lapse sketches of Vero. In the fast-forward flipbook version of this notebook, she scans left to right. She lifts her eyes, her shoulders rise, her mouth opens in a wide bray of laughter. I am terrified. She thinks California is a joke. But then, the fingers of her left hand curl into an unambiguous *okay* sign.

Hot damn tamale, we've made our wedding plans. I confess, this is not how I thought things would end up, with me carrying her across a continent in search of sunlight. Not that I mind. California, here we crumb.

Say goodbye to Charlene's house, goodbye to Keaton. I tidy up all the little messes I've made. I move thru the rooms like an astronaut, chomping hovering cracker crumbs and stray drops of water; I straighten the quilt on the bed; I gather empty shopping bags and apple cores and bring them outside and shove them into the trash barrel.

Under the bruised sky, I run my hands over the browning leaves of the bean vines as well as the last of this season's tomatoes, which will certainly freeze before they ripen. It is September and we are in Colorado. Soon, autumn will arrive.

I haven't yet eaten any of Charlene's garden bounty. I couldn't do that to her. But just one? I pluck a fist-sized tomato from one of her plants. It's still warm with the day's heat. I clamp my teeth and the skin pops.

Lord almighty, that was a tasty tomato.

On Vero's TV tray is the thin stack of paper that comprises our entire correspondence from the time I first went hyper. My ghostly dispatches from the blurred realm, her hurried handwriting, her absolute faith in me. If anyone is irrepressible, it is Vero. Seven minutes, maybe, have passed in her life and she's never once doubted the words of her poltergeist of a boyfriend. She kept her cool in Cookie's Palace Diner, she allowed me to carry her to Keaton, she read my notes, she accepted my marriage proposal, and she's agreed to a two-thousand-mile hike for our nuptials. This all happened to her in *seven minutes.* Do you see now why I love this woman?

I fold our correspondence into quarters and squeeze it, along with Charlene's diary, into the secret compartment within the secret medicine cabinet door and I close the latch.

I adjust Vero's body into travel plank position so she hovers feet first, level with my bellybutton. I press on her shoulders and she slides forward and we exit the backyard thru the gate and enter the dark streets of Keaton.

Before we leave town, I bring Vero to the grocery store, where I introduce her to Charlene. The lights in the store are on. I assume they've been on since I first arrived in town, although I don't recall noticing one way or the other. With the sun out, the lights make the building downright homey. I can practically hear the hum of the refrigerators.

I pose Vero upright so she faces Charlene, the dedicated, hospitable baby-finder who doesn't like to talk about the weather.

"This is the woman who saved my life." I say this to both Vero and Charlene. "You two would get along, I think."

I leave them like this and make a final walkthru of this store that has kept me alive for these many moments. I make sure all the doors in the frozen food section are properly closed, I tidy up floating candy wrappers, bread displays, straighten the cereal boxes, and, as a favor to Charlene, I remove all the expired cheese and milk and meat from the shelves and coolers and put them in a shopping cart, which won't roll, because things don't roll for me. I drag the cart into the stockroom, with the intention of bringing it out the back door and placing the expired products into the dumpster behind the store.

This is my first time in the stockroom, and I discover two things.

The store's back door is padlocked shut.

The store has a resident kitten, and it's adorable.

I am uncertain as to the legal status of this cat. Its presence here surely violates several health codes, being as it's a cat in a grocery store. So what? It's a kitten. Laws against kittens are laws against decency.

This kitten is black with orange stripes, an inversion of a tiger's coloration. The kitten, about two months old, I'd say, is curled up in a basket on a shelf above the computer on the desk. Next to the cat basket are a water dish and a food dish, the latter of which still contains a lump of well-licked tuna.

I touch the long hairs inside the cat's ear. The cat does not react. I stroke its fur. The kitty is warm and cuddly. I scoop her out of the basket. She fits easily in my palms. I hold her against my cheek and sniff her neck. The cat smells like clean laundry. I kiss her teeny wet nose. I peel back the cat's lips and run my finger over her cute widdle kitty teeth. I love this kitty. I wish I had found her a long time ago. I will put her in a papoose and carry her everywhere. I will be kind to this kitty and hug her and she will be my friend.

I will do none of this. Only an asshole kidnaps a cat. I return her to the basket and then I drag the shopping cart out of the stockroom and to the front door and bring armloads of expired milk and veggies and meat products around back where I shove them into the dumpster.

It's time to go. I stand next to Vero so we're both facing Charlene Morning, the woman who was nearly my mother, and I cry for several minutes, and it's thank you, but goodbye, my friend. So long, Keaton. You've been kind. So long, vast prairie of Eastern Colorado. You've fed me and entertained me and tolerated me and kept me calm when I should have been losing my mind. You are a space that tells us nothing, but which allows us, if we tilt our heads just right, to listen.

I hug Charlene and then run back to the stockroom and pet the cat one last time. Then I return to the front of the store where I horizontalize Vero and push her out the door.

I'm standing in front of the grocery with my fiancée hovering next to me. My headlamp scours Keaton's two roads and its various buildings. Across the street, kitty-corner from here, stands the Keaton State Bank. A bank, just sitting there, completely unattended.

I've never robbed a bank.

Here's what I'll do. I'll go in, find out where they keep the cash, bring a bag of money outside, check *Rob a bank* off my list of things to do, and then I'll immediately bring the cash back inside and check *Return stolen loot to a bank* off my list of things to do. And then I'll get the hell out of Keaton, I promise.

Deal? Let's go!

The Keaton State Bank is a ranch-style building made of beige bricks. A bizarre contraption is leaning against one of the outside walls. The contraption is an antique bicycle that's been modified to accommodate an engine that I presume was transplanted from a lawn mower. It's either a poor man's version of a motorcycle or it's another of Keaton's quirky lawn sculptures. There are three civilian-type automobiles in the parking lot.

I approach the bank's front door to peer thru the tinted glass for one simple, innocent look born of harmless curiosity.

Hey there, what's this? A flash of light has erupted from within the bank. The flash grows bright and stays bright, illuminating the lobby. There are several people inside, which explains why there are still cars in the parking lot so long after closing time. They had to work late, maybe, celebrate a birthday, maybe, and now it's time for a group photo with the whole gang.

That sure is a big, bright flash. Perhaps, rather than taking a group photo, the gang has gotten drunk and decided to shoot off some roman candles in the lobby. The gang certainly isn't *posed* for a photo. They're spread around the room as if they're in the midst of a game of Smear the Homophobic Slur. But why the roman candle, and who's holding it? I can't tell because *thon* is obscured by the flash, which is just now starting to shrink back into itself.

With my hands cupped around my face, which is pressed against the tinted-glass door, I daresay it appears as if some sort of solid projectile has escaped from the mysterious flash and is now traveling across the lobby, toward me.

The lighting situation is not ideal for the identification of the projectile, what with the flash turning everything into a silhouette, so I'll just wait here until either the flash has completely diminished or until the projectile comes close enough for me to make it out, whichever comes first.

While it does appear to be traveling blazingly fast in the normal time stream, in my time stream the mysterious projectile is creeping along at significantly less than one mile per hour, so don't worry about me. I'm perfectly safe.

Several moments later, the mysterious projectile butts up against the tinted-glass door, at which point the glass bulges, at which point I back away from the door, at which point a hole appears in the glass and a bullet emerges, spinning, distorting the air itself.

This is not a post-work birthday party, this is not a fireworks-laden game of Smear the Homophobic Slur. There's some lunatic in that bank and he's fired a gun.

Goddammit. Why hasn't anyone called the cops?

There are no cops. I'm the cop. I'm the hero. This is why I'm here.

Before I go in, I drag Vero around to the south side of the bank, away from the bullet, and sit her on the ground with her back against the brick outer wall. She's safe, I'm safe. I watch for several minutes until I'm certain the bullet's trajectory will send it harmlessly over the roof of the Keaton Cooperative Grocery, into the starry sky.

Time to kick some ass.

I lean into the bank's front door and push at the puckered web where the bullet has passed thru. I pound my shoulder against it until the glass starts to bend away and the hole grows until it's large enough for me to step thru.

The first person I see as I point my headlamp around inside the bank is a thin piece of white trash with bad teeth and stringy hair. He's standing splay-legged in the lobby, holding the AK-47 from whence the bullet has recently emerged. His pupils are pissholes in the snow, his face is flared nostrils and homicidal intent. Let's call this man Johnny Sunshine.

Johnny Sunshine is doing his courageous best to ignore the man who has leapt onto his back. Let's call this man Dom DeLuise. Dom DeLuise is balding, early sixties, dressed in black slacks and a white business shirt. One of his loafers is missing and his hands are duct-taped together. His thighs are cinched onto Johnny Sunshine's hips. Dom has reached over Sunshine's head and is leaning rearward so his portly weight draws his bound hands into Sunshine's throat.

This act has compromised Sunshine's aim, such that the bullet from the AK-47 has, as we know, exited thru the bank's front door and flown out of town rather than piercing the flesh of the brown-suited man who is currently kneeling on the floor, his back to Johnny Sunshine, and with his fingers interlaced behind his head. Although the brown-suited man is in what would be called a "pose of execution," he maintains the cocksure expression of someone who considers himself too important to die.

Given the look of things, I'd wager that the brown-suited man is affiliated with this bank in a significant administrative capacity. Several framed photos of him, brown suit and all, hang on the walls. In each of the photos, he is shaking hands with various dour-faced farmer-types whom he's probably defrauded out of *thon*'s land. In one image, he's shaking hands with an old man in front of an airplane that looks suspiciously like the one I mistook for a one-legged seagull and which is currently putting on the airshow above Cookie's Palace Diner in Holliday.

I'd bet the brown-suited man drives a pickup shaped like a yacht and I'd bet he's an asshole. If any of his employees were to suggest that the bank adopt a cute little kitten, he would fire that employee immediately.

Or, hell, I don't know. He could be a fucking saint. Let's call him Brown Suit Balthazar.

It would seem that Brown Suit Balthazar has said something inappropriate to Johnny Sunshine, such that Sunshine is taking action steps toward hastening his death. It also seems that Balthazar would be dead were it not for the heroics of Dom DeLuise, who I suspect is one of Balthazar's brave employees. I sincerely hope Dom gets a raise when this is all over.

There are several other humans—hostages, innocent bystanders—here in this dark-paneled, shaggy-carpeted small town bank lobby. Among the other humans:

A balding man, middle aged, slouched in the corner. He's alive, unharmed, eyes downcast. We will not discuss him any further.

A man, very tan, lying on his face on the ground, his hands and legs spread wide. He, too, is unharmed. We will not discuss him any further, either.

An incredibly ancient, shriveled male human near the front entrance. He's lying on his back with his arms on his belly. His eyes are closed, perfectly content. It's possible that he's in the midst of a heart attack. I have no clue. It's not like I can check his pulse. We may or may not discuss him later.

So far, no blood. But it's probably wise for me to engage in some disarmament. I peel Johnny Sunshine's fingers away from his machine gun, confirm that the trigger is in its non-firing position, look for the safety button, fail to find the safety button, and place the weapon safely on the floor so it points away from human flesh. I leave Dom piggybacked upon Johnny Sunshine, arms wrapped around Sunshine's throat.

Situation neutralized. Thwarting robberies is easy. Nobody can control a situation like the man in the zebra skin shirt. I'm glad I checked this place out. Otherwise this town would be fucked.

To that end, I shall now gather a reward for my heroics. Let's have a peek down that darkened hallway over there. Surely, this is where I'll find the Giant Safe. There's gotta be a Giant Safe, otherwise, what's the point of a robbery. Already, I'm feeling less inclined toward my previous plan of stealing money and then returning it. A bag of cash would be a nice little nest egg for Vero and me when we get to California.

I walk toward the darkened hall. My headlamp will show me the way to the Giant Safe. It's a very dark hall. The lights are on in the lobby. You'd think someone would have turned on the lights in the hall.

There's a glow from deep within the darkened hallway, followed shortly by a flash, followed a few moments later by a bullet, which emerges in a flower of smoke. It appears that this robbery requires some more neutralization. If this bullet is allowed to travel unimpeded, its trajectory will come to an end in the ass of Dom DeLuise.

I hustle to the bullet, which is still a dozen feet from Dom DeLuise's backside, and press my thumb against it. This has no impact on the bullet's trajectory. I attempt a karate kick. My foot actually manages to strike the bullet, to no effect. Inertia, mass, force, speed, it all lines up to that bullet being stubborn as shit. I may as well try to deflect John Henry's pickaxe.

Fuck it. If I can't move the bullet, I'll move the people. I pull Johnny Sunshine and his human backpack out of the path of the bullet and watch as it travels over the head of Brown Suit Balthazar, across the lobby, and safely thru the gaping hole I created when I entered the glass door.

I must have a word with our mysterious new gunman. With my headlamp swooping wide arcs, I enter the darkened hallway, crouched, ready to dodge a bullet, should the gun fire again.

At the end of the dark hall, I find a malnourished woman pointing a pistol at the bullet that just went thru the door. Given the advanced state of dental decay, I'm going to assume that this pistol packin' mama is in cahoots with Johnny Sunshine. Let's call her Bonnie Sunshine. I remove the pistol from Bonnie's grip, successfully engage the safety, and press her face-first into the carpet. Situation neutralized, again.

Standing behind malnourished Bonnie is another woman, slightly less malnourished, and decidedly unhappy. I say the latter because she has tears on her cheeks. Let's call her Suzi Sadbags. Suzi's body is unperforated by bullet or blade. Her right fist is gripped around something that glitters between her fingers.

I peel her fingers away. She's holding a gold coin, a nifty one. Made in 1878, three dollars. Ah, the nineteenth century, when gold was worthless.

I extract from my pocket the silver dollar that I had retained from the kids' bag o' coins that I'd stolen from the ol' Riles Place. I give the silver to Suzi in exchange for her gold. I've just saved multiple lives. You're welcome, people of Keaton. Consider the debt repaid.

With the exception of the old coot, who is either sleeping or dead, none of the other characters seem to be in grave physical danger.

Let's find that vault. No, first, let's get rid of these guns. I don't want them in this building.

I bring Bonnie's pistol to the lobby, pick up Johnny's AK-47, and step thru the broken front door and into the calm embrace of Keaton on a late summer's eve. I wind up and chuck the weapons as hard as I can toward the roof of the bank. Of course, once they leave my hands, they get stuck in the air. But we all know they're moving. Before any of these people know it, the weapons will land on the roof where they will remain until they rust and die, or until somebody cleans the gutters.

God, damn. I'm a hero! This is all so life-affirming. And it wasn't scary at all. I'm as calm as if I'd just gone shopping for batteries.

Life becomes less affirmed, and I become less calm, when, kitty-corner across the intersection, I see the front window of the Keaton Cooperative Grocery begin to flex inward.

The bullet from Bonnie Sunshine's pistol has crossed the street in a trajectory that is far from harmless. It's pressing the glass in the center of the grocery's front window. Due to the persnickety nature of nighttime reflections, I cannot see thru the window clearly. It's just a warped darkness with street light reflections crossfaded into a blurry, amberish suggestion of a grocery store within. Translucence issues aside, based on where she's been standing for the past several weeks, that bullet is on a collision course with the back of Charlene's head.

The glass flexes, caves. The bullet appears to slow down, and then it pops thru the other side of the window.

The glass, meanwhile, florps back and forth twice and then shatters. This ain't no safety glass, kids. Silicate slivers bloom into an hourglass explosion.

Thank Jesus for Vicodin. If I weren't a little loopy right now, the quantity of adrenaline that just squirted into my bloodstream would make my eyes explode. As it is, I sprint toward the store like a man with a lobster attached to his ass. The shattered glass is drooping inward. I can't bother with the door. I pull my shirt so it covers my head, and I leap and spin ass-first and fly thru the galaxy of glass dust and shards.

I thereby enter the establishment, skid, gain my balance, suffer no wounds.

Good lord, things are really picking up around here.

Looks like Charlene has heard the gunfire, the first round, at least. She has finally turned her head away from her tabloid and now she is looking toward the bank. In doing so, her upper body has shifted about ten inches to the left. With great relief, and just a hint of disappointment,

I watch as the bullet slides thru the air just to the right of Charlene Morning's left ear. The relief is obvious, the regret is ridiculous; I had hoped to save her life.

Still, I am overwhelmingly happy. I hug Charlene tightly, watching over her shoulder as the bullet continues unimpeded down the frozen foods aisle.

With all parties now completely, unquestionably safe, I slide to the floor and rest for a moment with my back against the checkout counter. I congratulate myself for my heroics, I rub my ankles, I replay the recent events. Veronica is safely seated outside the bank, the bank robbers have been neutralized, the two stray bullets have been accounted for.

Oh, for the love of God. The fucking bullet that I left cruising down the frozen food aisle is heading directly toward the goddamned stockroom, and in the goddamned stockroom there's a shelf with a sonofabitchin' basket on it, and curled up inside that sonofabitchin' basket is a darling, sleeping, innocent, widdle kitty.

I'm on my feet before you can say "Insufficiently thorough," and I propel myself over the checkout counter and I'm sprinting down the frozen foods aisle staring at a hole in the wall directly adjacent to the door that leads to the stockroom.

Here's a small sampling of the thoughts that enter my mind as I take the eight strides necessary for me to reach the storage room:

This is just like the time I ran twenty-four miles to try to save Vero from a bullet.

This is not just like the time I ran twenty-four miles to try to save Vero; in this case, it wasn't me who pulled the trigger. And cats aren't girlfriends.

Can a bullet from a handgun pass thru a wall?

I skid into the stockroom door, turn the knob, and open. To answer my question, yes, a bullet from a handgun can travel thru a wall. An armada of pulverized dust and gypsum chunks is billowing out of the sheetrock. The armada is already halfway across the shallow room, only a few more feet before it reaches the kitten. And a couple of feet ahead of that armada, leading the charge, is a misshapen bullet, still traveling forward, spinning head over heels, refusing, in spite of all common sense, to abandon its deadly purpose.

Meanwhile, the kitten is curled up in her basket, unaware that Death is churning the air just a few inches away.

Suck it, Death.

I dive forward and, you know how everything slows down when you're in a car accident? That's what happens. As I travel across the room stretched out like a temporary Superman, I wing my arm so as to knock the cat basket off the shelf. My hand makes contact; the basket and cat are airborne and out of harm's way. I, who remain airborne and practically horizontal, then shift my attention to the wayward bullet, with which my face is about to collide. I go cross-eyed as my momentum carries me directly toward the lump of lead. At the last moment, I squeeze my eyes, tilt my head to one side, and brace for impact.

I dream I am a good person.

I awake face down on the floor of the Keaton Grocery's stockroom. I'm covered with a powder of dust from the punctured wall. I touch my temple and there's a crust of dried blood from where I collided with the bullet. My fingers follow the crust to the wound itself. I can't tell without seeing it, but it feels like more of a scrape than a split. I'm fairly certain I will survive striking a bullet without any lingering aftereffects. There is a throb in my head, moderate disorientation. A variety of my ribs and knees are in various stages of discomfort.

My headlamp has fallen off in the collision with the bullet and it's now on the floor on other side of the room. I crawl upon my discomfited knees to the lamp and stretch its elastic band over my forehead and point it toward where I last saw the cat basket hovering. The basket has descended halfway to the floor. The cat is still asleep, still in bed. I wipe chunks of dust off the shelf and put the basket back in place, making sure the kitten is curled up comfortably. Cute kitty. I saved your life and you don't even know it. I reconsider and put the basket in the crook of my arm. I'm not leaving that kitten in this mess.

What has become of that accursed bullet? I can't rest until I know it's no longer trying to kill and maim. I scan with the headlamp until I find a pinkie-sized hole in a cardboard hat atop the head of a cardboard Twinkie the Kid store display whose sedimentary layers of dust suggest that it hasn't been out of this stockroom in several decades. The bullet itself is lodged into the cinderblock wall behind Twinkie's hat.

I feel my temple again, where I collided with the bullet. A nasty bump, some blood in my hair, no worries. I brush the dust off the front of my shirt and exit the stockroom and walk down the frozen food aisle and out of the Keaton Grocery.

My work is completed. Dom DeLuise: safe. Charlene: safe. Kitty cat: safe. Twinkie the Kid: mortally wounded. Guns: on their way to the roof of the bank. Narwhal Slotterfield: mildly concussed.

The people of Keaton can sort it out for themselves what happened. Charlene won't have to sort out anything. I brought her and the kitten back to her house and wrote a letter in which I explained the situation as well as I could. Then I placed the three-dollar gold coin atop the wooden box under her bed and then I went out to gather Vero from where I'd perched her next to the bank.

I said to her, "Yes, my dear. This time, we're really, really leaving," and we headed north to good old Route 36, California-bound.

I've learned my lesson about moving fast in a slow world. Thick air offers resistance, and resistance leads to overly-stressed connective tissue, which hurts. So we're walking, not jogging, to California. I wouldn't want to jog anyway; it's too dark out here; I could collide with a low-flying bird and break my nose.

Lifting my legs like a careful old man, and with my last three Vicodin dissolving in my belly, I push Vero along the highway, drawn perpetually onward by the next set of taillights of the next car up the road. The stars have grown brighter, the horizon is dotted with yard lamps from the various homesteads. The cars all have their headlights on and I can see grasshoppers being flayed in radiator grills. Some of the drivers have pulled over and are wondering what happened to their cell phones.

We've made camp at the House of Pronghorn, under the hellfire storm, south of the tornado. The Mister still hasn't come home for dinner. The Missus looks concerned. Perhaps the Mister is a truck driver with a watermelon fetish.

My first order of business was to visit the bathroom and open the medicine cabinet. The closest thing I could find to a painkiller was a bottle of *Acetaminophen, With Codeine*. Prescribed by Dr. Elijah Shepard for shoulder pain for Mr. Austin Tucker. Hey-o, my hosts have a name. The House of Pronghorn is now the Tuckers' House of Pronghorn.

The back of the bottle warned me that Codeine is habit forming and potentially abusable. That's promising.

I swallowed two pills and put the bottle with its remaining ten pills into my backpack. I wasn't hungry, so I left the last of Mrs. Tucker's pot roast roasting in the pot and I went to bed in the guest room with Vero floating by my side. Even with the Codeine, I slept poorly, expecting any moment for one of the bullets from Mr. Tucker's twenty-one-gun salute that I'd way-back-when fired into the sky to fall thru the ceiling and crack my skull.

After several endless, unchanging hours, I gave up on sleep, got dressed, and ate two more Codeine pills. I tell you what, Codeine is not in the same drug-league as Vicodin. I honestly can't tell if it's doing anything. But it must be doing *some*thing; I haven't yet detected any withdrawal symptoms from coming off the Vicodin.

The lights are on in this house; it's nice here, if not entirely to my style. I find the Tuckers' aesthetic, with the guns and dead animal heads and dark paneling, to be more ominous than it is appealing. Still, thanks for the food and all.

Alas, I shall now remove myself from this place, just as I've done with Cookie's Palace Diner and the town of Keaton. I give Mrs. Tucker a kiss on the cheek and I place Vero in plank position and push her out the front door. We retreat from the glow of the Tuckers' House of Pronghorn yard light and we venture north into the hellfire storm, which has lately begun flashing lightning every few hours.

You didn't think I'd go to California without a detour to the Riles Place, followed by a quick visit to the tornado, did you? There's still a part of me that wants to find my birth parents, and another part of me that wants to throw sticks into that tornado one last time. I will satisfy both of those parts.

I opted not to explain the side-trip to Vero in one of my notes, as the reading and answering process would take too fucking long. She probably won't notice the detour anyway. It'll last, like, one second.

I walk the gravel road. No sound, no cars to guide me, the stars hidden behind the hellfire storm clouds, my headlamp casting a private, finite, subtractive dream which I inhabit like a bathyscaphe creeping about the ocean floor.

My light reveals a road, some fence posts, my feet, my fiancée floating before me. If I look straight up, my headlamp bounces light off the grey-white churling cloudbottoms.

I sit in the road cross-legged with my sketchbook on my knees. I draw the shadows and the curves of the clouds. I can't make them properly loom, so I point my headlamp at a fencepost and attempt to capture my sense of confinement, but I only manage a sense of smallness. How about I darken the entire page except for a tiny thumbprint of light in the bottom right corner? Show the smallness of my world. No luck. I tear the page out of my sketchbook and rip it into pieces and leave them floating.

I walk until my headlamp is reflected back to me by the broken windows of the Riles house. The house, the whole homestead, has grown more ominous with the onset of night. The ghostly, sagging buildings of pale wood, the lingering doom of the dead brothers, it tugs downward like angry gravity.

A red light glows from beyond the swaybacked barn, smoke hovering above, the air fragrant with combustion.

Tugging Vero by the ankles, I peer around the corner of the barn. Remember the two kids fighting over the bag of coins? They appear to have ended hostilities. They're seated at a campfire made from chunks of wood torn from the rotting barn. The girl is staring into the flames. The boy is using a broken shingle to scrape pudding out of a large can whose label reads "Tapioca Pudding." The shadows of the firelight are doing a fantastic job of emphasizing the kids' hungry, hollowed flesh. I cannot imagine what led them to this ghostly place. They're just two more clumps of dust in my journey beneath the living room couch in the townhouse of lost souls. I leave the kids a handful of granola bars, courtesy of the Keaton Cooperative Grocery, and then I move along.

Creeping past the barn, away from the kids, I stumble over the half-buried Riles family basketball hoop, its orange paint eaten by rust. I squat next to it and try to pull it out of the ground. It won't budge. I scrape dirt away with my fingers and wiggle the hoop. I lean back and pull and pull and it comes away with clumps of dirt and yucca needles attached to it.

I float the hoop as high up in the air as I can, which is pretty high since I'm six-eight, and then I step away and find a clod of dirt. I run and jump and dunk the dirt thru the hoop. I land hard and I lay on the ground on my back, hugging my legs. My headlamp shows the hoop and the dirt clod hovering together nine feet above the ground.

Goodbye, Riles Place.

*

As we cross the north grassland, my knees and back and shoulders and everything else settle into a state of all-encompassing achiness. I eat two more Codeines, but they don't touch the pain, so I eat two more. And then two more. Hell, I only have two left. Might as well get it over with. I finish them off and wait a few minutes. Trick done. I embrace the numb and push Vero ahead thru the night, stumbling on small mounds of dirt. Sometimes, for the variety, I walk around front and tug her along by her feet, but that tends not to work because I can't walk backward without veering to my left.

Deeper into the storm, we cross into the curtain of rain and then into the hail. We follow the contours of the land. Vero's feet become wet from bouncing into raindrops.

How does one locate a tornado in this silent darkness?

I should have followed my old footprints from the last time I came up here. But I didn't and so now I'm walking without crumbs. Too much rain, too little light. I'm not gonna find the tornado unless I walk directly into the fucking thing. This is dumb.

In our short relationship, Veronica and I had quickly established a set of rhythms, traditions, rituals. One of those was "Tuesday Night at the Old-fashioned VCR". It was our way of looking at the past thru the eyes of the past. The basis for VCR night was Veronica's extensive Collection of Last Episodes, as recorded live off network TV in the 80s and 90s. Her family had been taping them for years. *M*A*S*H, Newhart, Friends, Cheers, Island of Hair, The Witch and the Whistler*, etc. Tuesday evenings, Vero would fill a bowl with licorice and beef jerky and we'd wrap ourselves in a quilt and watch from 10 to 11 PM, without fast-forwarding thru the commercials.

These final episodes—also known as series finales—were a parade of high drama and fond farewells, especially when a lead character would get burned to a crisp while saving his family from a ball of fire, as happened to Kelvin Blatmore in *Island of Hair*'s thrilling conclusion. Even the comedies got heavy-handed in their death rattle, which is why *Party Line's Romeo and Juliet*-themed ending, with its lessons in interfamily kindness and tragic nipple piercing, resonates to this day.

Some of those final episodes were for programs that were canceled abruptly, without offering the writers a chance to wrap things up. The final *Star Trek* was, for instance, just another, slightly below-average episode. But even in cases like *Star Trek*, when the final episode isn't a celebratory event, when it isn't even acknowledged, the *viewers*, especially the two viewers at Tuesday Night at the Old-fashioned VCR, know this is the last episode. In those cases, it's like watching someone enjoy a big-chip day in Vegas while we snicker into our elbows knowing that *thon* is going to die in *thon*'s sleep that night. It's also like how, as you approach the end of a book, you simultaneously read faster and impart every word with more import than it probably deserves. Which is to say, anything can seem deep, secret, heavy if you're willing to invest the emotional time into it. At least that's what Vero said when I complained that I didn't like watching TV on Tuesdays.

With my light pointed upward thru the glittering raindrops, my eye espies a shape to the clouds, a large spiral, like a hurricane. I orient myself to the spiral and begin guiding Vero toward this center of depravity.

There, a glint. A scintillating glint. And another and another in a line that leads in an upward hyperbola to the center of the spiral. I follow the scintillations thru the rain curtain, pushing gently on Vero's shoulders.

Although I can't very well make out the details, these glints reflecting the light of my headlamp are, without a doubt, silver, as in, silver coins, as in, the same coins I'd poured into the tornado all those inches of hair ago. Hot damn, Gretel, we've got our crumbs back.

I continue forward, following the arc of coins. Step, step, step, and—

The ground disappears, my hands slip off Vero's shoulders, and down I fall.

I've landed hip-deep in a hole of the approximate diameter of an NFL offensive lineman. It's a coyote hole or a sinkhole or something. Although I've suffered no major injuries, both ankles, both knees, both hips, and every single one of my vertebrae are, more than ever, in need of a serious session of rolfing. I have no more Codeine, no more opioids. I'll deal with the consequences when they come.

I point the headlamp at the back of my fiancée's head. In falling, my flailing my arms had knocked her slightly askew. Still, other than looking like she's in the midst of an Olympic dive, she seems hale and hearty and deeply asleep.

I gaze upward at the cyclonic swirls in the clouds above. Illuminated in the lollipop blue of my lamp, the line of coins leads up and up and directly to a black wisp that's all that remains of my tornado.

I say to Vero, "A few weeks ago, that wisp of a cloud was a bona fide twister. I fed those coins into it and they led us here. Alas, the tornado is not the marvel of nature it once was. Nevertheless, by finding its mirthly remains and gazing upon them, I have satisfied any lingering desire to revisit this general area where Charlene Morning discovered an infant boy. I once thought I was that boy. But we all know I am not that boy, for that would be overly coincidental and utterly preposterous. And so, with no further delay, let us now proceed apace to California."

I place my palms on the upper rim of the hole. I brace myself to hop out onto the ground and remove myself and Vero from this poorly-thought-out tornado chase, whenupon I see a movement.

It was a bright glow, maybe thirty yards down the hill. Initially, I supposed it was one of the tornado coins, somehow flitting about at a speed enormous enough that I could register it in my personal time warp. But, hey. Coins don't glow, they reflect. When I held my hand over my headlamp, the not-coin continued to shine.

It hovered several feet above the ground and wobbled back and forth like a hypnotic fob watch. But not like a fob watch. It glowed. It was Tinker Bell, an orb, dazzling and soft, and it behaved as if it were watching me.

It had been ever so long since I'd seen anything move—*really* move, I'm not talking about my own limbs or airplanes that crept or tornados that stirred, or even bullets that bulleted—that my brain quickly ran out of processing power and went directly into standby mode. Overwhelmed and growing gradually under-medicated, I became so dizzy that I had to squat back down into the hole in order to avoid falling over. Vero remained above, vulnerable, oblivious.

After some deep breaths, I regained a sense of equilibrium and chanced my head over the lip of the hole.

The orb had either grown larger or it had grown closer, I couldn't tell. Either scenario was worrisome. It's common knowledge that not all sprites are friendly. I watched it for another moment and then it disappeared. Then it reappeared, unmistakably larger and closer.

I once again squatted in the hole. I pushed my headlamp's off-switch, which I knew wouldn't work, and it didn't. So I removed the headlamp and stuffed it deep into my backpack. I was in absolute darkness now, which was terrifying. But I was also no longer broadcasting my presence to the orb, which was comforting. And Vero was still up there, still askew, still vulnerable, and I didn't see how I could possibly fit her in the hole with me, which was disconcerting.

Keeping an eye on the orbic faerie, I climbed myself up and out of the hole and stood on the grassy earth. I reached forth, searching the dark for Vero. My hand squished into her beehive haircut and I reached until I could grasp her by the shoulders.

I would walk backwards with her in the dark until I was sure we were safe. Then I'd pull my light out of my backpack and, opioid withdrawal or not, I'd run like the dickens over the Rockies and thru whatever states lay between Colorado and Yosemite National Park. And then we'd spend a month in a cave under a waterfall, dining on salmon and bears before we moved on to Hollywood.

The sprite light moved eerily thru the raindrops, still approaching, but now twisting left and right, as if it were confused. Then the light disappeared and I couldn't see a goddamned thing.

I squatted next to Vero and took shaky breaths in the darkened silence. I didn't know if it was possible to outrun a sprite, but I knew that I had to move myself away from my current location, even if just a few feet. Otherwise the thing would know exactly where to find me, and it would squeeze itself into my head via one of my nostrils and it would devour my brain.

I did my damnedest to relax, had very little success, and confessed to Vero, "Perhaps we should not have come here."

I tugged on her shoulders in the same manner I'd tugged on her shoulders a dozen times before. This time, however, she didn't budge, because this time something was holding onto her.

In bold defiance of my body's demand for fight or flight, I chose fright, which is to say, I froze. I maintained my grip on Vero's shoulders. My heartbeats pounded like underwater earthquakes, squeezing my brain tighter with every *ka-thoom.*

Here it comes, the inevitable, unimaginable, blood-spattered conclusion to my life as the Flash. I've served my purpose. I've done my duty, the bank is safe, and, no longer necessary, I shall be consumed by a ghastly, ghoulish, glowing sprite.

I will not let go of you, Vero.

An impossible thing happened. On the opposite end of Vero, beyond her feet, at around waist-height, a match flared. It happened so quickly it felt like an explosion, and yet I recall every moment. First, my world was black and empty of anything but fear and paranoia. Then, a tiny yellow glow appeared and it blossomed into a cloud of gas, disorganized, heedless of gravity. The blossom drew into itself, found its core, and erupted into a single wavering, vertical flame, balanced upon a wooden match gripped by the fingers of a human hand.

The hand moved the match toward another hand, which was holding a helmet. In the faint matchlight, I sussed that it was the kind of helmet an old-time coal miner would wear. Tarnished metal with a miniature lamp mounted on the bill. The match approached a steel nipple in the center of the lamp's parabolic reflector and ignited a glow, soft around the edges, delicious. Perfectly sprite-like.

75

The hands raise the helmet and place it upon a human head. My dilating pupils can't make out any features because the glowing lamp obscures everything behind it.

The helmet tips forward and alights upon Vero's face. Her eyes remain closed, her mouth remains in her grim smile.

The helmet tips upward, watching me watch it.

The hand releases the match and lets it float and then pinches it out.

I remain in place behind Vero, quite aware that I'm being scanned by a human. I hold my face still, blinking only when necessary.

The match hand raises itself in front of the headlamp, palms facing me, all five fingers splayed out, ready to stop traffic. Then the tips of index finger and thumb draw together and they make the sign of *okay.*

Both hands reach up now and grip the sides of the helmet. They remove it from the head of the human and the human takes steps to the right of Vero and approaches me. I remain still, my hands resting on Vero's shoulders. The human bows toward me. I see outlines of a face, of a body, shadows cast by the chest. This is a woman. The woman's hands offer the helmet to me and I accept.

I place the helmet upon my head and regard my guest in the unwavering light. She is a small, bent-backed woman, very old, with pale eyes that hop back and forth between me and Vero. She's wearing a pair of overalls with an unwashed long-sleeved shirt underneath. Her wrists are small. Her whole person is small, except her knuckles, which are too big for her fingers. Her skin has a swarthy tone, the texture of leather.

Under sagging lids, her eyes latch onto my face, or the darkness of where my face would be if the light weren't blinding her. The woman draws closer, squinting one eye. It's an expression of curiosity. Not a drop of fear in this one. She is considerably less surprised to see me than I am to see her.

She moves her mouth into a smile, as if she hasn't done this sort of thing very often, as if her mouth is a pair of toddler's legs and they're taking their first steps toward an expression of contentment.

I trust this woman; she's moving at my velocity, she gave me her hat, and she hasn't yet attempted to eviscerate me. I smile back at her, and my face, too, feels like toddler's legs taking their first steps toward contentment. It's been a while, apparently.

Her shrunken apple of a head motions forward in an expression that could be either a nod or a Parkinsonian tremor. I nod back and then I take my hands away from Vero's shoulders and, cautiously—so cautious it's comical—I remove my backpack from my shoulders. With the woman watching, I unzip the backpack and extract my headlamp and offer it to her.

She shakes her head, *No thanks*, and makes the okay sign again. I offer her the helmet back and she waves her hands, *No*. She points to me, *You keep it*.

I make the okay sign now. *Thanks for the cool hat, mysterious human*. I put the electric headlamp in my pocket, where it glows thru the fabric of my sweats.

She makes two thumbs up in that way that, when an old lady does it, you can tell this was a newly popular gesture when she was a kid. I mimic the sign.

This is the best conversation I've had in a long, long while. I hope it doesn't end with the lady peeling off her face to reveal that she is actually a reptile.

The woman points at Vero and makes the okay sign.

I nod, uncertain. The woman points at me and then at herself and then at the hole I've just climbed out of.

I point at myself and at herself and then at the hole, to indicate that I'm paying attention.

She points at Vero and then me and makes a sort of yanking motion, as if to indicate that I'm supposed to pull her, Vero, somewhere.

I mimic this as well, not entirely certain where this is going, but moderately secure that it won't conclude in in my death. So what if it does? This is a *person* and she can *see* me.

The woman, satisfied that we're on the same page, walks past me and hops into the hole and disappears. A moment later, her head pops up and she nods, definitely not a tremor this time, and beckons me to follow and *Oh, and please bring that floating fiancée of yours with you.*

There isn't room for the three of us in the little hole. The lady doesn't care. She beckons with her knobby fingers, her face annoyed at me for being stupid.

I shrug. *Fine, I'll follow.* And then she's gone again. I draw Vero to the hole and peer in. It's not just a hole, turns out. One side opens into a tunnel and there's an old lady's skinny butt crawling down it.

Hey Vero, let's get some subterranean homesick blues.

Wearing a carbide lamp on my head, I ease into the hole and squat and peer into the tunnel down which the old lady has crawled. I gaze upward at the back of my fiancée's beehive. I wonder how a tunnel got planted into the wall of this particular hole in this particular valley. I pull my fiancée into the hole and, tugging her by the wrists, awkwardly crawl ass-first into the tunnel. I think, in the voice of my fiancée, "The only thing we have to fear is a gruesome death at the hands of a shape-shifting sprite."

Taking care to not to bump my fiancée's hair against the smooth walls of the tunnel, I crawl backward for several feet until I encounter a series of steps that have been carved into the subterranean stone. The tunnel opens up here, allowing me, even one so tall as I am, to stand upright.

Tugging my fiancée's smallish wrists with my largish right hand, I steady myself against the wall with my left hand. I descend the stairs, seven of them, and then reach the floor of a cave. I am seriously creeped out to be in a silent, dark underground cavern into which I have been led by a senior citizen in overalls. I turn around and cast my carbide lamp light about the cavern. I judge it to be large and empty. I see no sign of the old lady.

You'd think I'd grow accustomed to crazy-ass crazy shit, but every time I think I've raised my tolerance to the max, the shit expands into a new realm of crazy-ass.

I'm in an underground cavern and the woman who led me here is as gone as gone can be. Neither hide nor hair. Either she disintegrated or she's lurking at the other end of this room where the darkness steadfastly refuses to reflect any light from the miner's lamp.

I should, of course, make like a bat and get the hell out of here. But, no. The Irrepressible Narwhal Zebra shrinks from no challenge. I saved the Keaton bank. I do not turn back. I saved the kitty. I do not turn back. I'm here, here's queer, get used to it.

My head has begun to ache. The first flush of opiate withdrawal. Let it be. I will not turn back.

The cave is deep. All I can see is the illuminated area in which I'm standing, which is roughly the size of a dual occupancy recovery room in a hospital. The walls are a fresh, glossy white. I reach up and brush my fingers against the ceiling above my head and the stone is not as cool as I'd expect. There is nothing else to see except, to my right, on the hardpacked floor, there's a blanket, grey wool, roughly woven.

Vero remains tilted from our climb down the stairs, her head lower than her feet. I pull her fully into the room and render her horizontal and hover her over the blanket. I tidy up her beehive. She continues to look content.

Where in the dickens has the old lady gone?

I point the helmet lamp at the far end of the cavern. The lamp's photons go into the shadows and they don't come out. This is a big room, kids. I extract my electric headlamp from my pocket and allow it to join forces with the carbide lamp and together they reveal not a goddamned thing.

The LED flickers on and off and goes out. I press the *on* button and nothing happens, of course, because I can't turn lights on, because. Because I don't know why.

I release the dead light to float and I walk forward. As I proceed into the depth of the cavern, I turn back frequently to make sure Vero is still there.

The protective bubble of light cast by the carbide lamp stretches along with where I'm going and peels away from where I've been. Vero becomes faint as the cavern gets deeper. White stone walls, hard floor, nothing to see. With my next step, Vero will be gone to shadow. I take the step and Vero blends away. I'm alone inside my bubble of light. I do something nutty. I remove the helmet and mess with the lamp until I find a knob, which I turn. The lamp dims and then sputters out. I blink my eyes until the afterglow of the lamplight fades and all I can see are the sifting flakes of my retinal snow.

It's dark, I'm in a cave, I have no means of re-igniting the lamp, and my battery-powered light has quit working. Vero is back there somewhere.

With hands outstretched, I take steps. Here, what's this? Straight ahead, a teeny flickering light. I take more steps and the light grows and it's a candle, floating at shoulder height. The flame is flickering. The candle is hovering near a sort of shaft where the room pinches off into a tunnel. The tunnel is roughly the diameter a Galapagos turtle shell. I squat and look into the darkness of this new tunnel. As my eyes refocus, I spy another light, a candle, which I follow on hands and knees. The glow of this second candle leads me thru the tunnel and into another room, much smaller than the last. It's maybe the size of an adult elephant. The ceiling pinches off like the inside of that church in the Red Square with the ice-cream cone towers.

There's another tunnel at the opposite end of the room. I squat and peer into the tunnel. Here there's an actual glow, with shadows. I crawl thru the hole and follow the glow until the tunnel opens up wide into a very fucking large underground cavern.

It's lit by candles shaped into foot-high cones. There are maybe a dozen of them, spaced evenly on the floor along the outside rim of the cavern. There's a bacon smell in here and I conclude that the candle cones are made of lard or something. The flames are aflicker, but the air in the room still doesn't conduct sound. The tulip-shaped flames leave black smudges on the curved walls above. The light reflects faintly off the ceiling, which must be at least—holy shit—twenty-seven feet above me. As with elsewhere, every surface is whitewashed.

Can you see this? Little old six-foot-eight, former basketball official Narwhal Slotterfield standing in a ginormous underground cavern, looking about in wonder. Like a kid who snuck into a gymnasium after the arena has been closed for the evening.

Little old Narwhal elects to keep on walking.

I come to the center of the room, where the ring of conical candles reflects neatly off the bright walls. Here's something. A cluster of small bones is resting on the floor. Poked into the ground in the midst of the bones is a knife with a shiny wooden handle and a polished blade. I lean over this strange exhibit. The bones include a skull with a beak. The bones belong to a bird. I'm no ornithologist, but suspect this was once a chicken. Murder most fowl.

There you have it. Somebody stabbed a chicken to death in an underground cavern. I begin to suspect that this whole adventure has been put together courtesy of a group of smart-ass Satanists.

Stomach cramping. My brain's growing blurry. I hope this place has a medicine cabinet.

I tiptoe to the far end of the room, which is, seriously, big enough to house Batman's entire underground operation, and by gum, I reach the entrance to yet another of these tunnel passages. Directly in front of the passageway is another cone candle. Floating inches away from the wick is a carbonated match. This candle has been lit recently and I think we all know who lit it. My apparition, who, now that I think about it

Not possible. Nope. My apparition is leading me to a glorious fate. Evil beings do not employ the *okay* sign.

I peer into the new passage. It's dark as shit and narrow as fuck and Christ knows how far it goes.

Onward and downward.

PART FOUR

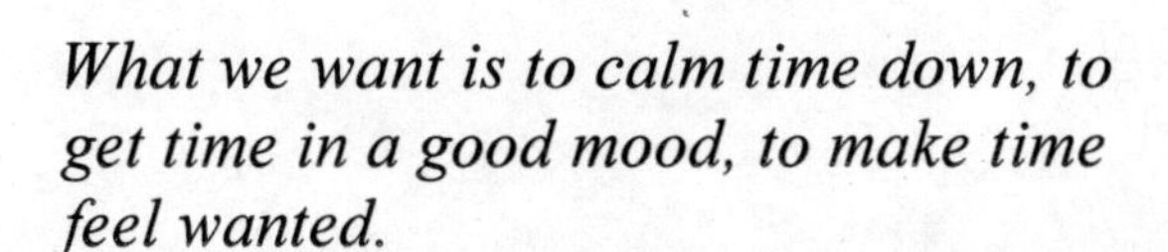

What we want is to calm time down, to get time in a good mood, to make time feel wanted.

— Tony Hoagland,
What Narcissism Means to Me

78

Dark, dark, dark.
Crawl, crawl, crawl.
Shimmy, shimmy, shimmy.
Scoot, scoot, scoot.
Twist, turn, slide.
Keep yer wits about yer.
Rest a moment, just a moment.
Don't be fallin' asleep, Narwhal.
Squirm it like you mean it.
Breathe until your ribs press against the walls of the shaft.
Use yer fingers and toes.
Wiggle like a dolphin.
It's easy. It'll happen.
Ignore your tummy.
Ignore the shadows of agitation.
There's an end to this thing.
Lookee, a light.

I wriggle my beanpole body out the end of the tunnel and plop into a cramped, spherical room, maybe eight feet in diameter. The white-washed walls gleam in the meandering light of a skinny wax candle which is being held by the little old lady, who has somehow managed a costume change, out of her overalls and into a white muslin gown.

She sits on the opposite side of the room with her knees tight to her chest. She's staring at the body of a naked man, which rests on a pedestal in the center of the room. The pedestal looks like a stone tongue molded from the stone floor of the room. The naked man is on his side, curled into a ball. He is not a big man. The skin on his back is pale, his arms and neck are sleeved in a deep tan.

I'm hunched with my spine pressed against the curved wall. The little old lady doesn't acknowledge me, she just stares at the man with pitiful fondness in her eyes, as one would stare at a tombstone after one had laid flowers upon it.

Keeping her eyes on the body, the woman nods, as if to say, *You may gaze upon him.* I settle to the floor and, in imitation of the lady, I bring my knees up to my chest and I gaze. The man on the pedestal is completely still, and has apparently been here a while, as he is covered with a layer of dust. We sit and gaze, me and the little old lady, for quite some time, long enough for the candle to burn down to a nubbin. I can see the man's back and neck and one of his ears. His tanned arms are wrapped tightly around his pale knees.

Even though it's cave-cool, I've begun to sweat. My stomach is cramping. I've an urge to vomit. Oh, dear God, why did I eat all the Codeine? Hold it in. Be present.

The woman blinks, as if she's just concluded a dream, and stands with her back curved against the wall. This room is *small*.

The woman beckons me to sit next to her. I slide my beanpole body around the pedestal and do so. From here, I can see the man's face. His chin is tight against his knees; his eyes are closed; his mouth is a close-lipped smile that sags to his left, toward the earth. His eyelids are pale. I can't tell his age, but he's definitely not old. His hair is brown, flattened against his head as if he'd recently been wearing a hat. His nose is odd. Depending on how I focus, it's long and flat and broad, or pointy and small and round. A Roman nose, via Pinocchio. I'm familiar with this type of nose, having spent many hours looking at one just like it in the mirror.

I know who this man is. And who he is, is John Riles, older brother of the legendary basketball prodigy, Kitch Riles. I've seen his picture in the paper.

With no warning, a cramp begins in my right ass muscle and climbs up my back along my neck and over the top of my head. I hug my knees tightly as the cramp creeps over my forehead, tugs every muscle in my face and then shoots all down my torso and arms and legs. I'm a wound-up ball. My muscles are so tight I fear they will shatter my bones. My chest won't breathe. Bitterness rises in my throat, claws for opiates.

The little old lady bends forward, places her hand on my forearm. Her fingerprints calm the bile. My muscles relax, I breathe, I swallow my saliva. I offer the lady a grateful lift of my eyebrow.

She makes a slight nod, and points at the naked man. Then she points at her crotch. She makes the okay sign with her left hand and then pokes her right index finger thru the circle of okay sign. The old in-out-in-out, she's saying. She's saying she and the man on the pedestal boinked each other. She points at the floor of the sphere room and makes the in-out sign again. They boinked each other right there. This explains John's smile.

Her old lady face goes wistful at the thought of all this inning-and-outing.

The lady uses both hands to mime the shape of a swollen abdomen. I nod. *You got pregnant.*

The lady points at her imaginary swollen belly and then points at me. Then she does the double thumbs-up sign from earlier.

Goddammit, fuckers, I was right. I *am* the boy from under the sagebrush; my father *is* John Riles, the dead cowboy brother of Kitch; and my mother is a withered old woman.

Okay, I didn't foresee that last part.

I scoot closer to the lady, my mother, and pat her hand to let her know I'm on board this train of implausibility. We're inside a hole, my naked, dead father is on that tongue pedestal, and I was conceived on the floor right there.

Mother leans forward and puts a hand on my dad's shoulder. She waves me closer, takes hold of my hand and places it next to hers on the man's skin. There is no heat in him. His face is younger than mine. He has been here for a long time, long enough that he ought to be a pile of bones.

I take my hand away from his arm. There remains upon his skin a red handprint, as if I'd slapped him. I look at my palm; still the same old Narwhal swarthy-off-white. The woman, my mother, nods, as if all is as it should be. Then the woman points at the tunnel-tube that led us into the room. Carrying the candle, she scurries around the pedestal and leans her head into the tube. She beckons me to stand next to her. I maneuver my body and poise myself on my knees and look into the tube. She points to the ceiling of the tube, as lit by her candle. The tube is covered with little red handprints. She points at her crotch and makes a downward sweeping motion. Then she points at me. She takes my right hand in hers and rubs my palm with her thumb. Then she points at the handprints. Then she points at me. Then she points at the handprints again.

Translation: *After you slid out of my womb, you walked out of here and slapped bloody handprints all over the place.*

I nod, *Sure, absolutely.*

She gives a thumbs-up. I give a thumbs-up. Then, still holding the shortening candle, she plunges head first into the tube and I, not wishing to remain alone in this chamber of death and conceptualism, follow.

The return trip is not nearly as uncomfortable as the arrival. Either

I've gotten skinnier or the tunnel has gotten larger. I am able to take full breaths, I can twist my hips as I shimmy.

We slide out the tunnel, once again in the cathedral room, where we stretch our legs, roll our shoulders. The conical candles continue to burn here. The room is. The room is. The room.

I'm beyond reaction. This roller coaster, rather than dropping into the big dive, as it should have done long ago, this confounded contraption just keeps dragging me up the hill.

Together, we make our way across the room's vast floor. Halfway, we pause at the knife that's planted in the chicken skeleton. Here, the woman, my mother, pauses. Her calm is replaced by sternness and the sternness is replaced by red-faced anger. The presence of the knife here is an obscenity. She squats and grabs the knife by its handle. Tugs until her knees start to shake, but she can't extract it from the floor. I squat next to her and reach my hands around hers and squeeze gently. Together, we wiggle the knife and pull upward. It loosens from the hard stone floor and I let go of her hands.

Her face beams. She grasps the knife by its blade and presents it to me, handle first. I take it, uncertain of what I'm to do. There's a folksy, handmade feel to it; it was clearly made for someone with smaller hands than mine. The knife is not mine and I do not intend to keep it.

Mother kneels next to the bones and leans forward and kisses the skull of the chicken. I cannot begin to guess what happened here.

As Mother stands herself up, I place the knife on the ground next to the chicken bones, and now both it and the chicken are content, the obscenity forgotten. Mother is beaming. For the first time in our lives, she hugs me and I hug her back. In our embrace, the accumulation of trauma, dread, and darkness that lurked down here are mutated into glittering fondness.

This roller coaster is never going to stop climbing.

I follow Mom as she, with a straight back and a skip in her step, crosses to the far side of the room. We crawl thru the next tunnel-tube into the Russian ice-cream cone room, then we crawl thru the final tunnel-tube and emerge back in the foyer where my fiancée, Veronica Juanita Embajadores Vasquez, remains prone, hovering above the blanket on the floor.

Mom strokes Vero's cheek with the arthritic knuckles of her right hand. She raises Vero's left hand and points at the place where a wedding ring would be.

Good lord. I've known the woman for less than an hour and she's already bugging me to tie the knot. I put my hands on my heart and nod vigorously in the hope that Mom'll understand that I've proposed to Vero and we intend to get married as soon as we can get to California and find Lauren Bacall's house.

Mom gives me a wary look and then gently presses upon Vero until she's resting flat upon the blanket. Mom admires her future daughter-in-law, lingering over the beehive hair, and then points at me and to herself and to the exit. We are to leave now.

I point to my fiancée and rise my eyebrows, *We're bringing her, too, right?*

Mom flattens her palm toward Vero, *She'll be fine here, kiddo.*

We've got this sign language stuff down.

She hands me a candle and I follow her to the stone-carved steps and we crawl upward. She's limber, this old lady, and she scuttles far ahead of me. My knees are grinding, my wrists are grinding, my teeth are grinding.

I stop feeling sorry for myself when I realize three things:

My urge to vomit has passed.

My stomach is no longer tied up in knots.

My eardrums are vibrating.

I scuffle forward, led by the candle in my hand, chasing these vibrations on my eardrums. It's ticklish, as if people are blowing in my ears, and they make me giggle. When I giggle, the vibrations grow more powerful. And then, the vibrations become intensely uncomfortable. They metamorph into a platoon of tiny militiaman lunatics who invade my brain cavity and begin firing tiny machine guns at my ear nerves.

I lose my grip on the candle and I curl into a ball. I gasp shallow breaths. The air slides in and out of my throat, as if it, the air, were losing its viscosity. I concentrate on my respiration. Don't hyperventilate.

The machine guns in my ears become less insistent. The militiamen's ammo is running out. And then the final militiaman fires his final bullet into his own forehead, and the pain ends.

In the absence of pain, there's a thrumming. A thrumming *noise*. I'm still lying on my side. I open my eyes. A thin rivulet of water is approaching me along the bottom of the tunnel. It moves at lightning speed, probably an inch per second.

I come to all-fours, spreading my arms and legs into a bridge so the water will pass underneath without touching me. There's something wrong. Water can't move like this on its own. Nothing can move this quickly on its own. *I* do the moving.

And there, look at the candle, floating where I released it a moment ago. Not floating. It's slipping earthward even more quickly than the water is coming at me. It lands on the floor of the cave and bounces a little and then settles sideways in the water. The flame flicks and dies.

I'm staring between my crawling hands at this candle that's expired in this demonic trickle of water. There's a flash at the end of the tunnel. I look upward, and I'm clobbered by a sound so violent that I think I will disintegrate. It's like being awoken from a coma courtesy of an atomic bomb.

The sound continues, rumbling, shaking my guts, wiggling the hairs on the back of my thighs. I want to crabwalk backwards, return to the cavern, grab Vero, and dive deep into my daddy's death chamber. But the rumbles cease and soon it's just me in this quivering tunnel with an extinguished candle floating between my limbs.

And now I hear—this is what is happening, I'm hearing—a voice. It's the voice of a cassette player with a dying battery. Slow, low, indecipherable.

"*Kooooooooooooommmmaaaaaaaaaaaaawwwwn.*"

I say, "Pardon?"

My voice emerges from my mouth and I swear I can see the sound ripple thru the air and bounce off the cave walls and fly back into my ears: "*Paaaaaarrrrddddoooooooonnnn?*"

The cassette player voice repeats, "*Kooooommmaaaaaaawww-wwnnnn.*"

Diffused light pours in from the tunnel's entrance. It spills along the floor and walls, devouring the shadows.

I am irrepressible, goddammit. I crawl forward and forward and now I'm squatting at the entrance, looking upward at a daylit, clouded sky. Raindrops are diving right at me. They land in my eyes and my hair and each one makes me flinch as if I'd been stung by a wasp. I hug myself, let the water flow into my skin and my shirt.

A withered, big knuckled hand drops out of the sky and dangles in front of my nose. "*Koooooom. Oooooon.*"

I grasp the hand and I'm pulled out of the hole and up to solid ground where I'm embraced by my elderly mother.

It happened, you see? I slowed down.

I raise my arms and, lo and unfold, my hands fly upward without resistance. My clothes slide against my skin. I hear wind and splatting raindrops and the sound of my own voice shouting wordless nonsense. The arthritis flees my joints. I am strong and lithe. I leap up and down and up and down and up, huge leaps. I'm an astronaut on the fucking moon.

With her arms crossed and a bemused look on her face, my mom watches me bounce and shout until I collapse on the ground on my back to let the rain fall all over me. Each drop becomes a gentle surprise: the motion of the water as it runs down my cheeks, the splashes on my teeth, the dirt sliding away from my zebra shirt.

Walking softly on the grass, Mother squats and then lies down next to me, not touching, just near. I think, *This is marvelous, absolutely marvelous.*

We remain still even after the last of the raindrops has fallen.

The sun appears and shines as if a god had done something worth remembering. Blue sky, distant birds flying. Wind gliding over the gentle hilltops. Wet blades of grass shifting underneath my back. It's humid here, in this post-rain. Let the water evaporate from my clothes. Smell the shift of air, the dank of the earth and the musk of life. The buzz of flies all around.

Mom speaks. Her voice is magic. I say nothing because I can't understand, because I've forgotten how to hear. She speaks again, more slowly. I dig the sound, can't hear the words. I watch a *V* of birds cross the sky. They look like seagulls.

Some time later, and this time I understand, my mother says, "What is your name, boy?" Her voice is soft, with a twisted Okie accent. The accent is a surprise. I would have figured her to talk more like Mary Poppins.

I say, "Narwhal." My voice comes out too loud and the word is lumpy. It's the voice of a deaf person. I try again, concentrating on my consonants, and Mom understands.

She says, "Narwhal is an odd sort of name."

"I agree."

We're side by side, staring up at the sky. The pauses between our sentences are very long. I have to interpret what she's saying and then I have to practice what I'm going to say before I say it.

She says, "When's your birthday?"

"September first, thereabouts." I'm mimicking her accent.

"What year?"

"1976."

"Who raised you?"

"The Slotterfields," I say. "They're professors." Then I say, "You're my mother."

She reaches and touches the tip of my nose.

I say, "My father is John Riles."

"Johnny Riles. A fine boy."

Mother calls him Johnny, same as Charlene from the Keaton Cooperative Grocery. I like that. I say, "And that was him down there."

"Yes," she says. "That's where he died."

"He's a young man."

"The cavern doesn't let go of the dead."

"It's an odd spot, that cavern."

She waits a moment, two. She says, "I'm not accustomed to talking."

I say, "That puts us in the same boat, I guess."

"Well."

I say, "Down there, where my dad is. That's where I came from?"

"You came from fucking."

This mother of mine is no lilyflower. I say, "Mom—can I call you 'Mom?'"

"You may."

"Mom, Vero's still in that hole. And I—"

"Vero is your friend?"

"Wife, eventually. Short for Veronica. You'll like her."

"I hope that is the case."

"I want to see her."

"Wait here with me for a while."

She looks at me with slow-blinking eyes. I'm dying to see Vero, to see if she can see me, to hear if she can hear me. But I will obey my mother.

My mouth is coming back. I hazard an extended phrase. "Can you maybe give me some context with respect to, you know, my existence? Just a quick summary. Eight sentences."

She exhales for a good long time.

"What do you know, son, about yourself?"

I say, "I know that on January first, 1976, a basketball player named Kitch Riles, who may or may not have been dealing cocaine to half of the players in the ABA, drove to eastern Colorado to the ranch where his brother, John, lived. After that, neither one of the Riles boys was ever seen again. And then, eight months later, a woman named Charlene Morning found a baby somewhere in the vicinity of this valley here. Charlene wanted to keep the baby, but she couldn't, so she left it on the courthouse steps with my name—Narwhal—pinned to its blanket. Eventually, the baby was adopted by Mr. and Mrs. Slotterfield of Denver, Colorado."

My voice has returned.

I say, "Many years later, Veronica and I were eating hamburgers in a town called Holliday and I went to the bathroom and when I came out, time had stopped. But it didn't actually stop. I was just moving really fast, turns out. And now, due to various other circumstances, I am here. That sums it. Your turn."

Mom reaches forward and pinches my sleeve. "Your shirt."

"I'm a referee. I referee basketball games."

She likes this. "That makes sense."

"In so many ways. Tell me about me, please."

Mom says, "Johnny Riles ranched and he worked hard and he loved whiskey and horses. He had a poodle and he gave me a chicken."

This woman is not terribly concerned with conversational continuity. I rotate my neck so I'm facing her. She's blinking nostalgia out of her eyes.

She says, "Your father collected arrowheads. He smoked cigarettes and he loved a girl named Charlie. She's who found you."

I say, "Charlene."

Mom looks at me askew and says, "Charlie's a good one. I wish your father could have seen her tits." I keep my trap shut. This conversation is difficult enough already. No use sending the lady down any additional detours, especially when she's doing such fine job of it on her own.

Mom says, "I like your girlfriend."

"Fiancée."

"She part Mexican?"

"She's got four names, and her last one's Vasquez."

Mom is silent for a good long while.

We roll our faces back to the sky. I say, "Were you there when my dad died?"

"I was."

"What did he say, in the end, about all this?"

"He didn't say anything. We were both holding our breaths at the time." She continues. "You'll want to know how we met. First, there was a blizzard. I killed his horse and I ate it, but that was because I had bowel problems and there wasn't any food and it was blizzarding. He was pretty upset about losing his horse. After the blizzard, he hunted for me for a long time. When he found me, he waved a pistol so I threatened to cut off his testicles. But he started bringing me food so we became friends. He gave me one of his chickens. We spent Christmas together in those tunnels, me and your dad and my chicken and his poodle. It was a happy time."

Story-wise, Mom's not one to linger on details. And now she's stopped talking altogether. I wait a bit, figuring she's arranging her next batch of thoughts. Soon, she's snoring.

I roll over and poke her shoulder. She says, "But then, a week later, that loathsome Kitch showed up and he dragged us and the poodle into the tunnels and everything went bad. Kitch was filled with madness. He murdered my chicken with Johnny's knife. And then he made us all crawl into the deep room. Johnny and I made it thru without any problem, but Kitch became trapped. He was fat and the tunnel squeezed on him. So he died there. But his body plugged up the tunnel. We were corked in. At the time, the air in that room was bad. Just me and Johnny and that dead brother, sticking halfway out of the tunnel. We couldn't pull him in and we couldn't push him out and we couldn't breathe."

She stops again, swallows hard. As scenarios go, this one qualifies as overtly horrifying.

I say, "What did you do then?"

"I gave Johnny a gift."

In lieu of speaking, I tilt my head.

Mom says, "It was the thing that led to you."

"In the cave down there."

"Yes."

"And then?"

"And then he died from the bad air."

"But you didn't die."

"I didn't."

"How's that?"

"I thought the tunnels were angry because I'd brought strangers. I was trapped in that hole with your father's body and his brother's body. It was dark and the poodle was out there barking on the other side of Kitch. I couldn't sleep. I told the tunnels I was sorry. Eventually, the poodle stopped barking."

Her face is pained and then calm again. She says, "Johnny Riles never went ripe, never got stiff. He stayed soft and pretty. Kitch, he stunk. Every time I awoke I'd grab his arm and try to pull him out of the tunnel. One day, his arm came off in my hands. I stopped tugging on him after that. Meanwhile, you were growing inside me.

"And then you came out. You were a tiny baby. I held you to my bosom, but I had no milk. I could not let an infant child suffer in that hole. So I put my hand on your mouth and held it there for a long, long time. And I took it off and you were still breathing. You didn't cry. I put my fingers around your throat and I squeezed and I started crying and then there was a slurping, birthing sound and Kitch's body slipped out from where he'd been stuck in the tunnel and landed in the room. I took my hands away from your throat and you were still breathing. I carried you in one arm. We crawled over Kitch's body. He had gone soft, like grey mud. We crawled over him and thru the tunnels and rooms and up to the outside world, right here, in fact. I left you on the ground here and I went back into the caves, to my shelves. I used to have shelves with food and drink, and a table and a bed and a stove. But they were all gone. Disappeared. So I came back to you, but you were gone so I climbed back into the hole. That's the end of my story."

I say, "It's an unlikely story."

She says, "You don't believe it."

I say, “I do. Every word. Except.”

She sighs. “Except what.”

“What happened to the poodle?”

“The poodle ceased its barking while you were still a bump on my belly. I concluded that he was dead. But he wasn’t. You want to know how I know this. I know this because, ever since, the coyotes in this land are small. Because they’re part poodle.”

Mother chuckles.

I say, “That strains plausibility.”

She says, “Son, everything’s a strain.”

Pause.

I say, “Just one more thing.”

“You want to know how I came into possession of a carbide lamp.”

I say, “Well, that, I guess, and how you found me and how you were able to move fast enough so I could see you and why any of this is going on and if I’ll ever get to talk to Veronica again.”

She says, “Those are some good things to wonder about.”

Mother touches my temple with her ugly fingernails. She says, “You might use a nap.”

I close my eyes and listen to the moving world and smell the wandering air.

The sun has migrated across the sky. The world is still moving. Sounds are still sounding. How 'bout that, Toto? It wasn't a dream after all.

I sit up. Mother is nearby, sleeping on her back, her hands crossed over her belly. On the horizon, an elk grazes in the grass. I remark at the size of his antlers, which are big. Moose-like, actually. I didn't know there were moose in these parts.

There's a sound from the ground beneath me. I roll onto my belly and snake myself to the rim of the hole. From behind me, Mom says, "Wait, boy. She'll come to you."

I do as she tells me. A moment later, my sweet, darling, funny, patient Veronica pokes her head out of the earth.

Her beehive is squished flat and goofy, her eyes are cloudy from waking up. She exhales and her breath is onions and ground beef. After so long, so long with nothing, this is. It's like. Maybe Adam felt this way after God turned a lump of garden soil into Eve.

My first word to Vero is, "Hey."

Vero's first words to me are, "Nice shirt."

I tug the hem of my zebra skin so I can look at the dirty stripes running down the front. I say, "Ever the professional."

She reaches a hand up and I reach down and help her out of the hole. Her fingers are warm and wet and full of motion. She moves like an oil spill, smooth and fluid and full of rainbows. We watch each other like a couple who've recently endured mutually bizarre but entirely different experiences.

I say, "How's your tailbone?"

"It hurts."

"I didn't mean for that to happen. I thought time had stopped. I read your diary, 'cause I figured we'd never talk again. I was upset. I pulled your chair out from underneath—"

"Nar, I don't care about the chair. I don't care about my diary. I don't know where we are. I don't know what you've been doing since you went into that bathroom. All I know is that the last ten minutes of my life have been absolutely bonkers. You go into that bathroom and it's like, what the fuck? Then I'm on the floor and that waitress is pointing a gun at me. And those two assholes, the guy with the coffee and the cook, they were psycho. And those messages that appeared out of nowhere. I said to myself, 'Ride this sucker out, Veronica. You're in the middle of some truly bizarre shit. Treasure it.'"

She says, "Those people were dicks, except the waitress, who turned out to be nice. Thanks for getting me out of there. I liked that pretty yard you brought me to. Sometimes I'd see this blurry moving thing."

I say, "That was me, I bet."

"My own private poltergeist."

"I thought of myself as a superhero."

She says, "Thanks for proposing to me, by the way. What'd you think of my response?"

"It took me a while."

"Yeah. I'm clever. And then you said we could get married in California, which made sense since the sun had gone down."

I say, "You put all that together? You *are* clever."

"So I closed my eyes and I knew that pretty soon I'd open them and we'd be in California." She looks about. "This doesn't look like California."

My mother says, "We are a damned good distance from California, young lady."

Vero tilts her head toward the strange woman. "Where'd you get her?"

Mom says, "I'm the boy's mother."

I lean toward Vero and whisper, "She's my mother."

Vero, oh, unflappable Vero, says, "Cool beans." Her eyes move, her nostrils flare with each inhalation. In her flip flops, her big toes start to snap idly against her long toes. Vero is right in front of me. I stare and listen and love her.

Considering that this is the first meeting between my fiancée and my mom, things are proceeding nicely.

Vero's eye catches a movement on the far side of the valley. She says, "Where'd you get the moose?"

Mom stands and turns her head toward where the big-antlered

elk-moose is grazing out yonder. The beast lifts its head. It makes a bugle sound and starts galloping toward us. Although the animal's hauling ass, we're at least a quarter mile away; there's still plenty of time to dive into the hole if things get hairy.

Which is precisely what happens when a saber-toothed tiger crests the hill behind the elk. With feline leaps, the cat catches up to the elk and launches itself at its neck. Cat and elk go down in an explosion of dew. The cat writhes over the writhing elk until it stops moving. The tiger opens its jaws wide and then plunges its monstrous canines into the belly of the elk. At less than two hundred yards away, we hear the entrails slip out. Apparently, so do the tiger's offspring, because once the elk's guts are spilled, three saber-toothed kittens bound over the rim of the hill to join their mother in slurping up organs and flesh.

Vero says, "Holy shit."

I agree.

Mom says, "Don't bring attention."

The tiger and her babies stop gorging long enough to regard the three of us and then they get right back to it. When they finish, they cuddle near the corpse and fall into fat-bellied slumber.

I suspect that I've not yet seen the end to crazy-ass crazy shit. This suspicion is compounded when a camel crests the hill, takes a look at the sleeping tigers, and turns back.

I say to my mom, "I think perhaps this is a different hole from the one we came in thru." After receiving no response, I add, "Like, this landscape bears very little resemblance to the one we exited. Take the prehistoric animals, for instance."

Mom, ignoring me, reaches a hand to Vero. "My name is Jabez Millstone."

Vero takes Jabez's hand. "Veronica Vasquez. I intend to marry your son."

I rest my hand on Vero's shoulder, with its soft flesh and living bones.

Because it's been a good two minutes since anything nutty has happened, a wooly mammoth crests the hill and marches past the elk corpse and the sleeping tigers, who barely crack an eye, and approaches us. The thing is magnificent, with its swaying fur, preposterously curved tusks, and generally cuddly appearance.

My mother, Jabez Millstone, claps her hands and shouts, "Go on! Git!"

The mammoth watches us, idly waving its tusks.

Veronica says, "It's like it wants those tigers to eat it."

I say, "Since when did mammoths become suicidal?"

In another of her incongruent utterances, Mom points to the mammoth and says, "Do you think you could draw one of those things?"

I say, "It's funny you ask. I've been doing some sketching lately. There's a notebook in my—"

Out of the cloudless blue, a single small piece of hail falls and bounces off the bridge of my nose.

"Well, shit," I say.

Then more hail and more, little harmless spitballs of ice, showering from the heavens, covering our hair and shoulders, clattering the teeth in our wide-open mouths.

The hail grows larger, mouse-sized, and pummels the earth. We cover our heads with our arms and huddle together. Vero tries to cover my head and I try to cover hers and Jabez presses the two of us into a squatting position and leans over the both of us and lets the hail bounce off her bony back.

This all happens extraordinarily quickly. Perhaps I giggle. Vero may giggle as well. Jabez, with her hands on her knees and her back bent, snorts and spits a glob of phlegm onto the grass, which is quickly disappearing under the assault of hail. The cooling air puckers goosebumps on my arms. It's delightful, feeling things, suffering alongside other, breathing humans.

The hailstones grow even larger, bouncing like lumpen rats upon Jabez and, where she can't protect us, Vero and I. The sound is a rockslide, our bruises are already beginning to turn purple.

Jabez, sensibly, shouts, "Hole!"

In a more or less orderly fashion, we dive into the hole and scoop away ice and we are out of the storm.

Hush now.

The three of us will sit at the mouth of the tunnel as the hail pours in from above. We will rub our sore arms and backs and attempt uncomfortable laughter. We will watch as the entrance to the tunnel slowly fills with clattering stones. Light will grow dim, but continue to glow thru the barrier of ice.

Amid the racket, Mother will tilt her head and say, “Listen.”

We will hear a mammoth trumpeting in the distance.

Time will pass and the hail will slow until there are only occasional plops, like the last kernels in a bag of microwave popcorn. We will remain inside the tunnel, unwilling to retreat further into the caverns. We will not speak during this interval. We will merely look at each other, eyes roving from one person’s to the other’s, each of us gauging the degree to which we fear for our lives. Jabez will not fear for anything. Vero will shiver in her tank top, the top of her left ear swelling from a hail strike. As for me, I have been living on a planet of nonsense for so long, all I can do is wait for the next pile of crap to land.

When it is calm, when we are calm, Jabez will begin pulling handfuls of hail from the accumulation that blocks our exit. She will pass hail to Vero, who will pass hail to me, who will wing it further on down the tunnel. It will be a pleasant exercise, throwing chunks of ice and watching them bounce and skitter on the hard floor.

Once the exit is cleared, we will, the three of us, climb forth into a new world, twelve inches deep in hail. In our own ways will each of us say to ourselves, *What the fuck*.

The dead, gutted elk-moose will be completely buried. A white mound on the distant hill will shake itself free of the ice that has accumulated upon its shoulders and reveal a mammoth underneath.

The skies will be clear and blue and the sun will glare brightly off the polar landscape. No sign of the saber-tooth tigers.

Vero will hug me and I will hold her, both of us cringing from where the hail has struck us. Jabez will beam happily at this embrace. Then she, Jabez, will tilt her head back and say, “Yonder comes something.”

Up we'll gaze to a glow in the sky, not unlike that of Jabez's Tinker Bell gas lamp, except this will more closely resemble a comet plunging out of the heavens, white with blurred edges. At first, it will be the size of a pinhead held at arm's length. As it descends, it will grow to the size of a thumbnail, a golf ball, a bowling ball, a Volkswagen Bug, a comet.

We will stand directly in its path. The falling, glowing comet will be making a great deal of racket at this point. I will lean against Vero and the two of us, still staring upward, will engage in a sideways kiss, the kind where you have to drag your mouth to the side of your face while you continue to gaze forward at the comet that's flying toward you. We have never kissed in this manner before.

The falling object will be trailing steam or smoke or something. Parts of it will flake off like the ice chunks that fall off the space shuttle thruster tank when it launches. The chunks will drift away from the rest of the mass and evaporate into the glowing tail.

In a very short while, the three of us will be extinct.

Just as I and Vero and Jabez brace for death, the falling space rock will come to a grinding, midair halt, and then it will ease itself before us, gentle and steaming onto the hail-strewn landscape. The rock's final descent will bear more than a passing resemblance to that of a giant, frozen teardrop lowered from the heavens like a flying Sandy Duncan being wired back down to the stage in the production of Peter Pan, which I still will not have seen. Or, in less confusing terms, it will ease to Earth like the first snowflake of winter.

The mammoth and any other nearby prehistoric varmints will have made themselves scarce by this time, the only suggestion that they ever existed being the lump of hail that covers the elk's remains.

The teardrop-shaped space rock will loom before us, dripping water, hissing steam, sinking and melting into the hail below. As space rocks go, this one will seem to be on the large end of the spectrum, roughly the size of a condominium. It appears to be composed entirely of ice.

We will wait silently, observing the clunk of hydraulics and the seep of gas as the airlock is unsealed and the gangway slides out of the mouth of the vessel.

A creature, probably four feet tall, shaped like a grey Q-tip, no eyes, no limbs, no problem, will glide down the gangway and come to a halt in an ankle-deep pool of melting water with hailstones floating atop. The critter will shift in color like a cuttlefish, patterns appearing on its surface, mostly of the plaid and paisley variety. The coloration will settle into a series of black stripes on a white background, as if *thon* has deemed this interstellar denouement an occasion worthy of a tacky zebra-print outfit of the variety that one would encounter at a cocktail party on the Nassau end of Long Island. Or it just likes my shirt and wants to mimic me.

Here, now, the Q-tip will cease all motion—freeze, as it were, like a statue. Many minutes will pass without any further development, except for the fact that the mammoth will now be showing its head over the lip of the hill. And the camel's hump will be visible now and again.

Let me digress briefly. The audio will be incredible. I will have only been hearing things for a few hours at this juncture and the sounds will include the melting of thousands of hailstones, which shift and tumble upon themselves in the warm, sunlit afternoon. The breath of Vero and the breath of Jabez will mingle in a low harmony. I will sense a nearly invisible respiration in the upper and lower bouts of the Q-tip's body.

Here, Jabez, who is to my left, will reach across my torso to Vero, who is on my right. Vero will take Jabez's hand and Jabez will lead her a few steps toward the Q-tip. The Q-tip will be float-standing twenty yards away from us.

Vero will release Jabez's hand and she, Veronica Vasquez, my fiancée, will walk in her typical slouchy unconcerned manner directly up to the Q-tip and engage it in a conversation that I can't hear.

While Vero speaks to the Q-tip, Mother Jabez will stand in front of me, hands clasped in front of her belly. I will assume they are clasped. I won't be able to see them, as I will be behind her.

Jabez, at least from my perspective, will be in a state of contentment, yogic breaths, sloppy hair glowing in the light of the late afternoon sun.

I will not be in a state of contentment. I will be terrified that the Q-tip will begin probing, mutilating, vaporizing, or otherwise compromising the structural integrity of my fiancée. I know I shouldn't be anxious. Vero knows how to handle herself. This is the woman who didn't bat an eye while my hypertemporal self was dragging her all over the countryside and writing notes, and issuing marriage proposals. She can handle a space Q-tip.

Vero will appear to be calmly explaining something to the Q-tip. Her calmness calms me.

I will whisper ahead to Mother Jabez, "What are they saying?"

Mother Jabez will turn her head slightly and speak aloud, "Talking about the weather, probably." She will then say, "Shut up."

I will say, still in a whisper, "Is it just me, or does that thing resemble a Q-tip?"

Mother Jabez will say, "I'm uncertain as to what a Q-tip is."

I will say, "You clean your ears with them."

Mother Jabez will turn to me and say, "You should only clean your ears with garlic water, son." Then she will look disappointed.

I will persist. "A Q-tip is like a toothpick with cotton balls on either end."

Mother Jabez will say, "We used to call them cotton swabs. Be quiet. Your girlfriend is negotiating the survival of a civilization."

Whereupon Vero will bow gently to the Q-tip and skip back upon her wet feet to where Jabez and I will be standing. The Q-tip will remain where *thon* is.

*

I will say nothing.

Vero will say, "Her name is Pinta."

"Right," I will say.

Vero will wave jauntily at Pinta. Pinta's upper body will sway back and forth like a piece of seaweed.

Vero will say, "She just arrived, from Pluto. Apparently, their suicide rate is off the charts. Life is cold and depressing. As you can imagine. She's wondering if Earth would be an acceptable place for her fellow Plutons to settle down."

I will nod knowingly, because I sort of do know what she's talking about.

Vero will say, "Pinta says the earth is the loveliest thing she's ever seen. She thinks it'd do the Plutons a great deal of good to get a little sun. She doesn't want to cause any problems, but she'd like to know if she can invite the rest of her people to come stay here. Especially since the three of us," she will move her hand in a circle to indicate herself, Jabez, and me, "are the only humans within four-thousand miles."

I will say, "What kind of planetary scanner is *she* using? These parts are rural, but there's people all over the place. Believe me, I've been eating their dinner."

Jabez will say, "Not yet, there ain't."

I will say, "Mom?"

She will say, "The tunnels have brought us to the olden times."

At this point, I will concede that the roller coaster has reached the top of the hill and it has flown off into the wild blue yonder.

Vero will nod enthusiastically. "She's right, Narry. Kansas isn't even on the map yet."

"This is Colorado."

"Colorado isn't on the map, either." She will look to Mother Jabez. "What should I tell her? Her spaceship is melting."

To prove the point, a pointy cone of ice will snap off the top of the vessel and slide down the side to splash in the hail slush.

Questions will burst forth from my face: "What about Sandy? What about Charlene? What about the game I have to work tomorrow? Am I ever gonna get to see a coyo-doodle?"

Vero will touch my hand, "Look, babe. Did you not recently see that saber-tooth tiger eat a giant elk? Do you not at this very moment see that mammoth rolling delightedly in the hail over there? We're here, and here's a whole different place from where we woke up this morning."

The Q-tip will continue waving its top like seaweed.

Vero will say, "Remember when we were at that diner a few minutes ago and it was hot and we were hungry? And all that shit happened with the waitress and the gun and that asshole guy and the other asshole guy? And then that message appeared and it said, 'Please wink IMMEDIATELY.' I trusted myself to trust you. It was this feeling. And those blurs, I knew they were you. I knew it and I said to myself, 'This is Narwhal's perfect game.' There's nothing to change, nothing to judge, just watch. I will not blow a whistle. I will watch and it will amuse me, like those little kids did for you at your perfect game. I winked for your blur. I closed my eyes, and when I opened them a moment later I was in that little garden. And even though that blur snooped in my diary, asshole, I forgave you. And, even though you presumably found out about The Blad, you forgave me, presumably, so we became engaged. And now we're here, you and me and your mother." Vero will nod in the direction of the Q-tip, "And Pinta, the fair maiden of Pluto." Vero will place her hands on my shoulders. She will look at my eyes, say, "I *adore* you, Narwhal Slotterfield."

I will say, "I adore *you*, Veronica Vasquez."

We will embrace.

From the corner of my eye, I will see Jabez squirming with maternal pride.

Vero, who, one assumes, will have just needed to get that off her chest, will extract herself from my clutches and say, "I'd like to tell Pinta she can stay and that she can bring her people. She's being very polite."

The Q-tip will be stretching itself tall and shrinking back down, like an excited child.

Vero and Jabez will look to me. I will say to Jabez, "For a long time I had no idea why any of this was happening. Then I became of the opinion that all this time-fuckery was orchestrated so I could thwart a bank robbery in a town called Keaton. That's a hell of a magic trick just to stop a crime that, in the big picture, doesn't rate highly on the list of horrible things people do to each other on a regular basis. But now I'm beginning to think that this wasn't really about me at all. I was summoned here so I could bring Vero here so she could parley with a space Q-tip. Is that the case? Because if it is, I suddenly feel a whole lot less important than I did a few minutes ago."

Jabez will say, "A raindrop can't form without a fleck of dust."

After a polite pause, I will nod toward Vero and say, "You should see that raindrop swing an umbrella."

Vero, beaming, will say, "I'm going to tell Pinta it's okay. That she can bring the rest of the Plutons."

I will say, "Just a minute. How do you talk to each other? Did you take Plutonese in high school?"

Vero will giggle. "You won't believe it. She speaks perfect Spanish."

Vero will hug Jabez and then me. Then she will stride the ankle-high melting hail toward Pinta the Plutonic Planetary Adventurer.

Pinta will bow to Vero and Vero will bow to Pinta. They will speak for a few moments. At one point, Pinta will bounce up and down several times in what approximates ecstatic joy in the body language of Plutons. Vero will hug Pinta and kiss her on the side of her upper Q-tip and then Pinta will bow and rotate and hover to her melting space ship.

Before Pinta floats up the gangplank, I will shout to Vero, "Vero! Vero!"

Jabez will put her hand on my shoulder, as if to tell me to shut up. I will ignore her. I will shout to Vero, "Tell her about winter. She needs to know about winter. Tell her it only lasts a few months."

Vero will shrug and turn back to Pinta and, in a voice loud enough that I can hear, she will shout, "*¡El invierno es frío, pero será terminado antes de que usted lo sepa!*"

Darling Veronica, you know how hard I will laugh when I hear you say those words.

EPILOGUE

> *It seemed that, at the moment that the enormous narwhal had come to take breath at the surface of the water, the air was engulfed in its lungs, like the steam in the vast cylinders of a machine of two thousand horse-power.*
>
> —Jules Verne,
> *Twenty Thousand Leagues Under the Sea*

After Pinta the Pluton's half-melted spaceship launches into the sky, Vero and Jabez and I will watch as the mammoth on the other side of the valley raises her furry trunk and then trumpets loudly. She will spread her rear legs and a protoplasmic bag will bulge from a hole in her belly, and then with a loud *slap*, the bag will slide out and fall to the ground, splashing into a crater of hail. A pink geyser will flow from the hole in the mammoth's belly and redden the ice below her. The geyser will stop. Steam will rise.

The mammoth will kick the bag and tug on it with her trunk until the bag peels away to reveal a baby mammoth, covered in thin brown hair. After more persistent kicking, the baby mammoth will roll onto its knees and, slipping several times in the bloody hail, gain its legs and reach its wet mouth to the swollen nipple dangling from its mother's breast.

Ω

ACKNOWLEDGMENTS

As usual, I received a great deal of great advice from friends who read various non-great early drafts. Maureen, of course. Mom, of course. And the rest of the gang: Marrion Irons, Eric Allen, Lucas Richards. Terry Welty for narrating the audiobook in exchange for a few crummy guitar lessons. Paul Handley was especially helpful. Special thanks go to Tony Parella, for surviving two different drafts.

MVP goes to Brett Duesing, who not only read multiple drafts, but who double-checked my time-conversions and helped me clear up some muddy scenes, all while using sentences like this: *A logical argument will have clear, unambiguous language, while the narrative will have many elements open to interpretation, since the object of a narrative text is to have the readers use their imagination to create their own text, and build a subjunctive universe.*

Exponential bonus to Mike Lindstrom, for double-double checking my time-conversions (the man created a spreadsheet complete with "speed of AK47 bullet" and "rotation rate of average tornado" for crying out loud) and for finding that issue with the decimal point.

It's nice having friends.

To Kurt Svoboda, dedicated president (and sole member) of the Gregory Hill Fan Club. Thank you for your years of wacky correspondence.

Also, Mark Stevens, Carrie Breitbach, Euan Hague, Zack Littlefield, James Ford.

The gang at Genghis Kern did a terrific job on the covers.

Finally, thanks to Caleb Seeling of Conundrum Press for bringing all three of the Strattford novels together. It's great to be back home.

New bands: Manotaur MK II, The Super Phoenixes, and The Rural Roots Ad Hoc Country-Rock-Improvisational Music Experience, whom you can see the third Saturday of (virtually) every month at Grassroots Community Center in Joes (I recommend you confirm this before you make the drive).

ABOUT THE AUTHOR

Gregory Hill lives, writes, and makes odd music on the Colorado High Plains. His previous book, *East of Denver*, won the 2013 Colorado Book Award for Literary Fiction.

Visit his web site at www.gregoryhillauthor.com

A STRATTFORD COUNTY YARN

Three volume collection

BY AUTHOR GREGORY HILL

Now for the first time, Gregory Hill's humorous, often poignant, tales of life in fictional Strattford County on the plains of eastern Colorado are presented together. The trilogy starts with award-winning *East of Denver*, a story about a senile father, his son who moves back to the farm to care for him, and a half-baked plan to rob the bank that is stealing their land. *The Lonesome Trials of Johnny Riles* recounts the struggles of the "good" son living in the shadow of his brother, an eccentric ABA basketball star, while trying to keep the family ranch going on his own. *Zebra Skin Shirt* concludes the series when time stops for everyone except an unorthodox referee, whose decision whether to right the wrongs of the world may have cosmic consequences.

***East of Denver: A Strattford County Yarn Volume* 1**

ISBN 978-1-942280-45-3 | $17.00

***The Lonesome Trials of Johnny Riles: A Strattford County Yarn Volume* 2**

ISBN 978-1-942280-48-4 | $17.00

***Zebra Skin Shirt: A Strattford County Yarn Volume* 3**

ISBN 978-1-942280-51-4 | $17.00

CONUNDRUM PRESS
AN IMPRINT OF BOWER HOUSE

For More Visit gregoryhillauthor.com & bowerhousebooks.com

AVAILABLE AT YOUR LOCAL BOOKSTORE